The Rules of Engagement

The Rules of Engagement

ANITA BROOKNER

VIKING

an imprint of

PENGUIN BOOKS

VIKING

Published by the Penguin Group
Penguin Books Ltd, 80 Strand, London WC2R ORL, England
Penguin Putnam Inc., 375 Hudson Street, New York, New York 10014, USA
Penguin Books Australia Ltd, 250 Camberwell Road, Camberwell, Victoria 3124, Australia
Penguin Books Canada Ltd, 10 Alcorn Avenue, Toronto, Ontario, Canada M4V 3B2
Penguin Books India (P) Ltd, 11 Community Centre,
Panchsheel Park, New Delhi – 110 017, India
Penguin Books (NZ) Ltd, Cnr Rosedale and Airborne Roads,
Albany, Auckland, New Zealand
Penguin Books (South Africa) (Pty) Ltd, 24 Sturdee Avenue,
Rosebank 2196, South Africa

Penguin Books Ltd, Registered Offices: 80 Strand, London WC2R ORL, England

www.penguin.com

First published 2003
2

Set in 12/14.75pt Monotype Dante
Typeset by Rowland Phototypesetting Ltd, Bury St Edmunds, Suffolk
Printed in Great Britain by Clays Ltd, St Ives plc

A CIP catalogue record for this book is available from the British Library

ISBN 0-670-91436-3

I

We met, and became friends of a sort, by virtue of the fact that we started school on the same day. Because we had the same Christian name it was decreed that she should choose an alternative. For some reason – largely, I think, because she was influenced by the sort of sunny children's books available in our milieu – she decided to be known as Betsy. When we met up again, several years later, she was Betsy de Saint-Jorre. Not bad for a girl initially registered as Elizabeth Newton.

How much nicer children were in those days than the adults they have become! Born in 1948, we were well-behaved, incurious, with none of the rebellious features adopted by those who make youthfulness a permanent quest. We went to tea in one another's houses, sent each other postcards when we went on holiday with our parents, assumed we would know each other all our lives . . . The Sixties took us by surprise: we were unprepared, unready, uncomprehending. That, I now see, was why I married Digby: it was the right unthinking thing to do. That was why Betsy took it upon herself to have a career, out of despair, perhaps, at not being provided for. Choice hardly dictated our actions. Yet I suppose we were contented enough. Certainly we knew no better. And now we know too much. Discretion veiled our motives then, and perhaps does so even now, even in an age of multiple communications, of e-mails, text messages, and news bulletins all round the clock. We still rely on narrative, on the considered account. That is how and why I knew Betsy's story, though I cannot claim to know all of it. There were areas of confusion which it seemed better not to disclose. But she was always painfully honest, rather more so than prudence might advise. That quality made itself felt when we were still children; her desire to explain herself, to be known, was perhaps really a desire to be loved. That too was discernible, and it set her apart. In later life, when I knew her again, that quality was still there, obscured only slightly by the manners she had acquired, and always at odds with her mind, which was exacting. In other circumstances she might have been remarkable. But her hopes had been curtailed, and in the years of her adulthood one sometimes saw this, in the odd distant glance directed towards a window, or the eagerness with which she smiled at any passing child.

Her initial demotion from Elizabeth to Betsy was thought to be justified, given her uncertainty of status. She took it in her stride, thinking it gave her permission to assume an altogether different character, someone more lighthearted, skimming the surface, responding always with a smile. She longed to be superficial, with the sort of ease that I and my particular coterie took for granted. Adult responsibility, of an altogether unwelcome kind, had already come her way, in the shape of her widowed father and the faded aunt who kept some sort of primitive life going in that flat above the surgery in Pimlico Road. She was unfortunate: that was generally agreed, and it made her something of an anomaly in our midst. My mother professed sympathy for her, but viewed with dislike Betsy's attempts to be winning when she came to our house in Bourne Street, on the rare occasions when I was obliged to invite her. The enthusiasm with which she greeted my mother's teatime offerings (meagre enough in those days of austerity) and the attention she paid to the contents of our drawing-room were not attractive, and my mother was not tactful in acknowledging the evidence of Betsy's social awkwardness. I had many years in which to reflect on my mother's harshness. Even when young I was aware of a desire to depart from this, to be less brittle, less proud, less conformist than my mother. Now I see that I have not quite managed it. My only victory is that the harshness has been internalized. My judgements even now are sometimes less than charitable.

There was another reason for my mother's dislike, and that had to do with the cause of Betsy's profound disenfranchisement. Her father's negligence, or incompetence, had led indirectly to the death of one of his patients, who happened to be an acquaintance of ours. Pity and dislike, first manifested by my mother, affected Betsy even more than her father's disgrace, which she inherited. It seemed ordained to follow her through life, for there was nothing she could do to rectify it. His error was, I dare say, a common one: a lump in the breast which he assured his patient was a cyst revealed its malignancy in due course and led not only to that patient's demise but to his own, after a year of brooding and of unpopular comment in the neighbourhood. I met him once, when I went home with Betsy, the only time I did so; he entered what I suppose had once been her nursery, where we were discussing our homework, turned off the electric fire and opened the window. I found this insensitive, though it may have been protective, but there was little in his demeanour which struck me as kindly. I thought him completely inadequate to fulfil the role of father, but I think he was simply indifferent to children. His better manners were reserved for his patients, in particular for his female patients. Maybe a desire to reassure, or even to comfort, came uppermost in his professional armoury. There was no whisper of impropriety, or none that I was aware of. His greater failure was his dwindling reputation in the year that followed our friend's death, and his own death, from a heart attack, while sitting at his desk in his consulting-room, an irony he was spared. Irony was not a quality much appreciated in the 1950s. Now of course it is all-pervasive.

Sympathy was expressed, condolences were offered, and then the incident was forgotten, though not the fate of the patient. It was thought fitting that he should disappear, and that Betsy should be consigned to her aunt. This aunt – Mary to her niece, Miss Milsom to everyone else – was even less promising than her brother-in-law. Tall, thin, colourless, and obviously virginal, she inspired a vague repugnance even in those unliberated days. 'Poor thing,' said my mother, with a rich show of sympathy, but here again her dislike, or more probably her distaste, was evident, perhaps justifiably so. Miss Milsom had come to keep house after her sister's death, shortly after giving birth to Betsy, and she did so in a conscientious but defeated manner, so that it took her all day to prepare a meal which was no doubt unpalatable. After commiserating with Miss Milsom, or more probably for Miss Milsom, my mother would laugh, showing all her sparkling teeth, as if to demonstrate the difference between Miss Milsom and herself.

Nowadays, of course, we would assume that Miss Milsom and the doctor indulged in sex of a sort, but then we assumed no such thing. Those were innocent days; sex had yet to become the commodity on offer to all that it is now. By the same token there was little show of love between the aunt and the niece, neither of whom had been able to envisage an alternative to their present arrangement, but they were both loyal and obedient people, and they sustained an undemanding harmony, which, though honourable, provided little joy. Betsy

4

proved to be a clever girl, who was obliged to keep her cleverness to herself, except at school, where she developed a passion for the drama, and was given to declaiming lines from Shakespeare and even Racine (we were doing *Hamlet* and *Bérénice*); it was her one opportunity to deliver herself of aspiration (and it was aspiration rather than frustration) and to make contact with adult emotion.

The solution Betsy and her aunt made to their mutual lack of comprehension was their weekly visit to the cinema, usually on a Saturday evening, when they enjoyed a timid contact with the crowd. An early supper, the cinema, and a cup of tea on their return to the flat satisfied Miss Milsom's sense of a justified indulgence, both for herself and for her niece. She viewed the films as an outsider: not for her the extravagance, the licence, the romance. Even so, something in her disciplined soul responded, whereas Betsy remained faithful to the grander concepts in her favourite Racine. '*Que le jour recommence, et que le jour finisse/Sans que jamais Titus puisse voir Bérénice . . .*' These lines became prophetic, so that at the very end, when I visited her in the hospital, I would see her eyes widen in her thin face, and hear her murmur, '. . . *sans que de tout le jour . . .*', and then fall silent.

However, she naturally gave no sign of this when we were children, even adolescents. She was a pretty girl, though there was no one to tell her so. Our friendship in those early days was largely a matter of propinquity, and that only at school. My mother discouraged it. 'Can't you find someone more suitable?' she would say, meaning someone richer, more fortunate, more useful. She envisaged a life for me exactly like her own, marriage to a professional man, a comfortable establishment, licensed idleness, licensed amusements. Betsy's general lack of all these prospects ruled her out of what my mother, even in those days, thought of as an appropriate social circle. And she had noted, and condemned, Betsy's ardour when she came to our house, her slightly too emphatic good manners. Maybe she had also noted Betsy's appraising eyes, which had, for one or two significant moments, been trained on herself. Brought up in circumstances of bleak rectitude, Betsy was inclined to view any departure from that state with something like surprise. My mother was a frivolous woman but she had a well-developed sense of self-preservation; any hint of criticism offended her. Not that Betsy was critical; she was too well-mannered for that. But she was wide-eyed, no doubt with some sort of admiration, at the display my mother put on for any sort of witness, even one so very unimportant. I could intuit exasperation in the way she tapped her cigarette on the lid of the silver cigarette box before lighting it with a flourish. 'Do you want to show your friend your room?' she asked, after a brief silence. 'And show her round the garden, why don't you?' We were dismissed. In the garden Betsy said, 'Your mother's very beautiful, isn't she?' I saved this up to tell my mother after Betsy had left, hoping that this would propitiate her. For she was slightly annoyed; I knew her too well to miss the signs. And Betsy tended to have that effect on others, certainly in later life. Through sheer incomprehension she would fail to administer the right platitudes. This may have been a sign of virtue, one she had no doubt absorbed from her reading of the great dramatists, who only deal in virtue, and of course its opposite.

This is not to imply that Betsy possessed any recondite powers of divination. It is rather that those who have meagre beginnings are obliged to study the world more stringently, looking for clues. And there was much to learn, not only for Betsy but for girls of our generation, too old for the Fifties, too young for the Sixties. We were still bound by the rules laid down by parents and teachers, obliged to be obedient, respectful, with little understanding that we were entitled to make choices that had been denied to the generation that had preceded ours. In this matter I was as ignorant as Betsy, but perhaps more secure; my parents had a strong influence on me, largely because they were both decisive characters who abided by certain social rules which they saw fit to pass on to me. I now see, with all the wisdom of hindsight, that I was given the wrong instructions, as were my peers. Today I look at the truly liberated young (and the even more liberated middle-aged) and marvel at their insouciance, their apparent lack of anxiety. Even now I wonder if there are no penalties for what I still regard as bad behaviour. We were untroubled by desire, though timidly aware that the world was changing. On our excursions to the King's Road on a Saturday morning (the morning being safer than the afternoon, given over to householders, shoppers) we discussed the future in terms of what work we would do. This did not much interest me, whereas Betsy was considerably exercised by the prospect of a future for which no provision had been made. In that way she was more realistic than I was, for my grandparents had left me some money, and although this was controlled by my father I received an allowance which would enable me to postpone any far-reaching decisions. My mother had mentioned a cookery course, a year in Florence; this possibility I kept in reserve. In all innocence I mentioned these matters to Betsy, as we sat drinking milky coffee out of glass cups. She looked at me, perplexed. 'But don't you want to work? Or go to university?' she asked. 'You're good at English.'

'I wouldn't mind being a journalist,' I said, but this in fact was only a conversational counter. 'What about you?'

'Well, I'll have to get a job, won't I?'

'You're the one who ought to go to university. You're good at languages. Your French . . .'

'There won't be any money for that. And I need to look after Mary. She's not strong, you know. She has anaemia. It makes her tired. That's where you're lucky.' She blushed, as if she had committed an impropriety. It was the only time – the only time – I ever heard her refer to the imbalance in our fortunes. To be envied simply because one had parents, after all a natural endowment, was not something I could understand. I had read stories about orphans and I knew that they were to be pitied. But I could not see that her father was much of a loss, and in any event she had the sort of courage that enabled her to look towards the future, a courage in which I was strangely lacking. For the moment I was content to drift, to live out my last school years, and then perhaps to light upon a solution, or to have one arranged for me.

'Do give my love to your mother,' she said, as we shrugged on our coats.

It was perhaps an attempt to retrieve an earlier *faux pas*, a reference to my good fortune in possessing parents, but it revealed her concomitant weakness, a need to go too far. Too far in politeness, in accessibility, in offers of service. I was to witness this on many occasions, particularly as we grew older. Those evenings at the cinema, watching the fabled lives of others, had done nothing to persuade her of the necessity of dissembling, of holding back her assent, of flirtatiousness and unreliability, such as attended the heroines of those Holly-wood romances her aunt favoured, and whose trickiness, whose feistiness always brought about the desired, the honour-able result. Betsy never mastered that art. Her eyes would widen with something like shock if she encountered anything less than the plainest of speech, the slightest deviation from the truth. I could see that this might make her something of a burden; I could even see that there might be some things one would have to conceal from her, but at the age of fifteen, of sixteen, I put it down to lack of a mother who could instruct her in what was appropriate. She never entirely lost that faculty, and whatever one knows to be the desirability of honesty, one lives long enough to regret its persistence in others, particularly in those who knew one when one was just as honest oneself.

What I did not tell Betsy – and this was one of several related matters that I was obliged to conceal from her – was that my parents did not get on, and that I had become used to hearing angry voices issuing from their bedroom far into the night. My one desire was to get away, and to live my life far from the contamination of these adult matters. I valued a sort of innocence, or more probably ignorance, which I feared might be destroyed. My confused feeling at the time was that I should be allowed to make my own mistakes and not be harnessed to those of others. Instinctively I resisted my mother and her plans, thinking, perhaps correctly, that they did not have my best interests at heart. In this I was probably wrong, but I did not know then that two people could hate each other and still live together. I was aware that my father had a friend, but a girl is more likely to forgive her father than her mother. My mother, as far as I knew, was faithful, but fidelity had merely sharpened her tongue, her powers of criticism. Her scornful bitter voice in the bedroom filled me with horror, even with terror. I thought that parents should be sweet-natured, self-effacing, and some children are lucky this way. My plans were non-existent, but they centred around some form of escape. My one comforting thought was that I had my own money and could at some point run away, even go abroad. At sixteen this was unrealistic. At the same time I was sufficiently ruled by my upbringing and the codes of my class to know that I must lodge no complaint, express no dissatisfaction, and carry on as if all were for the best in the best of all possible worlds.

That I did not take Betsy into my confidence was perhaps an enactment of this code, which has somehow stayed with me, and also perhaps because I could not face the look of sympathetic horror in her unwavering gaze. I did not see how I could inflict that outrage on one whose innocence (or ignorance) had not yet been compromised. That was why I deflected all questions that had to do with my future, even with the putative choice of a profession. Our friendship depended on a sort of mutuality: she must not be told that I was already in touch with the sordid truth of which she could have no knowledge. She was only too willing to admire my parents; she would not be able to understand that they were not necessarily admirable. I thought that she should be protected from sadness, since she had most certainly endured the sadness of not having known her own mother. She had done well, so far, and I had no wish to cloud her horizon. It was not that I had any special loyalty to her beyond the limits of our childhood friendship. Had I known what was to follow I think I should have behaved no differently. Again, one respects those qualities one does not possess oneself.

This was to be the pattern: I must protect her because she had so few people in whom to place her trust. Miss Milsom, a broken reed at the best of times, could not carry out this function. I thought that Betsy behaved superbly in accepting Miss Milsom as she was, without a hint of impatience or criticism, enduring the insipid food, the formulaic conversation, the weekend visits to the cinema, as a version of family life with which she had no quarrel. It was clear to me that when the time came she would support Miss Milsom in her declining days, which might not be far off, and not even suspect that the Miss Milsoms of this world would contribute very little to those whose care and training fall within their remit. Betsy owed her schooling to scholarships; she would undoubtedly win a scholarship to university, yet Miss Milsom and her disorder might stand in her way. Betsy's loyalty, which extended to everyone she knew, including my parents, was no doubt the result of a truncated childhood, but it was no less impressive for that reason. In time that loyalty turned into a form of desire, as I was to witness. There was not then, and never would be, a wish on my part to damage that bright trust, even when it took on a damaged quality, or rather a dimension of longing, of distress, which at last revealed the original wound.

Already our association was conducted along certain lines, and strangely, or perhaps not so strangely, this was how it continued. On one level we knew each other very well; on another I was obliged to keep my own counsel. I was able to sustain this because I was proud, but I now see that there is no pride without some underlying shame. I felt this shame rather more than my parents appeared to do; I felt it even more when I was with my peers, most of all when Betsy outlined her artless plans: a job that would enable her to care for Miss Milsom, whom she had no reason, as she saw it, to abandon. In comparison with such transparency I knew myself to be opaque. Although we were both quite unawakened – we were, I suppose, the last virginal generation – I knew that I had glimpsed complexities that were not available to Betsy, for whom everything was straightforward. I kept in mind my plans of escape, though the thought frightened me. I was young enough to want everything to stay as it was, even if I were to become a hostage to my parents, their one point of contact. In the King's Road we wandered thoughtfully, making our way to our respective homes for lunch. We walked on in silence, until Betsy whispered, 'Did you see that girl?' I nodded. 'Wasn't she pretty? You could have your hair cut like that. It would look lovely. You've got such good bones.' Of her own bones there was no mention. It was as if she could only envisage certain advantages for others. Herself she treated with a stoical good sense that even then I perceived as rather fine. I wished that I possessed something of that quality, yet I also knew that without it I might make rather more realistic progress through life than if I had been blessed, or rather cursed, with all the virtues.

2

Naturally I saw less of her once we had left school and gone our separate ways, but news reached me from time to time from other friends who were still in touch with her. As I had anticipated she had gone to university, where she read French and German. What I had not foreseen was Miss Milsom's legacy of ten thousand pounds, making Betsy independent for the first time in her life. She was still in Pimlico Road; at some point she intended to sell the house and purchase a small flat for herself. She used Miss Milsom's money to go to Paris to further her education. 'Furthering her education' meant freeing herself from the constraints of her upbringing, attending a few lectures and classes, but also getting her hair properly cut, acquiring a modest wardrobe, and generally learning how to be part of a group of young men and women who, flushed with the success of the student protests, spent their days in informal discussion groups before dispersing to one another's lodgings to continue talking long into the night. This emancipation, modest though it was, for I did not suspect undue licence on her part, completed her progress into adulthood, on the surface at least. When I next saw her, at my wedding, I was impressed by the change in her appearance. Only her eyes, shining with happiness at what she perceived to be my good fortune, beamed forth her habitual messages of confidence and candour.

'You look lovely,' she said, pressing my hand.

But it was she who looked lovely, as if she were in some

sense fated to be blessed in the same way, the way signified by this reception in a London hotel, my parents' last throw of the dice before they divorced and abandoned me to my new destiny.

'Are you happy?' she went on, her hand reluctant to let mine go.

'Yes, of course.'

'What a pity we can't meet. We've got so much to tell each other, haven't we? You're going away, I suppose?'

'Venice. Tomorrow morning.'

'Lovely,' she said again. 'Will you get in touch when you get back? I'll leave it to you; I expect you'll be busy. Where will you be living?'

'Melton Court. Those flats in South Kensington.' My replies were becoming abrupt, uninformative.

'Oh.' Her eyes widened. 'Will that be nice? I imagined you in Chelsea, somehow. Do you remember how we used to have coffee in the King's Road?'

I did indeed remember, almost nostalgically, as if harking back to a time before I was overtaken by adult concerns. In this hotel ballroom, with its tired waitresses who had seen it all before, I felt compromised, and, worse than that, without resource. I should have liked to have sat down with her, but my mother, whose own wedding it seemed to be, kept calling me to order, to greet another of her friends, to whom I had to repeat my mantra of Venice and Melton Court. In a way the extreme tedium of the occasion was a blessing in disguise; Betsy was not a person to whom I could give an unvarnished account of myself. And in any case she would not have believed me.

I married Digby Wetherall because I was bored and unhappy, because my parents' disaffection had eventually

14

resulted in their separation, prior to divorce, because our house was to be sold, because I was drawn to anyone whose attitudes and affections were uncomplicated, and because he loved me. His size, his breadth, his expansive smile, would have drawn me to him in any circumstances; when he asked me to marry him (with tears in his eyes) I responded instinctively, although until then I had only thought of him as a family friend for whom my father acted as solicitor. And because without him, or someone like him, I had no future. I had drifted into the fatal habit of falling in with my mother's plans, had indeed taken that cookery course, and had made a fairly good job of cooking for private dinner parties, as was the quaint custom in those days.

I longed to be delivered from this chore, but was not trained to do anything else. The liberating climate of the recent past had not included me in any significant respect, though I was susceptible to the beauty of young men and longed to know them better. Digby was not a young man. He was twenty-seven years my senior, but for that very reason seemed to promise an extension of the parenthood and guardianship which my father appeared to have relinquished without regret. I knew that this father (no longer 'my' father) intended to remarry, a woman some years younger than my mother. This disparity in age seemed to me far more distasteful than the fact that Digby and I were separated by more than a generation. The divorce was to be 'amicable'; in other words my mother would be financially recompensed. Whether this would restore her temper, as the prospect of it seemed to do, could have no bearing on my future life. I would be free of her scorn and her disparaging ways, free of what I thought of as my father's indiscretions, and secure, if rather sad, in the knowledge that no more reasonable outcome could have been found to mark a change of status which I was convinced was necessary, both for their sakes and for my own. At the time I did not identify this instinct as fear.

I did not love Digby. What I felt for him was the gratitude that unmarried women in Jane Austen feel for a prospect that might, if fortune favoured them, bring about the sort of resolution considered to be appropriate. At that dormant stage of my life I hardly knew what love was. Digby was an attractive man in his way: I hazily acknowledged the fact that I would not object to his love-making. He was substantial in every respect, and this gave him authority. He was the director of an engineering firm across the river in Battersea. I might have taken note of the fact that I should be entitled to fairly uneventful days on my own when he was at his office. I could give up my job and spend my time largely as I liked. I should always be at home to greet him in the evenings. If I had had a lover I could have fitted him in without difficulty. But I had no thought of this. On the contrary, the attraction of this marriage was its utter seemliness. I was perhaps unduly influenced by my parents' growing hostility to each other, and also by the fact that they had entered with something like grim enthusiasm into the destruction of their marriage. I viewed the flat in Melton Court as a place of sanctuary. Its lack of poetry I could easily accommodate.

What was so nice about Digby was the energy he put into pleasing me. I did not consider the honeymoon in Venice as anything other than a rite of passage: what I liked was the fact that even if I did not wholly appreciate it there would be other holidays, other excursions, so that in time I would be agreeably broken in to a more expansive way of life. He had already suggested Christmas in Seville, a spring holiday in Sicily, anywhere, everywhere, until I was happy. That was the true quality of the man: unforced generosity. And that I did appreciate, for as long as we were married. I like to think, in retrospect, that I never let him down. Even when I compared his thickening frame with the sort of grace I occasionally glimpsed in others, young men whom I passed in the street, even, occasionally in the host of those dinner parties for which I provided the beef Wellington and the chocolate mousse most favoured in those days, it never occurred to me that sexual transgression was within my grasp, and indeed it took some time for this to become evident.

None of this I could say to Betsy, on this or any other occasion, though even at the wedding I had it in mind to wish for a return of our early confidences. I would ask her to tea, in Melton Court, and ask her about her experiences in Paris and her plans for the future, and would not divulge any plans of my own, for I did not have any. I should describe our holidays, as rather boring people do, and see her wide eyes, which had perhaps anticipated revelations, take on a tinge of puzzlement. I would be seen to have left her far behind, as perhaps I had intended to, for I knew that I did not have her sort of courage, the courage to live alone among strangers in a foreign city. She would forgive me for this, but she would regret it. I myself would regret it, perhaps more so than she would. But I would not let her know this. It was the old dichotomy of pride and shame: to let her into my life would be to invite confidences, and that I would not allow.

There was another reason. In that brief meeting at the wedding, when she pressed my hand so joyfully, I noticed something that gave me pause. She looked young, younger than I did in my finery. She was brimming over with all that she longed to tell me, with all the enthusiasm that I should have to eschew. The cause of this, I assumed, was a man, the sort of man I was not marrying, the sort of man one does not, perhaps should not, marry, the sort of man for whom marriage is not even a distant fantasy. I imagined that this was easily accomplished in Paris, for I was unduly influenced by foreign films at the time. I doubted if I could have managed the real thing. I had spent six months in Paris after leaving school, and had not much enjoyed the experience. I had lodged with a Mme Lemonnier in a gloomy flat in the Avenue des Ternes, in the so respectable seventeenth *arrondissement*, far from the excitements I thought of as taking place in the centre of town. Mme Lemonnier, an elderly widow, had no liking for me, nor I for her. She had expected a more lavish contribution than I was able to make, and consequently paid no attention to my comfort or wellbeing. I was expected to spend evenings quietly in my room and to be in bed by nine o'clock, or even earlier, after which time absolute silence would reign until the following morning. I was allowed to make myself coffee in the morning in her Stone Age kitchen, and after that I had to fend for myself. That meant eating out in the evenings, which I loved to do anyway, but rushing back to the flat shortly afterwards in order to beat the curfew. This was agreeable in that I got to know what the French liked to eat, and I made it a point of honour to order something different at every meal. This proved to be far more useful to me than any cookery course, and had the additional virtue of training me in some sort of independence.

This was significant, for another reason. I had not expected to be mobbed by admirers, and became used to existing on my own. I supposed that I bore the rigours of Mme Lemonnier's regime about me like some sort of aura of untouchability, but I also knew, or came to know, that I was not the kind of woman who sent out the right messages. This puzzled and saddened me, but I accepted it. I was quite nice-looking, and I thought I behaved like everybody else, but I began to suspect that women are either instantly recognizable as potential lovers or somehow fail the test in ways so subtle that there seems no possibility of adjustment. The result was that however many times I went to the same restaurant I was not greeted with any show of warmth and was left to eat my meal more or less unattended. I supposed that my habit of concealment made me seem self-sufficient, and my habitual pride enabled me to bear the solitude, to which I became accustomed. I spent my days in markets, learning to recognize what French housewives would buy, and those morning excursions were somehow companionable. '*La carotte est en baisse aujourd'hui, ménagères,*' would shout the stall-holder in the rue de Buci, and in the rue de Passy (for I walked from one end of the city to the other) cheeses exposed their nakedness to the ambient air. In the afternoons I went to the cinema, and studied the sort of passion from which I calculated that I must be excluded by some sort of biological misunderstanding. The hurt I felt was also concealed, but came back to haunt me in moments of discouragement, and has in fact stayed with me ever since.

This was no doubt the reason for my marrying Digby, without questioning the suitability of the arrangement. I knew that he was kind, and that I was more or less prepared to accommodate myself to him: my culinary skills and my untested propriety would, I thought, be adequate for whatever else might be required of me. But when I saw Betsy again, in that brief exchange at the wedding, I knew that she held the secret from which I was apparently disbarred. She had the sort of smile that went directly to the heart; it revealed not only her vulnerability, but her accessibility. I believed, or maybe I wanted to believe, that she was as untested as I was, yet I could see that there was a readiness about her, a propensity to trust, which I did not possess. A man would like her, as well as love her; intimacy would be no problem, for she would appeal to the tenderness, even to the remaining innocence of her partner. And I knew that she would instinctively reject the sort of arrangement I had entered into, in which the lover or husband is a sort of uncle, hearty and kind and protective, and the wife a perpetual niece or ward. Much as I longed to be taken in and sheltered I could see that the first sight of my husband caused Betsy's eyes to widen with a sort of surprise. Pride came to my rescue once again as I waved her towards one of our other friends. I did not much care whether she knew anybody else. I was obscurely assaulted, for the moment, by some of the regret and pity she obviously felt, until I summoned a smile and drank another glass of champagne. 'Careful, dearest,' murmured my husband, but he pressed my hand. He too had noticed what I had noticed, and he felt for me. As I say, he was a man of the utmost generosity.

And I could see from her untarnished gaze that she was still the girl who had declaimed Racine's lines – *'Que le jour recommence, et que le jour finisse/Sans que jamais Titus puisse voir Bérénice'* – and that she would, in the same exalted spirit, accept all love's challenges, and remain just as faithful as if she had committed herself from the moment her eyes had met those of her lover, whoever he was, and however unsuitable he might turn out to be. I could also see that her appeal would be to young men not much older than herself, that she would not suit a man like my husband who, at his age, knew what he was prepared to settle for. Digby would not care to rely on ecstasy as his principal fare. He preferred, as I had come to realize, a settled relationship in a suitable environment. He had been married before, in his thirties; his wife had died giving birth to their child, who had also died. Therefore I was able to concede that he too must be indulged, protected, never again exposed to tragedy or loss. He had, as the French say, assumed, taken it upon himself: he did not refer to those events except to inform me of them. During that exchange his expression had hardened, which warned me that this matter was to remain a secret. So that for ever after we were doomed to be on our guard. He trusted me and I wanted to be worthy of his trust. Whereas the woman that Betsy was, or was destined to be, would share such a secret and would be allowed to do so.

When I had learned that she was to be based in Paris I had given her Mme Lemonnier's address, knowing that she was just the kind of daughterly personality to make this bitter old lady happy. That was another odd thing about Betsy: she had all the daughterly virtues, although she had never in any sense been a daughter. This had not marked her, although it may have left her vulnerable to whatever affection she was offered. She too may have longed to be taken in – perhaps all women share this archaic longing. Given the opportunity she would treasure her position in some sort of hierarchy, some sort of household. This in no way derogated from her disposition as a lover; indeed the one might have enhanced the other. And yet I could see that she would not be suited to the sort of hierarchy I should soon be part of: settled, middle-class, respectable. Her aspirations would be more poetic, her chosen co-ordinates more ideal. She would be ready to embrace a family, but only if every member of that family were beautiful, rare, exceptional, enjoying a status far above the ordinary. Whereas my taciturnity would make me more adaptable, more realistic, able to call on those reserves I had perfected while sitting in those cafés and restaurants or wandering about the city, finding some sort of peace in the indifference of passers-by and the beauty of the material world. As far as I was concerned I was being given an opportunity to share in that world, and throughout that onerous wedding reception I reminded myself rather forcefully of this fact.

And yet whenever I thought of that room in Paris, as I sometimes did, puzzling over the fact that it had given me so little pleasure, I seemed to see Betsy in it, resolutely happy, as she always was, and, knowing that her good faith would at some stage be put at risk, I had an impulse to protect her, or perhaps to wish on her some of my own impermeability. I did not, until a much later stage, question the fact that in my mind's eye it was Betsy who inhabited the room and not myself. I was outside, in the lawless streets, while she, in her quest for a home, had accepted this setting, embracing what was handed on to her without the slightest feeling of discontent or incongruity. She was a romantic, as I was not; she was even a serial romantic. No discouragement could deflect her high hopes, even when it had been demonstrated that these were not appropriate.

I caught up with her again as I was circling the room to say goodbye to my wellwishers. 'How is Mme Lemonnier?' I asked her, attacked by a brief passing nostalgia for Paris where I had learned my lessons of self-sufficiency. Suddenly this absurd setting – the flowers, the dressed-up guests, my mother's high-pitched laughter – seemed intolerable. I longed to get out into the air, preferably by myself, and to take a long walk in the cooling evening.

'Oh, but I'm not there any more, or shan't be in a week's time. I'm moving to the rue Cler.'

'Alone?'

'No. I've met someone, you see. Actually I've known him

for a couple of months. A few of us used to get together to talk about the situation in the universities. There's a lot of that going on at the moment, now that we're looking for a way forward.'

'And this group, I take it, has a leader?'

'Yes, a former teacher. Well, I suppose he still is. He's a philosopher, a communist. Very prestigious, very charismatic. Roland.'

'And is he your friend? The one you're with? In the rue Cler?' This last I hazarded at a venture. It was hardly my business to interrogate her, though she was obviously willing for me to do so.

'My friend, as you so tactfully put it, is Daniel. And yes, we are together.' Her smile grew radiant. 'We might even get married. I'd like you to meet him.'

'Of course. You must bring him to dinner. We'll be back from Venice on the twenty-fifth. You'll give me a call?'

'I'd love to. I have to come to London to put the house up for sale, probably next month. Now that I know I'll be staying in Paris.' The smile seemed destined never to leave her face. 'It's only small, the rue Cler, I mean; really only an attic with a *cabinet de toilette*. But when I've sold the house we can look for something a bit more substantial.'

'You wanted to be an interpreter,' I reminded her. 'Has that all gone by the board? What does Daniel do?'

'He's still a student. He was very active in the protests. He's a year younger than I am.'

And you are twenty-five, I reflected. My age. I felt Digby's hand on the small of my back. 'Time to move on, I think,' he said. Maybe he feared an exchange of confidences.

'Don't forget,' I said, as he steered me away. We had both been dismissed. Girlhood friendships were no longer to be my lot. When I got to the door I looked round and waved to her. She must have been waiting for me to do so, for she raised her hand at exactly the same moment. Then I was moved towards the lift that would take us to our room, and to married life. I gave a thought to the discrepancy that Paris had brought about in our respective lives, and briefly regretted the lack of romance in Digby's veined hand unlocking the door.

'I'd love a cup of tea,' he said. 'I can't stand champagne in the middle of the afternoon.'

'I'll order it,' I said. That was my first attempt to make him comfortable, in what was clearly a relatively uneasy situation. He was tired, and it showed in his face. He looked nearly as old as my father, whom I had not managed to thank for all the fuss. As we drank our tea the strain we both felt slowly dissipated. We had baths, changed into simpler clothes, decided to go out for dinner, and let the rest of the day take care of itself. We were due to catch an early plane the following morning, and would probably appreciate an early night. That was what Digby said. I envisaged a succession of early nights, in which nothing very remarkable would take place. In this I misjudged him, and was pleasantly surprised.

But when I woke briefly in the night, or rather in the early morning, what filled my mental horizon was the image of love in a garret, in the sort of Paris that had not been disclosed to me, or rather that I had been incapable of seeing. This mental Paris was the Paris of those foreign films that had been the main feature of my solitary afternoons. It was those images that returned to me now, with Betsy's face imposed on that of the female lead. And for the next few minutes, or for as long as the scene lasted, I was aware of myself, a spectator, sitting in the audience, while outside the sun shone down on a Paris I had never known.

3

My mother embarked on what promised to be an endless series of cruises and my father decamped to an alternative domestic arrangement in Crouch End. I was left alone with my new husband, whom I continued to find perfectly agreeable though in some ways disconcerting. Given his age he was rather more old-fashioned than I was, and proved to be fussy about his personal comfort, seeming to view his wife largely as an adjunct to what was already a well-regulated life, his business taking priority over everything else. I had had a foretaste of this in Venice. Sitting on the steps of the Redentore while Digby took a nap in the hotel, I told myself that I was free to make plans of my own in the fairly long intervals when he was absent, either physically or mentally, but I had no clear idea what these might be. Reading the papers I could not help but be aware of the enormous strides women were making; they were vocal and radical in a way I knew I could never be, but there was a discontent, even among the most liberated, that I felt summoned to share. I was still young, young enough to wish for something fiercer than the life for which I had settled, or to which I had succumbed.

The attractions that this marriage had offered did not fade, but they receded. When Digby came home in the evenings he was tired (he seemed to me inordinately tired) and given to airing his business concerns. 'But you don't want to hear about this,' he would say. 'Tell me about your day. What have you been doing?' Or he would ask me whether I would prefer

Paris or Rome for a spring break. I respected his attempts to entertain me and summoned up an enthusiasm I did not feel. Or he would suggest a dinner party, again of an old-fashioned type, to which the same people always came, friends of his with whom I strove to find something in common. These people, the Johnsons, the Fairlies, seemed to know more about my husband than I did. They never failed to congratulate me on my cooking, and then picked up the conversation where it had left off during my absence in the kitchen. My role was a subordinate one. Fortunately my reserves of silence were sufficient to enable me to repress any awareness of boredom. But it was there: I felt it, and I knew that I must be on my guard.

In the daytime, when Digby was at his office, I walked, though I hardly saw my surroundings, those dull almost handsome streets and squares, where I might encounter a neighbour, on the same shopping expedition designed to furnish a quiet afternoon. After an unexpectedly radiant February the weather had turned cold and cloudy; there was no pleasure in these walks but they were my harmless way of damping down any incipient dissatisfaction that I might have felt. I was aware of the paradigm shift between my life in Paris and my life in London which might prove to be as uneventful in the future as it was in the present. In Paris, despite the solitude, I had been aware of my strengths: I had been mature then in a way that now threatened to desert me. In my empty stoical days, knowing myself to be excluded from more strenuous pleasures, I had at least formed a notion of how life might be, whether or not I managed to negotiate some sort of admission to it. I had been unawakened but incurious, thinking it better to concentrate my attention on the display at a flower stall or the smells of coffee and wine issuing from a café. There was a democratic illusion of participation that I could no longer find in my new surroundings, which were, after all, not so very new. In fact part of the problem may have had to do with a sense of having been returned to the scenes of my childhood and adolescence after a brief foray into adulthood. For the sense of exile I had experienced in Paris had a maturity about it which I had begun to recognize at the time: perhaps adulthood is a sense of exile, or rather that in exile we are obliged to act as adults.

Here in London, wandering by the river in a cold wind, and knowing that my time was my own until my husband returned and asked me what was for dinner, I could no longer summon any enthusiasm for my preparations, though these were as careful as ever. Throughout that spring I settled into a sort of benign numbness which I took to be contentment, or rather which I willed on myself. I too began to work up an enthusiasm for distant places, and presented Digby with travel brochures and books from the library which illustrated the beauties of Apulia or Turkey or Corfu. These served as conversational fare, and vague plans were made to visit all or any of these places. At the same time, as soon as the table had been cleared, I knew that Digby would take the evening paper into the other room, switch on the television, and fall asleep. He slept heavily, more heavily than I did, and seemed unable to invest any energy into keeping awake. I was careful not to disturb him; I laid aside the travel brochures and picked up a novel, *Vanity Fair* or *The Professor*. I thought that I might seek out a few evening classes, educate myself in something like the Victorian novel. Those I had read were a source of endless fascination. How brave the female characters were! How noble or resolute the men! I told myself that that was why novels were written, to give ordinary men and women a better idea of themselves, and, more important, to show how fate might take a hand even when the given circumstances appeared to militate against a significant outcome. On my walks I had noticed a school building which advertised some sort of programme of tuition for adults, and I had even lingered by the school gates, suddenly homesick for a much earlier time. To be part of an attentive group once again seemed to promise companionship of a kind in which I knew myself to be lacking. If this were regression I did not much care. It would be part of the general regression signified by my obedient childlike wifeliness. Even I knew that the submissiveness of those Victorian heroines had nothing to do with weakness; on the contrary they were fearless, those women, as perhaps I had once been, even in Paris, where there was no one to mark my heroism. There was a lesson there for me. I mentioned the idea of evening classes to Digby, but he demurred. 'I like to see you here when I get home,' he said. 'I look forward to it all the afternoon.'

It was true that he was an attentive husband. I was not able at the time to evaluate the limits of normal attentiveness before it spilled over into watchfulness. He needed to know where I was at all times of the day; I knew that even if I achieved his permission to attend evening classes he would insist on driving me to the school and no doubt be waiting for me afterwards. He did not quite believe me when I told him that I had spent the afternoon walking, and once I had even caught sight of the car which must have been following me. Though I did not know this at the time, there were moves at the office to demote him from his present functions and to make him some sort of honorary chairman. This enabled him to spend hours away from his desk, so that on certain afternoons we might even have been circling one another on our solitary excursions. When I became aware of this it struck me as exceedingly odd, even bizarre, but I gave no sign that I had noticed this behaviour. I knew that he was conscious of the discrepancy in our ages, that he feared and distrusted all the feminist propaganda which was so widespread at the time, and that in an unacknowledged part of his mind he even feared that I might seek pleasure elsewhere and betray him. I think that is what men most fear: betrayal. Therefore I made no mention of the fact that I had seen the car, merely welcomed him when he came home in the evening after what might have been a normal day. For we both maintained the fiction that he was returning from the office just like any other husband. I got used to this, but it made me uncomfortable.

He loved me. That was what had always impressed me. He loved me rather too much, in ways I could hardly accommodate. He was occasionally impotent, which increased his vigilance. Neither of us alluded to this; I knew that any such allusion would be a mortal affront to my husband, whose ardour was growing more desperate. Our nights, in that dark bedroom, were often silent, though not restful. I assumed that Digby had known physical passion for his first wife, had maybe not envisaged a resumption of it, but had substituted some form of ideal domesticity as a realistic alternative. He made occasional attempts to appear younger than his age, which was the age of retirement for most pursuits, and then gave up, and took a certain pleasure in giving up, disappearing with his newspaper, watching television until he dozed off, while I resignedly read my book and began to awaken to a sense of bewilderment, of dissatisfaction, even of resentment. Only in two different circumstances did Digby reveal a more interesting side to his nature. One was his attitude at our usual monthly dinner parties with the Johnsons, the Fairlies, when he would be genial, hospitable, generally admirable. The other, unfortunately, was in the course of those secret afternoons, when, out of the corner of my eye, I could see the car disappearing round a corner as I approached from the other end of a quiet street, with no sign of greeting or of recognition from either of us. This was Digby's hidden self, compounded of anxiety and suspicion. He seemed to be preparing himself for my eventual desertion. In this he was more prescient than I was. I never did desert him, but I think the idea was in his mind most urgently as we circled each other in the unsuspecting afternoons. His only reference to these activities was oblique and neutral. 'I don't want you to feel lonely when I'm at the office,' he would say, as if he had verified my solitude, seen it with his own eyes. 'Why don't you ask a friend round? One of your old friends?' I knew he meant safe schoolgirl friends. 'It would be company for you.'

But I had no friends. My neighbours in Melton Court were stately large-bosomed widows, or so they seemed to me; there was no possibility of my inventing a friendship with any of them. Nor were the Johnsons and the Fairlies any more approachable, though Digby thought them suitable companions for me. They were his friends. He had been at school with Alan Johnson, while Fairlie was his broker. Their unliberated wives were largely silent; they had learned their place. Margaret Johnson was always kind to me, complimenting me on the poached salmon or the navarin of lamb, and I responded to her kindness in a numb fashion, having no chance to respond in any other way. Constance Fairlie was rather different, and, I suspected, not kind at all. Small, dark, and sardonic, she was tacitly given permission to interrupt her husband, to demand attention, to wait with a cigarette between her long fingers until he lit it for her, and to view me with an amused insistence which seemed to me to hold little indulgence. I may have had hopes of the Fairlies, largely on account of their Victorian names, Constance and Edmund, which I thought sufficient pretext for a discussion of *Middlemarch* or *Pendennis*, but when I ventured a perhaps too hopeful introductory remark to this effect no notice was taken of it and I was made to feel foolish. Constance Fairlie considered me lazily through the smoke of her cigarette before informing her husband that they must not be late. She was rude, with the rudeness of a moneyed woman who was wealthier than her husband. Even though I was, I thought, better-looking, and with no stain on my conscience apart from that unhappy marital secrecy to which I should never refer, I felt diminished by comparison and more than ever conscious of my subordinate status. It occurred to me that she was fortunate in having Edmund for a husband, for even in my dormant state I could see that he was attractive. On one of these occasions I stole a longer look at him and conceded that he was almost handsome. But my gaze was objective, dispassionate. Surveying the wreck of the table as my guests moved into the drawing-room for coffee I concluded that the evening had gone well, as always, but that I still had no friends, more, that I was actively lonely, but so well trained that I gave no sign of this and at times was hardly aware of it myself.

For these different reasons I was extremely receptive to Betsy's voice on the telephone the following morning. She was in London to sell the house, she told me, and she was not alone. That was how she always put it: 'I am not alone.' Daniel was with her, and she would love me to meet him. Of course, I said: why not bring him round to tea this afternoon? By the way, what is his name? I've only heard you call him Daniel. Saint-Jorre, she said. Daniel de Saint-Jorre. We'll see you this afternoon. I'm so looking forward to it.

Great physical beauty is extremely rare. In those days, the days of which I speak, men were divided into the young and the no longer young. Now the middle-aged are spurred on to greater acts of youthfulness, as if the depredations of age could for that reason have no purchase on them. But Saint-Jorre was truly young, in a fashion that called into question any other category. And he was beautiful, with a lithe mythical beauty that brought to mind certain classical statues seen in reproduction, as if only now was I face to face with the real thing. If he lacked true classical qualities it was because he was never in repose. After greeting me, rather perfunctorily, I thought, he sat down for only a few minutes before getting to his feet again and roaming round the room while Betsy explained their plans, or perhaps her plans: she was selling the house, they were staying temporarily in the rue Cler until they were able to find something big enough for the comrades to gather every evening in pursuit of their nebulous ideals. I tried to get her to elucidate these ideals, and she may have done so, but I was too distracted to understand them, or perhaps she no longer understood them herself. Saint-Jorre was restlessly on his feet, and humming under his breath. 'Do sit down,' I said, exasperated. He ignored me. 'You have all this space?' he asked incredulously. 'For the two of you?' I saw nothing wrong with this. Of course he was a communist, or something like it. I pointed this out to him. A Marxist, he corrected me. And what does that entail, I asked him. 'Structures,' he replied. 'New structures. Long overdue. Don't you agree?' His tone was obdurate, as was his expression. I realized that I was not worth bothering about, not even worth converting. He obviously considered himself a leader of a sort, as his looks proclaimed him to be. It was clear to me that he had no thought of earning a living in a humdrum way, as my husband did, as everyone else did. He was the movement, the *Zeitgeist*, powered by the intoxication of recent events. This was in the 1970s, when those events were receding into the background. No doubt the money Betsy received from the sale of her house would solve immediate problems of subsistence. And no doubt she would find other ways of securing his wellbeing if and when that money ran out. As I was beginning to perceive, one pays a high price for a man as prestigious as he so clearly was.

Nevertheless I found him repellent. His activity, his humming deprived him of ordinary accessibility and removed any possibility of normal exchange of the kind practised in the circles in which I moved. I doubted, in fact, that he himself was normal. It seemed to me that for all his resplendent appearance he would not have much use for normal love or sex, for his energies appeared to be concentrated on achieving some impossible Utopian goal which might conceivably benefit the many, or at least those like himself, rather than any one particular person. And if he loved Betsy, which I had no reason to doubt, it would be as an adjunct to his wishes, ready to throw in her lot with him, less for love than for reasons of solidarity, even political solidarity. Much as I was able to admire him – but in the abstract, almost as a work of art – and to understand what that lithe frame, those effortless movements might inspire in a woman, I did not think that he would respond in the same way to that woman's own attractions, and that his volatility would militate against the sort of exclusive closeness that would be a woman's own wish. I even had time to congratulate myself on my own situation, which, in a way, I had contrived: my own will had not been subverted by a dangerous attachment of the kind to which Betsy had so willingly succumbed. We had both been born too soon for the freedoms currently claimed by women; we had assumed, perhaps wrongly, that safety lay in stability, that love and desire could have only one true end: marriage, and no doubt children. That this certainty was being attacked from all sides had not yet taken us over, changing us from what we had been and were still destined to be. We were innocent, like girls at school, waiting patiently for fulfilment, which would come to us in the guise of another person, and not a series of more or less random persons who might or might not have our wellbeing at heart.

My own marriage, with its tediums, and the solitude it inevitably brought in its wake, had given me one inestimable gift: the assurance of affection. I knew that Digby would never be unfaithful, would never torment me. In a sense I had the upper hand, though I had never desired this. I had wanted what my mother had assured me was priceless: fidelity. I reminded myself of this from time to time, when I was particularly bored; there would be no unpleasant revelations. Yet I knew that women of my age were in revolt against their mothers, that it was their mothers, and not men, who were the enemy. I was even grateful that my mother was, so to speak, off the map, for her sceptical discontented attitude might have found more faults in my situation than I was willing to do. I had vivid memories of my unresolved life in Paris and the time I had to fill there, knowing that this was not the destiny of a young person, but honing my skills to endure the lack of success that I already knew was to be my lot. I had achieved the kind of stasis that my situation demanded, and if I ever again wandered haplessly through uninhabited afternoons I should do so by my own decree, and with the assurance that I could at any time call upon the sort of companionship that would assure me dignity if nothing else.

Betsy was watching her lover with anxious eyes, as if she were his mother or his nurse. She was willing him to give a good account of himself, for to her I still represented a settled way of life, even a place in society that had been denied her. She could see that the afternoon was not going well: how could she not? Daniel made no effort to play his part, indeed made it quite clear that his part lay elsewhere, on those barricades that existed in his own mind and in the minds of others similarly convinced. I was all too clearly on the wrong side of the barricades, a bourgeoise, a member of a despised and obsolete class. He sat flung back in his chair, his teacup negligently clasped between his thumb and forefinger. I offered him a cigarette, from the silver box that I had been used to seeing at my mother's elbow; he refused the cigarette, but examined the box, as if appraising it for its monetary value. He was so extremely unaccommodating that I could only register this as a fact of nature, or of upbringing; his origins were a mystery to me, as was his formation. There seemed to be no way in which I could bring him into the conversation, or such conversation as Betsy and I were able to sustain. 'Would you like some more tea?' I asked him. 'Tea?' he said, surprised. 'No, no tea.' He stood up, ready to leave. 'Yes,' said Betsy. 'It's time we were making a move. You must come and see us in Paris.' Her tone was worldly, as if this invitation might hold some reality. We both knew that we might not see each other again.

She took his arm, and at last he broke into a smile. The smile transformed him, so that I could understand the bond between them. They found each other's hands, and, so joined, proceeded towards the door which I held open for them. Betsy turned to me with a smile that held a certain fatigue. I thought she must have grown thinner; either that or her eyes were wide, too wide, as if she were contemplating a great difficulty. She was faultlessly dressed; her hair was immaculate. She was becoming transformed into one of those Parisian women whose look of exigence, of stress, merely adds to their allure, and announces their readiness to deal with any possible criticism, if anyone were rash enough to offer it. Any difference of opinion would be dealt with combatively; I had witnessed this too many times to expect anything different. And I could see that Betsy would soon acquire this manner, if and when she were called upon to defend her lover, in whom hostile witnesses, such as myself, could see only idleness, wilfulness, a sort of innocent savagery, like that of an infant whose own wishes must be imposed on his surroundings. Yet as he turned to her he gave her a look of love to which she so naturally responded that I was left in no doubt that this was a genuine love affair, even if in my eyes it had little to recommend it beyond the fact that it seemed to have come about naturally, and that it therefore had nature on its side.

As I cleared away the cups and saucers (and I seemed always to be clearing things away in what was after all my own home) I wondered whether I should ever be able to attach myself to a man who promised little more than youth and beauty, and decided that I was too staid in temperament ever to conceive of such an arrangement. Yet the afternoon had saddened me: it is a terrible thing to lose a friend, and it was clear that I had lost Betsy, or rather that we had lost each other. I told myself that I could bear this, as I had learned to bear other absences in my life, passion, joy, rapture, escape from the destiny I had sought and had congratulated myself on attaining. I wandered into the bedroom and contemplated it for a moment. Then I shook my head, as if to dismiss unseemly thoughts, thoughts which visited me when I was low-spirited. I decided to write

Betsy a note, suggesting that we meet, just the two of us. I hoped that this might restore something of our previous friendship. If such a meeting took place I should not mention Daniel. I did not want to question her or to learn any more about him. To be an accessory to another woman's love affair is an invidious position, and I had no intention of becoming such an accessory, however much Betsy might wish me to become one.

I ran a bath, washed my hair, put the disruptive afternoon out of my mind. We were to dine with the Fairlies, in their rather grand house overlooking the river. This was the sort of entertainment I was used to, and it was very different from the sort of love in a garret which I imagined reserved for the happy few. The evening would be ponderous, and I might question my own tolerance of such ceremonies. And so it proved. I studied Constance Fairlie with some perplexity, as if newly open to her barely concealed malice. Edmund Fairlie saw my glance, and I turned to meet his eyes with a deprecating smile, as if to excuse myself. Digby's eyes were watering slightly in the effort to keep awake. Then it was time to leave. Edmund Fairlie helped me into my coat, then stood watching me as I held the collar protectively to my face. That instant proved to me that it was not the first, almost unemotional, sighting of a potential lover that was significant, but the second, the moment not of recognition but of confirmation, so that every other consideration is irrelevant, as if it might have mattered at some point in the past but no longer had any currency in the charged wordless exchange that seals the matter for ever, regardless of the dangers thus incurred and whatever the cost.

4

I descended into clandestinity with a gratitude, a relief, and an open-heartedness of which I had not previously thought myself capable. It was another paradigm shift, a change from one category to another, from the obedience I had once observed to something like a lawlessness which I found altogether more natural. I had a reason for getting up in the morning other than to make coffee, to pour orange juice, and to grill the bacon on which Digby insisted and which I had always found repulsive. All day I performed domestic tasks uncomplainingly, knowing that the days were a mere preparation for the evenings, when I should see my lover. I told Digby that I had found an evening class, a fact which he found mildly annoying but which he did not seek to check. Had he done so he would have discovered that these classes met at seven o'clock and finished at nine, and that they had moreover come to an end at the beginning of the summer, when the city began to empty and the students to disperse. From time to time I even regretted these notional classes, only to delight when the stately periods of the Victorian novel, which I still read, gave way to the crudest of language in the course of those evenings to which I now devoted my life.

I covered my tracks by leaving Digby's meal in the oven, having instructed him by telephone how to heat it up, and by assuring him that a friend would give me a lift home after the class. At first he demurred at this, but my expression was so innocent and so convincing that he believed me. My one cause for concern was that I might see the car, either following me or coming to meet me, but as I was in a part of the neighbourhood quite removed from the school in which the evening classes were held I thought I was safe. And, surprisingly, I was: I was protected by a new-found gambler's insouciance which was in itself a comment on the laborious good behaviour which I had exchanged for a fulfilment that I knew to be my birthright.

It hardly disturbed me that I was unfaithful to my husband or that Edmund was unfaithful to his wife. With eyes and senses newly sharpened I more or less knew that he made a habit of this, that he thought such adventures a legitimate part of a man's life. Why else did he keep a rented flat for this particular purpose? I was never so deluded as to imagine that I was the first woman to visit this flat or even that I should be the last. It was enough to know that I had rights of admission, and that for one or two evenings a week, sometimes fewer, and never at the weekends, I should meet him there, should linger after he had gone home, and luxuriate in the knowledge that our intimacy was a secret enshrined in this place, which, as far as I knew, had not yet been discovered by any third or fourth party. The day he gave me a key to the flat was the happiest of my life.

I knew very little about him. I knew that he was a welcome ten years younger than my husband. I knew that he had three children, twin girls, Julia and Isabella, and a boy, David, and that he was devoted to them. When he spoke of them, which was frequently, I felt a mild unease, a wistfulness which I tried to ignore. I was stoical enough to look the situation in the face, and at no point was I tactless enough to ask him if he loved me. His attitude was simple: his sexual confidence demanded that he employ that confidence in the most natural way. He was a man of pleasure, and I was a means of ensuring that pleasure. Nor did he give much time to rationalizing his behaviour, or indeed my own. 'Incredible,' was all he said. 'One never suspects . . . That, of course, is part of the fun.' 'Fun' was the only false note; it was the wrong word to describe what I was feeling. Maybe it did not adequately describe what he himself was feeling, but we did not talk about that. Our attachment was at its best when it was wordless. Fortunately, given the limited time at our disposal, it usually was.

I loved him, while never completely suppressing the knowledge that love was something quite different, that it was steadiness, constancy, familiarity, even availability. But I dismissed this knowledge, as I had to. I had only to watch the expression on his healthy face, see his eyes widen appreciatively, to acknowledge that what I had, or rather what I was given, was enough. I no longer thought in terms of lifelong allegiance. I thought of his strength and what I now perceived as his beauty. He was tall and fair, with a slightly heavy build, the sort of man one sees jogging in the early morning and to whom one pays little attention. Now I understood the message of such exercise: it was an element of courtship, a desire to remain attractive and fit for the main business of life. Edmund put in an hour of such punishing exercise before beginning his normal working day. This was one of the few facts I knew about his life. His wife I managed to forget for most of the time. Fortunately the dinner parties were in abeyance: Constance and the children were in the habit of spending the school holidays at their house in Hampshire, where Edmund joined them at weekends. Digby had more or less given up trying to tempt me with holidays abroad. I think he thought my new-found contentment an appreciation of our life as it was. In any event he was tired, more tired than he had been at the outset of our life together, and may have been slightly relieved not to have to make further efforts to entertain me. To his tiredness I owed the relative safety of my evenings. Perhaps he was grateful for my absence, though I could never quite rid myself of the need to choose unfamiliar streets, to take unnecessary diversions, so that I was in no danger of being sighted from the car, or, worse, being subject to that stealthy and unacknowledged surveillance which had so puzzled and alarmed me and which now, thankfully, seemed to be at an end.

The days took on a charmed quality. I would leave Melton Court when the sun was at its height, just after three. It seemed appropriate that these matters were taking place in the summer, in those long light days when nature adds its energy to one's own feeling of wellbeing. Edmund's flat was in a small street bounded on one side by a public garden, where I would spend the afternoon, almost innocently, with a book. There was a church, to which I turned my back, as I might not have done at an earlier stage in my life, for I knew that Dickens had married there. When the children appeared, at an hour when they were allowed to make a last use of the climbing frame in the play area, when the tired mothers wheeled their babies home after collecting them from the childminder, I would get up, put away my book, and cross the garden to the flat in Britten Street, let myself in with my key, and wait for Edmund, who would join me shortly after five. Our time together was brief, too brief, for he always tele-phoned his family, or was telephoned by his wife in the country at the same time every evening. He was frequently invited out to dinner: friends took pity on him for being left in town. I think that our evenings together held some poetry for him.

I was careful never to let him see my rapture, except in one particular circumstance; my former secrecy reasserted itself for my protection, and for his. I knew that he must not be exposed to the depth of my feeling for him, for that would spoil the 'fun', and he relied on me to accept this particular bargain. Thus he did not know that when he left I would wander round the flat, take a shower, fantasize briefly about a possible future life with him, and then slowly make my way home to my dozing husband, the television still on, the newspaper discarded by his side. He would rouse himself as sounds came from the kitchen where I would wash up after his meal, and hastily eat some bread and cheese. 'You must ask that friend of yours in,' he once said. 'It's good of her to give you a lift.' I made noises of agreement. Even I knew, even then, that there are some limits to duplicity.

I felt surprisingly little guilt; shame, perhaps, yes, almost certainly shame, when I looked at my husband's sleeping face and even at his ungainly aspect as he sat slumped in his chair, oblivious to the television blaring out its multicoloured attractions. But what I mostly felt was energy, and it was true that I was never tired. I identified with the young people I passed in the street, bare-armed, bare-legged in the beautiful summer light, rather than the slow-moving and so respectable women issuing from flats like mine at an hour when I had already done my hasty shopping and was willing to sacrifice the rest of the morning to the preparation of Digby's dinner. He complained that the casseroles I left in the oven for him were too heavy, that they gave him indigestion, but what little conscience I had left was appeased by the care I put into the composition of those meals, as if they would count in my favour at some hazy moral tribunal which might or might not take place. I was not sure about this, although it seemed likely that at some point a reckoning would be demanded of me by a higher power, albeit one with which I had long since ceased communication.

At other times I felt distressed when pierced by a shaft of unwelcome insight, for I knew that Digby was in many ways superior to Edmund, even knew that Edmund was a worldly character, aware of his entitlements and indifferent to any form of censure. His handsome appearance and attributes had in some fashion secured him permission to act as he pleased; this too seemed to me to be a law of nature. And he had after all not put anyone in jeopardy: his children were healthy, his position in life assured, his wife apparently complaisant. On this last point I chose not to ask questions, either of myself or of Edmund, who would, I knew, frown at what he would consider a breach of etiquette. At that same moral tribunal I would be obliged to acknowledge that her cynicism, her disabused indolence, might have been earned the hard way, that it was entirely possible that she knew everything, that the two of them were parties to an arrangement that I could hardly understand. I was relatively inexperienced, and remarkably stupid for my age. I was in fact older than those girls I passed in the street, but too young to identify with those other women with their shopping baskets and their no doubt spotless consciences. I was too busy living in the present, making my own calculations of occupation and urgency before setting out for Britten Street and the exalted time I was able to spend in the garden, as a prelude to the evening's fulfilment.

Therefore it was with a feeling of supreme annoyance, as if my movements had been unnaturally checked, that I was waylaid on the stairs to my own flat by Mrs Crook, whose invitation to coffee I could hardly refuse. It was after all eleven o'clock in the morning, and I had time to roast the chicken which I would leave for Digby. Yet I felt hampered and distracted by the invitation, and followed her unwillingly into her flat which was a mirror image of our own. I felt that my safety depended on my keeping my distance from this kind of woman, from the species of which Mrs Crook was an outstanding representative.

'One hardly sees you these days,' she said. 'Not that one ever saw much of you. Such a private little person.' This last remark was faintly disparaging, as if she had decided that private little persons were not qualified to provide much in the way of interest for persons such as herself, whose company she thought worthy of greater deference than I was likely to offer. Meekly I took my seat in her overstuffed drawing-room, while she occupied herself with the coffee (which I knew would be too weak) in the kitchen. I calculated that I had half an hour before I could be back at home to take Edmund's telephone call informing me of his own movements and of his availability that evening. He was not always free; demands on his time were numerous, and he sometimes had to see a client after work. This hardly mattered; though I was disappointed when we were not able to meet, the call reassured me that the connection was still secure, and I knew that his voice would power me for the rest of the day. I might go to the flat in any case: those afternoons in the garden were now a part of my life, perhaps the part I most treasured. They had an enchantment, a stillness of their own after the adjustments of the morning. They constituted a time in which I was free to contemplate my emerging and authentic self, a self which had been obscured by the years of careful living which I could now see for what they had been: erroneous, fallacious, and with a stifling quality I was ready to condemn unreservedly.

Mrs Crook settled herself in her chair and prepared to give

me her full attention, or rather prepared to let me give my full attention to the honour of this summons. She was eighty years old, an age which I was not inclined to contemplate. Large, slow, and formidable, she was something of a presence in the building. Few people found her sympathetic but all paid her a certain amount of respect, owing largely to her unshakeable conviction of her own importance. She was, like most of her kind, a widow, who probably spent lonely days but was careful to disguise any loneliness she might have felt and to dismiss the activities of others as unimportant. She had travelled widely with the second of her two husbands, and for a time, in the early days of my marriage, had queried me about our holiday arrangements: had we managed to find the hotel she had recommended, and if so had we remembered to give her best wishes to the proprietor? Remarks such as these had furnished what conversation we were obliged to have. My husband thought her admirable, as he did anything of a settled and recognizable nature, but I perceived a curiosity in her that I did little to encourage. My reluctance had been noted. She was not disposed in my favour.

'And how are you getting on?' she now said. 'Still going to those classes of yours?' This was dangerous ground. 'Not that I suppose I should understand a word of them,' she continued. 'I don't understand much of what is going on these days. The world has changed so much.'

I agreed. I recognized this for the rhetorical performance it was likely to be, and prepared to give her twenty minutes at the outside before making my escape.

'What has happened to manners?' she demanded, without waiting for an answer. 'Tradition? Standards? All those dreadful women clamouring to be heard, making fools of themselves. What has happened to morality?'

'I suppose certain changes are inevitable,' I felt emboldened to reply. 'More women working . . .'

'That's another thing. In my day women were looked after by men. I never saw any reason to quarrel with that. My mind was as good as my husbands'. Yet I would never have dreamed of protesting, of arguing with them, of demanding more than my due.'

'I think that women want more than that,' I said. I was playing into her hands.

'And what good will that do them? They will find out too late, when all the men have deserted them. I despair of my sex,' she said, with a complacent little laugh. 'Not that I have anything in common with this new breed. Women knew how to behave when I was young. Oh, do you take sugar? It's in the kitchen, would you be kind enough . . . ? You know where it is.'

On the kitchen table I saw the pitiable results of her morning's purchases: biscuits, a sponge cake, a small loaf, tea bags, instant coffee, a packet of ham, and a small oozing bag of tomatoes. Not enough there to give one an appetite for life, and yet she seemed vigorous enough, with a monstrous vigour that enabled her to condemn anything of which she did not approve. I could envisage her frugal lunch: a slice of ham and a tomato, washed down with more of the horrible coffee. She probably still had a few cronies, would venture out again in the afternoon to see one or other of them, would rely on an invitation to dinner which would satisfy her nutritional requirements until the following day. She retired early; we could hear her radio booming through the bedroom wall. At some point she would fall asleep until the sound roused her. Then we would hear her make her way to the kitchen for a cup of tea. Her irregular progress was audible until she settled down again, round about midnight. The thought of her life filled me with horror. I did not intend ever to become like her.

'At least you look after Digby properly,' she said, as I returned with the sugar. She took a proprietorial interest in my husband, as she would do with all men, asserting her rights as an unreconstructed woman of the old school. 'I dare say your mother brought you up properly. One can always tell. These women (that is to say, all women unlike herself) don't seem to have had that advantage. As for the young . . .' She lifted both hands in a helpless little gesture which nevertheless implied a wealth of condemnation. 'Not that you're all that young. But you seem to have settled down quite well.'

This was calculated to bring me out, as she would no doubt have put it. But it seemed that I was not of sufficient interest to engage her attention further. Either that or she was bored. She was certainly disappointed. My reticence was a sign that I was of negligible quality, unworthy of any sort of husband, let alone the one with whom she had exchanged playful comments before I had been imported on to the scene. Though I had occupied that scene for some time she seemed to view me as temporary, rather like a servant who might not shape up to the job. She was unaware that her dislike of me was quite plain. I was equally aware that she must never discover the reasons for it. For somewhere, at some undisturbed level of her brain, she recognized sexual activity on my part, though she might not identify it as the most significant of the differences between us. And I was not paying her homage. At a very deep level, even deeper than the first, she made the connection between the presence of the one and the absence of the other.

'Mrs Crook, you must excuse me,' I said, getting to my feet.

'This has been delightful.' I did not return the invitation. Instead I offered to shop for her on my morning outings. This may have been a kind offer, but it was not a genuine one. I was anxious to leave, but was aware that I should have to make some concessions to the spirit of the occasion. She viewed me with a marked lack of indulgence. In my imagination I could hear my telephone ringing unanswered.

The incident had unsettled me. I had been brought face to face with an unwelcome phenomenon, the prospect of a woman from whom emotional sustenance had been removed and who had settled for viciousness as a comforting substitute. Her flat had been filled with that particular miasma, and everything in it – the wheezing cushions into which she had sunk, the uncared-for kitchen, deemed fit occupation for a notional domestic, even the lowly shopping – had all signified an absence which she had tried to fill with her lofty observations about the decline of standards. That these were somehow directed against myself, still technically blameless, had not deceived me, though they may have deceived Mrs Crook. Sooner or later my secret would be uncovered, not by my husband but by the likes of Mrs Crook and her jealous perceptions. I feared the power of women, though I was one myself. The only harmless woman I knew was Betsy, whom I suddenly, acutely missed. Not that it would have done to have Betsy as a witness; she would not have understood the dreadful attraction that bound me to Edmund. For Betsy love was only admissible if it were poetic, a redeeming feature informed by the highest emotion. Her own love affair was, like all her endeavours, largely a matter of aspiration. There was no possibility of my sharing my thoughts with Betsy, although I should have liked to discuss my situation with another woman, a woman essentially uncorrupted, who might not understand but whose sympathy would be guaranteed by that very transparency which would honour my confession (for confession it would be), with all the natural simplicity she had managed to retain. She would no doubt do her best to dignify it with the appropriate classical quotation, out of loyalty, out of a desire to reconnect with matters so evidently absent from my own preoccupations. Or would my preoccupations more properly be identified as obsessions? My own nature must have held dark secrets, which were dark only because they were not shared. In the course of those evenings with Edmund all conscience dissolved and I possessed a conviction that I was acting in accordance with my true nature. In the intervals I was conscious of a fall from grace which I was obliged to register, though to condemn it seemed not to be within my power.

In the kitchen the air vibrated as if the phone had just stopped ringing. I had missed his call, and it was Thursday; on Friday he would join his family in the country and I should not see him until the following week. I dreaded the weekends, which were filled with subterfuges of the kind designed to uphold my stance as a loyal wife. I should be deprived of my afternoons in the garden, watching the children until they went home for their tea, waiting – and this was the only circumstance in which waiting could be counted a pleasure – for the time when I would slip my key in the door and will my waiting to end. The arrangement no longer seemed questionable to me, nor did the fact that Edmund had designed it, initially, for others, for anyone who might willingly join him there, become a partner in the kind of deception I had embraced. I had a moment of fear: was he therefore entirely cynical in his approach to me? This I dismissed: I had met his glance and sustained it, besides which there could be no other truth. Before I knew him I would no doubt have expressed disapproval of a man who kept such an establishment. Now in an odd way I approved of it as an indication of a man's sexual entrepreneurship. And the benefit was all mine. Nevertheless I was obliged to recognize the changes it had brought about in my own nature. For instance I no longer dreamed. My dream life, which had been vivid, had been cancelled by the vividness of events. If I dreamed at all it was in the daytime, sitting in that garden. Nor did I read as much as formerly, though my mind was still obstinately stuffed with Victorian prototypes. This had been kindly looked upon by my husband as a harmless quirk which did me credit. My attempts to introduce such subjects as I thought interesting at our dinner parties must have made me seem awkward, tiresome. I blushed now in retrospect at what must have been tolerance on the part of our guests.

I surveyed the flat, which had been Digby's flat, and there-fore part of my mother's plan for my future when our house in Bourne Street was put on the market. Despite her worldly opinions she was as unreconstructed as Mrs Crook, believing that a woman's principal need was to be looked after by a man. I accepted the dull flat for what it was, a no doubt enviable property to which, in some unimaginable future, I should not lay claim. At that time, and that could only be when Digby died, I should leave and go somewhere else, perhaps back to Paris, where my former morose habits would reassert themselves. This prospect no longer frightened me. I had been given a certificate of viability, and it would guarantee my future. I knew that, in comparison with Edmund, I had few assets of my own. This was the one factor that seriously divided us. Sometimes I felt poor when I was with him, and this was a genuine shadow on my happiness. I doubted whether this aspect of the affair was apparent to him, or, if it was, whether it would have made any difference to my status.

I could not spend the rest of this disappointing day indoors. I decided to take a book and go to the garden, out of loyalty, out of longing, not out of exasperation. Instead I went to a café round the corner and ate a full English breakfast in the guise of lunch, swallowing every greasy mouthful with something like genuine enthusiasm. This was another change in my behaviour, a preference for gross and speedy satisfactions. Uncomfortably full, I walked to the garden and chose a seat from which I could no longer see the windows of the flat. But I was restless; without the prospect of seeing Edmund I was reduced to pure vagrancy. Finally I went home, roasted the chicken, peeled the potatoes, washed the salad, and sat down to wait not for my lover but for my husband. That husband was agreeably surprised to find me sitting in my usual chair, with an open book in my hands.

'No class tonight?' he asked.

'Cancelled,' I replied.

After we had eaten he went into the other room as usual, and switched on the television. When I joined him I found him asleep, a scene of passion beaming out unnoticed. When two characters joined in a violent embrace I switched it off.

'I was watching that,' Digby protested mildly.

'No, you weren't. Your eyes were closed.'

'Oh, I knew what was going on anyway. One always does.'

I looked at him uncertainly. But there was nothing in his mild gaze to give me pause, and after a few minutes I went to bed, his remark dying quietly on the night air.

5

If I had learned anything it was that the highest virtue –
honour, dignity – can be subverted or negated in an instant,
given the right stimulus. Sublime behaviour exists now only
in the pages of Betsy's beloved Racine. I also learned that
nature, that great benefactor, exacts its punishment for all the
bounties hitherto enjoyed, without a thought of worth or
entitlement, and that all life ends badly. 'Peacefully, in his
sleep,' one reads, but what of the preceding hours or minutes?
Shakespeare has it over Racine here, and Hamlet's doubts and
fears speak for all of us. It is these rather than the statecraft
that the seventeenth-century classicists brought to the consideration of these matters that resonate in the mind. I also
learned that it is the gods who are in control, and that their
pagan indifference can be visited on any life, no matter how
correctly that life has been lived. I have come to believe that
there can be no adequate preparation for the sadness that
comes at the end, the sheer regret that one's life is finished,
that one's failures remain indelible and one's successes illusory.
I also believe that there occurs a moment of renunciation,
when one is visited by the knowledge that time is up, that
there is to be no more time, or that if a little time remains it
will be lived posthumously, and with a sense of pure loss. This
is also, conversely, an invitation to play Russian roulette with
one's life and affections while one has the time, to take chances,
to defy safety. But of course one no longer has the time to
do that. The ability – the capacity – to take chances has been

lost. All is subject henceforth to the iron decree of mortality.

The first of these propositions I had been able to verify for myself. The second came to me by way of information relayed by my mother during one of her brief visits to London from the villa in Spain she had bought with a further injection of money from my father and which she shared with a woman friend. I looked at her, perplexed, unwilling to accede to these morbid matters which she seemed to have embraced without prior warning. It was true that I no longer saw her on a regular basis; had I done so I should have been prepared for the change in her appearance, which I could not quite analyse. Her face seemed to have changed its shape, to be hollowed out on one side, and her lips were slightly puckered, like the lips of a very old woman. But she was not old, or rather she was old by my standards, in her late fifties, and still, as far as I knew, unimpaired. Yet the altered shape of her features, so different from the carefully nurtured appearance with which I had grown up, together with her doleful pronouncements, brought an unwelcome sense of danger, of further changes still to come, which I found unwelcome.

She smiled faintly at my inability to give her credit for her lately discovered wisdom, and put her hand to her face. 'You're probably wondering what brought this on,' she said. 'Such a minor thing, but it served as a warning of some kind. I had to have some teeth out. I'm afraid Spanish dentists aren't very good – not that English dentists are much better – and the apparatus I have to wear doesn't really fit. It's obvious, isn't it?'

'You'll come to terms with it,' I said awkwardly, not willing to be conscripted into this new intimacy. My mother had always exaggerated. I had thought her brave when I was a child, making light of my colds and scratches, my minor and not so minor accidents. Now I saw that her brashness hid terror, and that her defences against that terror were no longer adequate. I was particularly concerned to eschew any form of sympathy that would lead to the sort of identification she seemed to desire, as if we were no longer mother and daughter but one old woman commiserating with another. She seemed to have forfeited a sort of propriety, to be looking to me for reassurance, and again I could not help but perceive a loss of nerve. Once again I was glad that she was not there to witness my behaviour, though that behaviour was, I thought, discreet. But I feared her instincts, which had always been sharp. She was the kind of woman whose main attention is given over to other women, as if to calculate their assets, and if possible their disadvantages, with regard to herself. She had been expert at the subtle insinuation, the laughing dismissal, as if these matters were crucial to a woman's success with men. I now saw why my father had looked for love and comfort elsewhere. I did not exonerate him, but I understood him. Yet she had been beautiful, and was so no longer. I was able to regret that quite sincerely, while at the same time resenting the fact that it had been brought to my notice.

'You've changed too,' she said. 'You've got more colour in your face. And you're better dressed. Well, you can afford to be.' She laughed, with one of her old angry laughs that always accompanied any discussion of money. Yet I knew that she expected me to express gratitude to her for having steered me into marriage with a prosperous older man. At least he had seemed prosperous at the time, although in the light of Edmund's wealth his income was probably minimal. We lived comfortably enough, and I was happy to add my own money to his. I paid my way, as seemed only right to me, while Digby took care of the outgoing expenses. I realized that our holidays, in the early days of our marriage, must have been costly, and was glad for several reasons that these had come to an end.

My mother's presence was particularly onerous because I had several matters of my own to think about. The first and most important of these was Edmund, or rather his absence. He had taken his family to France, to a house they always rented in the Alpilles, and I should not see him for three or even four weeks. This enforced period of calm was unwelcome for many reasons, for I knew, or sensed, that if the momentum of a love affair falters one loses one's confidence in a good outcome. I could not help but contrast his circumstances with my own. I spent quiet days alone or with Digby, whose own holiday it was. He preferred to spend it at home, venturing out only for a ruminative morning walk, and sometimes not even for that. It was only too easy to imagine the physical splendour of Edmund's surroundings and activities, the lithe bodies of his children supplementing his own, as if they were a different race, and inhabited a different atmosphere to our own, to Digby's and mine, and now, tiresomely, to my mother's. Until she sat down, glass of whisky to hand, and started unloading her dire observations for my instruction, I had not actively minded our uneventful summer. Both Digby and I were preoccupied and did not converse much, yet there was a kind of harmony in our silence, and I had felt the faintest inkling of a distaste for Britten Street and a recognition that honourable behaviour does impress one and convince one of its validity. Yet, of course, as soon as I perceived this the counter-argument became active, and I was ready to issue hot denials of the importance of dignity and gratitude in human affairs and to claim rights that would in any case be rendered obsolete by age and infirmity. In this I was very much of my time, since women had long discovered the euphoria of protest, possibly because their own mothers, like mine, were uttering dire warnings, shaking their heads at the heedlessness of youth, willing younger people to observe their own constraints, without success. There was an envy there, which daughters perhaps intuited before their mothers did, and it served to sour relations for a time. Certainly I did not intend to compare myself with my mother, whose hand had once again crept to her sunken cheek. I willed my own hand to remain in my lap. Had I been alone I should have run to a mirror to make sure that my appearance was unchanged.

After weeks of blank and grateful sleep I had begun to dream again, and I had had two dreams that seemed oddly baleful, as dreams do when they linger in the mind. In the first I had been persuaded that all the lights in the flat had failed, and that I must remember to ask the caretaker to check the fuses. I was aware that I was dreaming this, that it was the middle of the night, and that I must telephone the caretaker as early as possible the following morning, yet the image of the lightless flat was so convincing that I actually got out of bed and went to the bathroom, where the light worked normally. I could hardly reassure myself by switching on the lights in the other rooms, spent perhaps a couple of minutes looking out of the window on to the silent street, and then got back into bed, where I immediately, or so it seemed, had another dream. This took place in a notional daytime, on a sunny afternoon much like the afternoons I had been used to spending in the garden. This time, in the dream, I was in South Kensington, not far from Melton Court, and about to enter a café, where Edmund was already seated. He appeared not to know me, but this disturbed me less than the fact that his hair had turned white. I could make no sense of this, for Edmund seemed to be guaranteed protection from age, until

I realized that it was not Edmund who had turned white but Digby.

'And Digby looks terrible,' said my mother, intruding into my mental landscape. 'Are you sure you're looking after him?'

'He gets tired,' I said lamely. 'He works very hard, too hard. I think he's quite looking forward to retirement.' Though what I should do when he was at home all day I had not yet worked out.

My mother's hand was at her face again. 'He couldn't remember my name,' she said, in genuine alarm. 'He called me Helen.'

'Helen was the name of his first wife,' I told her, though this made me sad. 'You must have reminded him of her.'

She smiled, with her new lopsided smile, as if this were some kind of compliment. Yet some instinct moved her to get to her feet and make noises of departure. She was staying at the Basil Street Hotel, where my wedding reception had taken place, and she was anxious to be re-absorbed into its benign atmosphere, after revealing too much, and indeed learning too much, in the course of the afternoon.

After clearing away the lunch she had been toying with from the kitchen table I went and surveyed Digby in the drawing-room, suppressing a wish (but registering one) that he would remove himself if he wished to doze unobserved and not do so in such a public space. My father had had the same unattractive habit, which he pursued as a deliberate strategy in order to defy my mother's angry remonstrances. It was his defence against her, and although clearly willed, it was also genuine. He seemed able to plummet into unconsciousness at a moment's notice, and this had soured the atmosphere at home and reconciled me to the various changes in my situation. Now, by an exquisite irony, I seemed to have been returned to my origins, the only difference being that my father's place had been taken by my husband. I did not think that men should behave like this, was annoyed with Digby for being too somnolent to wish my mother a sufficiently ceremonious goodbye, although I had sensed her reluctance to engage with him for longer than was necessary. She had seemed to want to confine herself to women's talk, largely in order to share what I now understood as her fear of the future. The woman with whom she lived, and whose contributions covered the villa's expenses, could not be counted upon to care for her. They had met on a cruise and had formalized their plan to retire to the sun without giving the matter much thought. Indeed my mother, who had not previously been known for her appreciation of female company, was no doubt regretting the arrangement but was unable to dismantle it. She may even have been looking to Digby as the man of the family who would know how to extricate her, cancel the friend, sell the villa, or, if not, advise her how to proceed and in a more general sense what to do.

Her need of support, in the broadest sense of the word, had not been met by any helpful suggestion on my part. I was embarrassed for her and by her; the hand that went repeatedly to her face served only to emphasize her altered looks. And I was embarrassed for and by Digby who had clearly not wished his afternoon to be disturbed, claiming a right to the peaceful enjoyment of his home in what he viewed as his holiday. Again the thought of Edmund's holiday intruded, not only with the inducements and embellishments that I was used to reading in the travel brochures that I had loyally brought home, thinking that by doing so I was demonstrating an enthusiasm that I knew to be acceptable, but with a clear and piercing vision of Edmund himself, enjoying the sort of intimacy to which I should never be admitted. There was nothing to be done about this, and at that moment I knew the situation to be unalterable, even irreparable. I took a book at random from off the shelves and prepared to sacrifice the afternoon to Digby's so-called holiday and to respecting his wishes. He liked to have me sitting near him, so that he could reach out and take my hand. In this way we were both appeased, for I was newly aware at such times of his goodness of heart. I lowered my expectations to meet his own, and in so doing achieved a measure of virtue.

The book I had taken at random, or so I thought, was unfortunately *Madame Bovary*, and the evidence of Emma's adultery seemed out of place. I closed it quietly and put it aside, exerting myself, as I often did, to observing everything in the room, as if to reassure myself of its validity. Digby took my hand and asked me whether I wanted to go out; I told him that I was perfectly happy for the moment but that we might take a walk later, perhaps eat in one of the local restaurants. I thought he mumbled rather, but put that down to his recent sleep: fortunately we had both eaten earlier, before my mother's inconvenient arrival, on which I now looked back with a sense of displacement. This, as always, I looked to Digby to disperse. But it seemed to me that his own face had become a mirror image of my mother's, with the same slight distortion. This was surely a projection. I walked to the window and looked out, but there was little to be seen that I had not seen before. When I looked back at him, in this different light and perspective, he seemed much as normal.

Digby had picked up my book and was leafing through it. 'You won't like that,' I warned him.

'I never have liked it. It's a woman's book, really.'

'Yet it was written by a man.'

'Yes, only a man would have killed her off.'

'She died because she had got into debt,' I reminded him coldly.

'I suppose so.' There was a brief silence. 'Are you making tea?' he asked. 'Deborah gone?'

'Ages ago. Yes, I'll make tea.'

I went immediately to the kitchen, suddenly anxious to avoid his presence. Yet I had warmed to him in the course of that peaceful afternoon, appreciated him, even admired him. Now my mood changed to one of weariness and incipient revolt. I played my wifely part adequately, and yet I could see it for what it was: a sham. And it was not only my married life that was a sham; my other life too did not, could not, bear active scrutiny. I saw the point of those grim days in Paris. They had been the means of preparing me for a life lived according to my own rules, rather than by rules imposed on me by other people. I had had a glimpse of the freedom available to the purely selfish, though that freedom could be limited by desire. Once again I wanted to roam the streets unobserved, my thoughts confined to myself rather than anticipating another's movements, another's wishes. I wanted everyone to die and leave me alone. I particularly wanted Edmund to die, for I knew that without him I should be myself again and not the person I had become once I had chosen him, or been chosen by him.

There was another area of discomfort. When we had exchanged that meaningful glance, and the recognition of each other that was to change everything, we had been in his house, in the presence of his wife. So great was the pressure of that moment that I had managed to ignore her. Now I wondered how much she knew about her husband's affairs, of his skilful arrangements. With increasing discomfort I could now see that she was fully aware – must be aware – of Edmund's manoeuvres, and that she was cynical enough to be amused by them. Either that, or they were so close that full disclosure was possible on both sides, that Edmund's adulteries were part of a marital game which engendered a sort of excitement they both found acceptable, even desirable. Maybe Constance too had lovers and could deal with them in such a way as to engender no remorse, no anguish, no soul-searching. Not every woman is an Emma Bovary.

Constance had always made me uncomfortable. She seemed to find me amusing in several minor ways: my careful cooking, my earnest reading, my obvious – obvious to a woman like herself – boredom, my acute self-consciousness in her presence. For she had managed to instil an uneasiness even before there had been any justification for such a feeling to exist. Her sly watchfulness across the dinner table had always seemed to expose weaknesses in myself that were not obvious to anyone else. I felt transparent in her presence, and had always done so. That was why I must never see her again, never go to their house, never ask about her children, once heard innocently playing in an upstairs room. I must never ask Edmund if he loved her, though, alone in my kitchen, I could see that he must be linked to her in several ways that survived love. Her value to him was obvious, almost as great as his value to her. It was a Faustian bargain, but who was to say that Faustian bargains never worked?

This revelation, which I had somehow managed not to confront, shocked me, as complicity, connivance, always shock one. I saw that I was merely an accessory, a minor character in a much grander plot, one I was not fully equipped to understand. I saw both of them on one side of a sexual divide and myself on the other. Now I should have to work out whether I wanted to join them in their knowingness or retain an essential part of my own ignorance. I was not clever enough to work out an independent strategy. Yet I was still not willing to forgo the experience. I even felt a certain unhealthy curiosity: what would come next? And if I did not like what came next what could save me, apart from flight?

When the telephone rang I almost dropped a cup, thinking that it must be Edmund calling from France, telling me when he was coming home. But it was a woman's voice, and my disappointment informed me that I was not yet ready to relinquish this adventure, however destructive it turned out to be.

I cleared my throat. 'Hello?' I repeated. 'Who is this?'

'It's Betsy.'

'Betsy! Where are you? How long are you here for?'

'For good, I think. Or for the time being anyway. I just rang to give you my new number.'

'Oh, you've sold the house, then? Where will you be living? Yes, give me your number. Have you moved?'

'Not quite. Not yet. I've bought a rather horrible flat that I haven't had time to prepare. It was the first one I saw.'

'Betsy, what is that noise? I can hear drilling. Are you still there?'

'Builders. The new owners are having a lot of work done. I had to ask if I could stay on for a month, until the new place . . . until I've sorted myself out.'

'What's happened? Of course I'm delighted that you're here, but . . . you don't sound quite yourself.'

'I've not been well.' The voice was monotonous, unin-flected. 'I'll tell you all about it.'

'Are you alone? Daniel?'

'Daniel died.' The voice was still neutral.

'I see,' I said slowly. 'Would you like to meet? I'd love to see you.'

I did want to see her, not only because I was intrigued by the change in her voice but for more general and more admirable reasons: she was a part of my past when the past was still relatively unspotted, not yet subject to alien influences. She was the friend of my youth, and therefore an essential witness. She had looked to me for protection, yet her blitheness was in itself more protection than I could offer. She had seen me as respectable, with a proper home and proper parents, not dreaming how fallible both could be. She had admired my mother, had felt a misplaced respect for our lives, for my life, which she viewed as fortunate. Not once throughout our mismatched childhoods had she manifested envy or resentment. I remembered, with a twinge of pity, of embarrassment, her evenings at the cinema with her aunt. Her staunch spirit seemed to have withstood the blandishments of those heroes and heroines, for whom everything progresses to a foreseen conclusion. Then I reminded myself that to let her down by confessing to my current behaviour would be a major solecism, almost an offence I could not bring myself to commit. And she had found a hero of her own, a man almost as unrealistic as herself, and who was now dead. This in a sense was appropriate, yet I could hardly point this out. It was somehow in line with her classical aspirations: Titus and Bérénice doomed never to be happy together. Did she still cling to those superhuman ideals?

'What about that tea?' called my husband.

'Just coming,' I said. From the telephone came noises of banging, as if the house were collapsing on top of her. 'Betsy,' I shouted, as if she could hardly hear me. 'Are you still there?'

'Yes, I'm here.'

She seemed unable either to say anything or to end the call. It was unclear why she had contacted me, for although we were old friends she had noted my dislike of her lover. Who was now dead, I reminded myself. And she herself had not been well, as was evidenced by her subdued and altered tone.

'When can we meet? I'm here all day at the moment. I mean, I'm not busy. Do you want to come over? Now?'

'Tomorrow, perhaps. If you're sure. I've got so much to tell you.'

'Come to tea tomorrow. It will be lovely to see you.'

I rang off, moved. It would indeed be lovely to see her.

'This tea's cold,' remarked my husband. 'Who were you talking to?'

'My oldest friend,' I told him. For she was, I realized, the one and only, the friend who follows one through life, and to whom one is bound by the very fact of life itself.

6

The children were going back to school. I could not help noticing this when I went out the following morning. They seemed excited rather than downcast, as if the prospect of order were a welcome change after the variegated activities of the summer holidays. They dominated the streets, or perhaps one's eye was simply drawn to them as a fact of nature, the new exerting its rights over the old. It was a sight to make any childless woman thoughtful. While never exactly wishing for children, and in any case knowing myself to be inept, I seemed suddenly to be conscious of a dimension that was lacking in my life. The sight of fathers holding the hands of chattering little daughters affected me now as it would not have done previously. From what I had gathered Edmund's attitude to his children was one of tacit devotion, not to be spoken of to an outsider, active only within the boundaries of his home, incommunicable to anyone in a position radically different from his own. One sensed that few people would be allowed into the jealously guarded intimacy thus observed, and that to attempt to do so would strike a false note. Even a neutral enquiry, such as I had attempted, would be met with a banality which might have answered my question, had it not been met with an instinctive turning away of the head, and a smile which merely emphasized the firmness of the mouth. After that I was careful to behave as if I hardly knew of his children's existence. It was an area from which I was excluded. My attributes were those of a woman whose sexual availability was guaranteed by childlessness, as if the same practices could not be visited on a woman whose status was enhanced by the kind of respect accorded to mothers. While I knew that this was an absurd suspicion on my part I was aware that I could not hope to share his experiences of life within a family, and it was perhaps the feature that separated us even more than the disjunction between our needs and wishes.

This was not the only sign that summer was coming, indeed had come, to an end. The mornings were cooler and the evenings longer than they had been; already leaves were changing colour and scents were sharper in the occasionally misty air. My afternoons in the garden would very shortly be curtailed and I should be obliged to spend more time at home. Oddly enough I had become quite reconciled to home during the peaceful days that were now concluded, when Digby and I had kept each other amiable company without exchanging anxious enquiries or forbidden confessions. For we both contained areas of secrecy. I suspected that he sometimes compared his first marriage with his second, and while never faltering in his loyalty to me must have regretted the intensity of feeling and desire that had died or been extinguished by his young wife's death. Such thoughts as he must have entertained were kept from me, and I respected his silence on such matters, for I had a silence of my own which must not be broken. I liked to know that he was in another room, that we were within reach of one another, that our tact would protect us from exaggerating a need which had perhaps become diffused but was no less valued. With Digby back at his office the flat would seem unoccupied, for in his absence my presence was somehow diminished. And on such a morning – the end of everyone's holidays – I was left with a sensation that time had overtaken me. The children on their way to school, and the new silence at home, signified a return to order, and I was obliged to consider the challenge of how to reconcile the disorder of my love affair with the resumption of daily life so clearly within the grasp of those I passed in the street, the eager children and the no less eager parents, all recognizably conforming to some mysterious normality of which I had lost sight.

Such social conscience as I still retained urged me to buy a cake for Betsy's tea, rather as if we were still children invited to one another's houses. I dismissed the idea, but children were on my mind, even the children we had been ourselves. It was hard to see how we had progressed to our present situations without bringing to the matter something of that earlier sincerity, yet we had both in our various ways attained a notional adulthood which, by comparison with our initial state of grace, appeared bizarre, even theatrical. My situation was no doubt banal, Betsy's more unexpected. And also more unexplained. I did not know if she had been married to this Daniel, and if so when and where the marriage had taken place. The absence of information (for one always advertises a marriage) convinced me that there had been nothing of this kind, wisely so, for few women, even women as unspoilt as Betsy, could bring themselves to take on a man who was essentially still an adolescent, placing his faith in a future to which he would contribute only in the most immaterial of ways. That she could believe that his nebulous discussions could constitute a credible career argued her devotion, which, to judge from the afternoon when she had introduced Daniel to me, was already making her unhappy. A man should grow out of his fantasies and devote himself to making money. And Betsy was my age: she must have humoured him beyond the point at which it made sense to do so. His death would have put an end to a process which had once involved them both but which would eventually have divided them. The wonder to me was that she should have remained loyal for so long. But then, I reflected, she had always been loyal. Loyalty was her besetting sin.

I also wondered how she would look, whether this rite of passage would show itself in outward and visible signs. She had been a pretty girl, with the slightly undifferentiated prettiness of very young English women, or indeed like the children on their way to school. When she had visited me with Daniel she had seemed half-way to being a French woman, thinner, more obviously cared for, rigorously focused, and yet distracted by her loving anxiety for her charge (for he was no less), doing her valiant best to reconcile her conflicting social duties to us both. I had discerned, above all, a desire to do the right thing, and in this she had not changed. Her quasi-maternal role flattered her but did not altogether suit her: she had been destined to be wholehearted and spontaneous, and perhaps she was aware of this. She was as disturbed by Daniel's moody presence as I was, but for more generous reasons. She wanted him to be comfortable, to be happy; I merely thought him rude. At the same time it was clear that I was still in some way her standard of respectability, as if I possessed certainties which had been denied her, and which the process of growing up had merely reinforced. She had had the same air of trying to turn a makeshift arrangement into a proper life, and, more important, into a proper home, a proper family. She had produced the names of friends – Vincent, Brigitte, Jean-Pierre – as if they formed part of her curriculum vitae, produced as an earnest of her and their intentions. Yet she had appeared isolated, as if she knew that what bound her to these friends was provisional, and as if Daniel's ability to take seriously an affiliation which was essentially not serious had only imperfect hold on her honest and forthright nature. She would have wanted all the comforts of marriage and I could see that these would be denied her. I had thought her performance courageous. As well as love she was already dealing with disappointment, and although the two are not infrequently linked I thought she deserved better.

When she was sitting in front of me I could see that further changes had taken place. She had lost more weight, and her larger eyes gave beauty to a face that had hitherto been a mere receptor of changing moods. She had gained a stillness, a languor; no longer did she exclaim with enthusiasm when presented with the slightest favour. Her hair had grown, and it was clear that she no longer dedicated much thought to her appearance. This, paradoxically, gave her a certain authority. It was as if her life were now properly adult and she herself had to deal with adult concerns, such as money, property, but also solitude, fear. She smiled faintly at my expression, and it was true that I was shocked. I wanted the truth from her, and I knew that she would give me nothing less, yet I did not want to intrude into such a private matter. All I knew was that her life in Paris was over, that she had returned, or had been returned, to her origins, to the old house, and by the same token to an old friend. I was determined to remain that friend, although I too had changed. Our friendship would now be measured by the success with which we managed such changes, and also by how much we chose to reveal of our changed selves.

'What has happened?' I asked, largely disobeying my need to be discreet.

'Well, I'm here.' She gave an unconvincing little laugh. 'I've bought a rather horrible flat off the Fulham Road, and I'll move in as soon as it's habitable. Which will have to be soon, because they want to get rid of me. The new owners of the house, that is. It's been bought by property developers, and they are not particularly responsive to my needs.'

'I mean, what happened to Daniel?'

'Well, he died. I think he wanted to die.' Her face expressed the most profound disbelief that anyone should want such a thing.

'Was he ill?'

'I think he must have been. I think he was mentally ill. I couldn't get him to relax. He was over-excited all the time. Sometimes he talked all night. And the flat was being repossessed by the owner, who wanted it for his son. That affected him badly. And the money was getting scarce.'

Her money, I assumed.

'One night he wouldn't stop talking, refused food. I tried to get him to calm down, but it merely made him more agitated. Then we had a row, our first. And our last. He ran down the stairs – I could hear him all the way to the street.' She became silent. 'He was run over by a police car. I heard it. Or rather I heard a woman scream.' She was silent again. 'The police were very kind. They took care of everything. I think they thought I might bring charges. The worst thing was when they asked me about him, and I realized I knew next to nothing. A friend, I said. I think they were relieved to be shot of the matter. They said they would look into it and let me know. But they didn't. I suppose these things take time. I never heard another word.'

'What did you do?'

'I had to find out more about him. It sounds silly, but I only knew what he had told me, and that was so little as to be meaningless. He wouldn't even talk about his childhood, and most people are willing to do that, aren't they? But I didn't know where to go, whom to ask. The friends I used to meet – I told you about them – had begun to disperse. Either that or they were doing other things. Or avoiding him.' She sighed. 'He had become very argumentative.'

'I thought you were all plotting the next revolution.'

'Oh, that was nonsense. We may have been interested in politics when we first met; well, it was hard to avoid such discussions after 1968. But in fact we were already drifting apart. It was Daniel who took these things seriously. Too seriously. And Roland, of course.'

'Who was he?'

'I may have mentioned him. Roland Besnard.'

I shook my head.

'He was an older man who sometimes joined us. He took an interest in us, and inevitably wondered how we saw the future. I think he just liked young people. He had been a schoolteacher in Angers. He'd come to Paris in his holidays and had stayed on. He was the only one of us who viewed the situation as something more than spectacle. He said it was a good time to be young. I think he was a little envious, in the nicest possible way. He and Daniel sometimes went off together. I don't know what they talked about.'

'I saw things quite differently. He seemed so . . . radical.'

'Yes, that was worrying. But I thought I could make things better for him, get him to settle down. But he wouldn't. Or couldn't. He was always serious: as if this were 1789, or rather 1848. I think what he really needed was a future for himself, one in which he could claim his rightful place. I wasn't enough for him. I could see that. But to tell the truth I didn't know what to do.'

'Were you very unhappy?'

'Oh, yes. But it was his unhappiness that upset me. And I suppose I gave him something. He did seem to rely on me.'

'Betsy, you are painting a picture of someone who was not quite normal.'

'That's what I had to find out about. Because if he was as . . . eccentric as he was beginning to become . . .'

'Or always had been . . .'

She ignored me. 'I had to see whether I had been mistaken all along. And yet I think he loved me.'

'What did you do?'

'I went round the various cafés where we used to meet. It took me a whole day. Then, when I had almost given up, I had a stroke of luck, if you can call it luck. I met Roland coming up the steps of the Métro station at Odéon. I must have been looking a bit odd. He knew what had happened. Word had got round, and I think there was something in the papers, though I deliberately didn't read them. I didn't want to know what they said about him. I wanted, if possible, to talk to someone who had known him. So it was really providential my meeting up with Roland in that unexpected fashion. And he was very kind. He took me to a café and made me drink some coffee. Then he told me things I never knew, that Daniel had never told me. That was part of the trouble. You do see that, don't you?'

I saw it all too clearly. What he had told her was dismaying even to a hostile witness like myself. Daniel de Saint-Jorre was a fabrication from start to finish. His name was Petitjean. Saint-Jorre was one of his mother's lovers, distinguishable from the others because he had taken pity on the child Daniel and bought him a toy boat to sail on the pond in the Tuileries. The child had fantasized that this man was his father and had appropriated his name. As the real Saint-Jorre had disappeared he had no knowledge of this. In any case he would have been anxious to leave no trace, and there had been no further contact. It had been easy to assume that Daniel was an orphan. In fact his mother still lived in the room in Asnières where she had brought him up, had earned her living as best she could, no doubt in the most banal way possible. Betsy, without knowing the reasons for Daniel's unbalanced outlook, had instinctively taken him under her wing. They were not and never had been equals. For all of Betsy's own sense of early deprivation her character rested on rock solid foundations. He had understood this as strength, and, like all the dispossessed, had looked for and found a protector. To a certain extent, and from a certain point of view, he was as innocent as she was. And social justice, of the fairytale variety in which he believed, would restore him to a place in life in which Betsy might or might not be invited to join him, depending on whether or not he still needed her.

I was profoundly shocked by this, Betsy even more so. 'Did you love him?' I asked, curious to know. My own life had managed to accommodate a number of unwelcome facts, and perhaps I took pride in my realism. I did not see how one could ignore such facts and preserve the simplicity of one's feelings. Perhaps it was that very simplicity that had saved her from the sort of corrosion to which even the least selfish are susceptible. She looked like someone who had survived a terrible ordeal, her eyes wide and her expression fixed, as if the telling of the story were some kind of physical re-enactment of that ordeal. 'Did you?' I prompted.

'Oh, yes,' she said tiredly, her shoulders relaxing slightly. 'Of course I loved him. I was very slow to fall in love; I had too many arrangements to make, and no one to help me make them. When I was in Paris I realized for the first time that I was young, that I had a little money of my own, and could be as independent as I wanted to be. And being the sort of student I was then – the sort of student who doesn't have to take exams – was enormous fun. That was how I met those friends I used to go about with. That was how I met Daniel. Someone brought him along at some point. And you saw how beautiful he was.'

I nodded. That at least was authentic.

'We started living together straight away, in his little room in the rue Cler. And at the beginning I was so happy. It was like *La Bohème*.'

'Which ends badly,' I reminded her.

'Yes, and we ended badly too. He died. There can be no worse ending than that.' We were both silent. 'And yet,' she said, 'I felt a certain relief. I felt it was my fault that he was unhappy. I blamed myself entirely. So that when I was alone once more, with little money left, and the landlord being very polite but very insistent, it was as if, in a terrible way, I accepted everything that had happened, that I knew that for me a certain kind of happiness was at an end. That's when I decided to come home.'

'No wonder you were ill. Are you sure you're all right?'

'I've got to be, haven't I? I've got to move. I've got to get used to living alone. And I'll need some sort of a job.'

'Tell me about this flat you've bought.'

She sighed, rubbed her forehead. 'It's a perfectly ordinary one-bedroom flat designed for a person with no roots. It's impossible to think of normal life going on there. I mean the sort of life lived by normal people.'

'I know exactly what you mean,' I said. 'But it needn't be like that. I'll help all I can.'

At this faint show of sympathy she let down her guard

and wept. Yet even as she did so she attempted to reassure me. It was a sign that her essential decency had not been compromised.

'Digby will be home soon,' I warned her. 'There's a bathroom down there if you want it. I'll make some fresh tea.'

I felt anger on Betsy's behalf, and also on my own. That I knew little about Edmund beyond what he chose to reveal was beginning to seem unnervingly close to Betsy's situation; we were both in love with virtual strangers, whose intimacy was a closely guarded secret. Like simpletons, or perhaps just like women, even here we had been seduced by outward form, and had made the mistake of believing that this outward form represented the truth. But truth is not so easily discerned, certainly not disclosed. I, in my hard-hearted way, was aware of this, but Betsy was so clearly above board that she was a victim of her own good faith. I regretted the fact that she was now enlightened, however reluctantly: her sad face, her wide eyes reflected her new condition. She had spoken as if she would never find her way back to the sort of innocent confidence that had been her most noticeable characteristic. And yet there was no shadow in her wistful smile, no suggestion of widowhood. It was as if she was still bewitched by some youthful amalgam of love and beauty, as if, in fact, she had been true to some ideal which she was not willing to abandon. And it was true that in appearance Daniel had fitted the stereotype of a young hero of legend, and whatever inner darkness he managed so successfully to conceal merely added an intriguing complexity to what was in reality a series of aberrations, to which no one meeting him for the first time could have access.

There was a dreadful pathos in all this. I thought of the boy and his toy boat, giving him parity with the other children watched over by mothers in the peaceful afternoons. Simply put, it had taken him a lifetime to recover from childhood and he had not managed the process, had in fact abandoned it, had perhaps had a moment of lucidity and known himself to be inadequate to the task. Whereas Betsy had not accepted that her circumstances had been unfavourable, and had only revealed her longing for love and friendship in a sometimes misplaced enthusiasm. That eagerness had now gone, replaced by something that was not yet maturity, was perhaps merely the dawning realization that all her efforts, her acceptance, and even the happiness she had known in the early days of her love affair, were all aspects of a reality, a complexity with which she had not reckoned, simply because it was not in her nature to look beyond the truth she sought, and had so far managed to find. That truth had revealed itself as unpalatable, and this constituted a moral problem. There was evidence of this in the way she had rubbed her forehead, as philosophers do in the statues of old. Enlightenment would not be altogether welcome. But then it so rarely is.

My situation was not greatly different. I too had given my trust to an unreliable partner. Digby, an entirely honourable man, had merely prepared the way. I thought, or thought I knew, that it was the intensity of one's feelings rather than any idea of merit that determined one's choice. Therefore love is a matter of pure solipsism. If that solipsism is in a sense exchanged with that of another the results are conclusive. Sentiment hardly enters into it, may not even be regretted. I had found myself entirely at home with this knowledge, and now barely thought to question it.

When Betsy returned from the bathroom she looked composed and refreshed, as if the mere fact of being in some-one else's home were reassuring. Some people can deal with solitude – I could myself – but not, I saw, Betsy. What she wanted was to be cherished. Ideally she would have liked to be integrated into a family, someone else's if necessary, where she would have various roles and would do her best to perfect them. On her own, in a small flat, she would not do so well. She seemed relieved to have delivered an account of herself, persuaded that she need not offer it again, that it had been dealt with, that I had evidently not believed that she had made Daniel unhappy. How could she? It takes a certain skill, a certain determination to make a man unhappy if one is frustratingly in love with him, and Betsy lacked that skill, though she was capable of determination, as her history to date had proved.

'The main thing now,' I said firmly, 'is the flat. Tell me about it.'

'Well, it's small, though bigger than the rue Cler. Oh, I don't like it. I don't suppose I ever shall.'

'You can move again when you want to. Find something more substantial.'

She smiled again, again faintly. That occluded smile was the only sign that she had survived a major misfortune. Her original smile, the one I remembered, had been open, undisguised, in tune with her candid nature.

'I don't see myself in anything more substantial, as you put it.'

'You'll have the money,' I reminded her, but it was clear that the money did not interest her. 'And you'll find something to do, make new friends.' This, at the moment, seemed beyond her. 'If I can help,' I repeated.

'Well, yes, I'd be grateful for some advice.' She glanced appreciatively at my pale green walls, a mistake I frequently thought, but pleasant enough. 'You've made it so nice here.'

'You'll have enough furniture, I take it. Though you can get rid of it if it's not suitable.'

The smile faded. 'Yes, all that stuff. Father's desk – I never got rid of that. Mary didn't want anything changed.'

'Change it now,' I instructed her. 'You'll feel better with new things around you.'

The sound of Digby's key in the door brought us both to our feet. 'Home!' he called, as he always did, and I went out into the hall to greet him. 'Tired?' I queried. That too was habitual. 'I have a friend with me,' I told him. Obediently he straightened his shoulders and summoned a smile. 'You remember Betsy,' I told him. 'She was at our wedding.'

Betsy held out her hand. 'Betsy de Saint-Jorre,' she said. She had appropriated both the aristocratic name and the married style. It was her one act of dissimulation, and I thought it entirely permissible.

7

Edmund's voice on the telephone sounded distant, patriarchal, as a voice does after an absence. I had not seen him for six weeks, and at times it had seemed to me that he had gone away, perhaps on a longer holiday than I had anticipated, or, worse, that he had gone away of his own accord, leaving me without an explanation, or rather with an explanation I was free to divine for myself. The agreement, or rather the agreement that had been imposed on me, was that we were two strangers who met from time to time for a specified purpose, but who did not otherwise intrude into each other's lives. In order to sustain my part in this bargain I had needed all my hard-won pragmatism, and this, so far, had not deserted me. What intimacy we shared was rigorously controlled, confined to the flat in Britten Street, and never referred to in a wider context. This tacit collusion had excited me from the start. Now, with the changes in the year becoming advanced, and consequently the alteration in my habits dictated by the colder weather, the darker evenings, I began to see the advantages conferred by a companionship that could be taken for granted, a middle ground in which references could be understood without explanation. This carefully contrived neutrality was something one observed with strangers, beyond the comfort conferred by true knowledge.

'Are you all right?' I asked, aware that my voice had betrayed an unwanted eagerness.

'My mother died. We had to go up to Scotland for the funeral.'

'Oh, I'm so sorry.' Again, this was too heartfelt. But surely the death of one's mother was a tragedy? I felt that it might be a tragedy for others, although the warring tendencies of my own parents had made their absence a blessing rather than something to be regretted, as I rather suspected their eventual deaths would do. Parenting responsibilities had long since passed to my husband, in whose care I remained safe. But I assumed that for a man who had had the confidence to establish a family of his own, while continuing to live as freely as he chose, such ties would inevitably be stronger. In fact it pleased me to view Edmund as a member not exactly of a class but of a caste, a man in possession of all the certainties that had come to him at birth and had never had to be relinquished. His assurance derived not simply from his untroubled physical expectations but rather from the conviction that he had obeyed all of life's norms, that he measured up to some ideal standard which he had never thought to doubt. His behaviour would remain unquestioned by those whom it affected, simply because there were no questions to ask, or perhaps because it was a matter of form not to ask them.

Privately it had occurred to me that such behaviour might cause anguish, bitterness, but from these dilemmas Edmund seemed inviolate. It was perhaps part of his natural endowment, this ability to please himself. He had given himself permission to do so by virtue of the fact that he had observed and paid the dues he owed to society, that he had acquired all those attributes that mark out the finished man: a fine house, fine children, honourable and amply rewarded work, considerable affluence, and the sort of health rarely achieved by those whose lives were plagued by anxiety or unhappiness. His ability to maintain an even body temperature in all weathers seemed to me to be part of this endowment: I myself began to shiver as soon as summer was over, and could, if I let myself, lapse into depression. Edmund, however, seemed untouched by such vagaries, untouched too by the melancholy which comes with the turn of the year and the approach of Christmas. He seemed, quite simply, impervious to any messages his nerves and susceptibilities might prompt, and thus gained an equilibrium that would no doubt be the envy of those not similarly favoured, myself included.

'I'm sorry for your trouble,' I said awkwardly, aware that this sounded quaint. 'I expect you'll miss her.'

'Well, she was very old, and she died in her sleep. The best thing that could have happened, really. We shall all go up again to look over the house, see what needs to be sold. We'll probably keep it, though.' There was a pause. 'The children were very fond of her.'

'And you? How are you?'

'What? I'm fine.' Another pause. 'Are you free?'

'Yes, of course.' But this sounded wrong too. I was being too simple, whereas I knew, from appreciative comments in the past, that what he preferred was a certain trickiness, a certain *savoir-faire*. I suspected that he preferred women who were as appropriately situated as he was himself, and from whom he need expect no sarcasm, no criticism, certainly no recriminations. It was all part of the bargain, a bargain which separated the initiated from the uninitiated. How one passed this particular test I was unsure, for I had thought ardour a worthy substitute for experience. Now I realized once again that my own experience was limited. What partners I had had in Paris were remembered with a certain discomfort, or indeed not remembered at all. That was why, like Emma Bovary, whose story does indeed seem to touch the lives of most women, I had been moved to exclaim, *'J'ai un amant! J'ai un amant!'* when undergoing the rite of passage that distinguishes true joy from mere acquiescence. That such pleasure had to be paid for was a notion that belonged to the Dark Ages. Or did it? Women of my generation were at last profiting from the freedoms of the 1960s and had not yet been punished for so doing. One likes to think in terms of rewards and deserts, or at least I did. I was aware that my conduct was reprehensible, and yet I had only to remember the loneliness I had endured in Paris (and indeed since then) to reassure myself that certain indulgences were permitted. And that even if they were not (here doubt persisted) I was willing to pay the price. That there was a price to be paid I had read too much, and had been too indoctrinated to ignore. But part of Edmund's gift to me had been to make me seem so fortunate that I might escape the penalties altogether. In short he had lent me some of his own glamorous freedom from the pangs of conscience, and I took this as further proof that I had matured in a way that had not hitherto been possible.

If I regretted anything it was that our time together was too brief, that there was too little conversation. I should have liked to ask questions, not only about his wife, his children, but about his antecedents, his childhood, his loyalties. While enslaved by the outward man it was only the inner man who would have satisfied my curiosity. The death of his mother might have furnished a pretext for such an enquiry, might have provided the answer to many questions, but I knew that I was duty bound to observe my rightful place in the gallery of his acquaintances. This would have been a slight torment if I had allowed it to develop into something like a grudge. Being obliged to keep my place I was aware of the inequalities of the relationship. This was one of the many unfairnesses visited on women by men, particularly resented by women of my generation whose anger had at last been given free rein. I had no desire to indulge in accusations, or even suggestions; instinct, or was it fear, had prompted me to apply only the lightest of touches. But a light touch can be a heavy burden. Only the satisfaction of desire, the confidence of shared pleasure, can mitigate the inevitable suspicions and dissatisfactions that come to the surface between opportunities for meeting. And sometimes those opportunities seemed too slender. I had managed my own domestic responsibilities as if by magic in my eagerness to make the greater part of my time available. Now I was prompted by a wish that Edmund would do the same, while conscious of the need not to voice this. So far he had managed to please himself without any hint of remorse. It was his lack of remorse that was his most perversely attractive feature.

Our meeting was perhaps more brief than usual. As I watched him dressing, with a rediscovered briskness, I thought he seemed preoccupied. Questions of the nature of 'Are you all right?' were, I had the wit to know, both clumsy and fussy, like the ardent 'How *are* you?' offered to mere acquaintances. 'Are you very busy?' I ventured, suddenly regretting that I had no job other than that of looking after Digby. I longed for an office, an enterprise that would absorb me and my daytime thoughts; I had observed, with respect, the girls on their way to work, briefcase in hand, one arm flung up to hail a taxi. I could see myself as a humble typist, a loyal secretary, anything so long as it gave a structure to my day and obliterated the long hours of waiting. Indeed I should have been more balanced, more reasonable, if I had had to compile an annual report, or – an even greater temptation, this – take part in meetings. Such activities would have palliated my isolation, and the loneliness which had survived my marriage and now threatened to disturb my love affair.

'Yes, very busy,' he said, in answer to my question. 'And we may be going to move.'

'From that lovely house?'

'What? Oh, yes, you came there once or twice, didn't you? Well, it's too big now that all the children are away. And there's a surprising amount of noise from the traffic. My wife finds it exasperating.'

My wife. Not Constance. A major error.

'Where will you go?' I said lightly.

'I've got a man looking out for me. We'll stay in the neighbourhood, I think. Probably move further inland, nearer Sloane Square. I really don't know at the moment. Look, I must go. I'll see you soon. Or at least I'll give you a ring. All right?'

'Of course,' I said, smiling. I was too imbued with the joy of seeing him again to be conscious of a desolation which had more to do with the threatened disappearance of cherished landmarks than with a sense of change. A feeling of displacement on my own behalf might increase not only any potential difficulties but also my ability to deal with them. I depended on a wholly artificial stasis: I liked to know, or to think I knew, where Edmund was, even if this were pure delusion. I did not care to think of him acting without reference to myself, enjoying a freedom that was somehow denied me. Even the fact that he had 'a man looking out' for him contributed to an air of suzerainty that was in his gift, as if it were entirely normal that he should have agents to do his bidding. I felt poor in comparison, quite literally so, as if my own naturally careful habits compared unfavourably with his largesse. I had genuinely admired my husband's departure from his usual thrift in his attempt to divert me with expensive holidays, and it had been with a sense of gratitude that I repaid him with my household management and the skills I had perfected in my erstwhile career. Now I felt as though these skills merely established me as ineluctably middle class, not dashing enough to ensure the continued interest of a man surely accustomed to grander associations. I determined to buy some new clothes, and wondered why I had not done so during the long summer break. I did not normally pay much attention to such matters. If I had any appeal it was because my entirely neutral appearance gave rise to a certain curiosity. Now I began to wonder whether I should not have been more calculating. But to bring such considerations into a love affair seemed to me to be so unworthy that I abandoned the thought almost as soon as it had formed. In truth it had half formed and thus qualified for further examination. This I determined to postpone until I felt less doubtful, less divided. For that was the way of it with another's obvious entitlements. They were genuinely envied, admired, even, but at the same time they left one feeling diminished. It was as if one's own entitlements were being depleted in order to make room for those other, more natural, demands. But no, demands were consciously formed. These were assumptions, all the more compelling in that they were entirely instinctive, almost a gift of nature. Or of the gods.

I was no longer anxious to linger in the flat, and yet it was too early to go home. I decided to pay a visit to Betsy, to see how she had settled into her new home. I found her surrounded by the overweening furniture that was *de rigueur* in the 1930s: a large glass-fronted bookcase, a nest of tables, and a standard lamp with a dull parchment shade. In the bedroom I knew I should find, and indeed did find, a bed with a sculpted walnut headboard and a dressing-table with a tilting mirror. The kitchen at least seemed to be free of influences, but her shopping – apples, cheese, coffee beans – proclaimed that here was a woman with little appetite and only a faint desire to go through the motions. A street light glowered through the window which was as yet uncurtained. It was, as she had said, so obviously a unit rather than a home, a unit designed for a single person, and one that gave out messages of loneliness, determination and suitability.

'You'll have to get rid of this stuff,' I said stoutly, with a conviction I did not altogether feel. My slight paranoia had diminished in the light of how Betsy now appeared to me: an orphan, surrounded by an orphan's furniture. She gave out an unmistakable message of loss. One advertises oneself in all sorts of unconscious ways: others are alert to the signals. A ruminative aspect, a hesitant walk, a less than responsive smile, all betoken facts about oneself that one would not necessarily wish to be known. Any assumption of busyness is immediately seen to be fallacious by those who know how to look. And Betsy's large eyes were so obviously turned to the past that her ugly surroundings seemed almost appropriate. How would she live? And in this new context how would she see her recent history? It seemed more than unfair to me that she should be cast adrift in this manner. A woman in our time is far from helpless; she can work, earn her own money, surround herself with like-minded friends, join protests, even constitute a one-woman protest in her own right. But if there is no love in her life she will know herself to be an exception, an anomaly.

I could see, or thought I could see, what the future held for Betsy. She would become one of those selfless volunteers who devote themselves to others, simply because she had more in common with the dispossessed than with those who were rightfully her peers. She would drop out of their ambience, take refuge in books, become so accustomed to being alone that she would be an awkward guest, unfamiliar with social norms, and soon cease to be a guest altogether. She had the courage of the survivor, but survival of this sort is a grievous condition, beside which I had to count myself fortunate. She was subtle enough to make comparisons with whatever she perceived about my life, yet too good-hearted to feel envy. What in fact would she envy, even if she knew the truth? Certainly not the fact that I had a lover, for this would surely have shocked her. Her own dream of love, unrealistic though it had been, had in many ways reflected her true nature, which yearned towards the impossible of attainment. She may have understood the various chimeras she had encountered, but she would not have avoided them in the name of prudence, of practicality. Such behaviour had served to isolate her even further; the fact that she had brought nothing back from her adventure was not quite apparent to her, as it would be apparent to others. I hoped that she would come by such knowledge slowly and if possible gently. And yet there was a strange beauty in her abandonment. She had kept her integrity, had forfeited nothing of her original innocence, had committed no fault. My own conduct in comparison seemed shabby, compromised, yet adult in a way that Betsy might concede, but would not understand.

Naturally I told her nothing. That this isolated me, and perhaps at a further remove from what we both once had been, was a matter for my private contemplation. I could not regret what had taken place, although I had certainly experienced flickers of disquiet, as recently as this evening. In retrospect I saw Edmund's behaviour as grandiose but flawed, as if he were a representative of a conquering race and I one of the conquered. I found this exciting, but knew it was questionable. Yet the endowment was not one I was willing to forgo. In giving me access to my own licence, my own lawlessness, Edmund had made me know myself, and in doing so I had gained a liveliness and even a courage that had not previously been within my reach.

'What we should do,' I said, 'is go to Peter Jones and look at their stuff. You'll soon see what you like. And you can afford it now; you can please yourself. I'll help you; we'll go next week, have lunch there. Like ladies.' We both smiled, as if at a picture of those ladies we could not yet hope to become. 'And eat something,' I urged her. 'You're far too thin. And your looks are too good to waste.'

It was a relief to be in the street again. It was a beautiful evening, soft, warm, and dark, with a rising mist. It had been a truly golden October: sharp mornings, mellow afternoon sun, the pungent smell of leaves. It had been easy to ignore the portents of winter and the shorter days, and with them my own reclusion. I had no wish to go home, and for once I had a perfectly valid excuse to offer for my absence: I had been with Betsy. I should have liked to stay out in the air, to take a long walk, as I had done in the early days of my marriage, before the instinct to escape had led me into aberrant behaviour, yet had already been felt in the blood, along the nerves. I was impatient with myself, with my tendency to dwell on recent pleasure, as if it were a singular endowment unshared by other women. My thoughts were if anything coarse: I could have this and more if I so wished. I regretted my circumscribed life in Paris, my only opportunity for eman- cipation, and my refusal then to seize it. Like Betsy I had come to love late in life, and I knew that a longer apprenticeship would have served me better. But I had received the wrong instructions, had thought that marriage was the answer. And no doubt it was the answer, for I did not really want the sort of independence that is more often forced on one than truly desired. Betsy's independence was assured, and yet I knew that she would have been the sort of wife who was going out of fashion. We both had had that picture in our minds when we were girls. But we were no longer girls, and now I understood the regret in those lovely songs I used to hear in Paris, in the odd café, or through an open window. *Le Temps des Cerises* is a land of lost content, whatever one's condition, a realization that what has gone will never return, whether it be love or a vision of love which has somehow failed to materialize.

I was surprised to find the flat empty when I got home, particularly as it was nearly seven-thirty. Digby was rarely late. He was a man of settled habits who frequently cited routine as a principle. I looked in his desk diary to see whether I had forgotten a meeting he was supposed to attend, but the pages were blank. Indeed all the pages were blank, the desk diary an annual gift from a Canadian colleague which kept company with the other accoutrements of his small desk, the old-fashioned fountain pen, the paper knife, his telephone extension. His study seemed so empty, so inscrutable, that I determined to turn it into something else, and yet it was too small for an extra bedroom, and Digby did occasionally use it when he wanted to write letters. The life he lived in that room was closed to me; it had been there before he met me, no doubt held secrets that were not to be disturbed. I found it sad, perhaps for that reason, yet the room was perfectly ordinary, summarily furnished, benefiting from the morning sun. But blank, like the diary.

I wandered into the kitchen, made myself a cup of tea. The

flat seemed very quiet. I was more tired than I realized, resolved to take a bath before Digby returned, yet was reluctant to move. When the doorbell rang I jumped. There were confused sounds from outside; when I opened the door the first thing I saw was Mrs Crook, standing outside her flat, her face a mask of horror. Then I saw what had caused this: Digby, leaning against a wall, supported by his secretary, Jean Thompson, one hand useless at his side, the other dragging Miss Thompson's sage green jacket from her shoulder, as if to get a last purchase on something tangible while it was still within his grasp.

'He was taken ill at the office,' explained Miss Thompson. 'At first it looked like a sort of seizure, yet he seemed to recover from that. He even told me not to be alarmed. Fortunately he had someone with him at the time; otherwise I might not have disturbed him till I left. I made some tea and took it in to him. That's when I saw what had happened to his face. And he seemed to be deaf in one ear. I thought I should call an ambulance but he stopped me. He could still speak at that stage, told me he wanted to go home. So I waited half an hour and then called a taxi. My father went this way. You'll probably want to see your own doctor.'

We took him into the drawing-room and sat him in his chair. His face seemed to have been divided into two halves, the mouth distorted, one eye closed. We all knew what had happened. Digby certainly knew. Yet we were determined not to name it, all three of us.

'If you could just help me get him into the bedroom,' I said. 'I'll look after him. I'm most grateful to you. I think this is what he would have wanted.'

I did not call the doctor. I understood what was taking place. I wanted to keep him with me.

We laid him on the bed. This was the signal for Miss Thompson to leave. The kindness of strangers, I had time to reflect. I wrestled with his clothes, wrapped him in his bathrobe, and pulled the covers over him. At some point, much later in the night, I undressed and got into bed beside him. He seemed to know that I was there, although I doubt if he knew exactly who I was. I took his hand, but it was not his good hand, and it slipped from my grasp. He slept, a stertorous breath informing me that he was still alive. That grew quieter in the course of the night, and I thought he slept almost naturally. When it became light again I examined his face, to see if there had been any further alteration. But it was beginning to relax, to become more recognizable. I had a moment of hope, but when I spoke his name he appeared not to hear me. I spoke his name repeatedly through the course of the day, but there was no response. I knew what I had to do.

I washed his face, combed his hair, took up my position by his bed. At some point I must have unplugged the telephone, but I had no memory of having done this. Again I took the heavy hand in mine and held it. I did not speak, since he could no longer speak. The day progressed, without my participation. I retained enough awareness to see that it was a fine day, a beautiful day, like the one that had preceded it, yet I was anxious for it to be over. It seemed as if the night were more appropriate for a vigil. And so it proved. Once again I lay down beside him. This went on for two more days and nights. I tried, on the following morning, to spoon some yoghurt into his sloping mouth, but it ran down his chin and I was indignant for him. On the third day I felt faint and went into the kitchen to make some tea. When I went back to him I saw that he had died. I felt a sadness so pure, so untainted by immediate concerns, that it was as if I had joined him in his new condition, and that this would be my inheritance, not only in my waking hours but for the rest of my life.

8

In the days that followed it seemed as though I were fighting death myself. I had letters to write, yet my handwriting wandered about on the page, no longer obedient to my intentions. I saw this as an omen, prelude to a larger disintegration that might already be under way. When I looked in the mirror my reflection showed a creature with dull eyes and a pursed mouth. I was hungry for sleep yet was unwilling to enter the bedroom. I had stripped the bed but not yet remade it. I spent the nights in an armchair and thought I might do so until such time as I was able to behave normally. I trusted in the natural order of things to restore something like instinct and appetite. I had no idea how long this process would take.

And yet I behaved efficiently, or efficiently enough, felt a moment of relief after the undertaker's men – subdued tactful creatures – had left, felt able to refuse the sedatives the doctor offered me. Miss Thompson, also tactful, said she would contact Digby's business associates as soon as I gave her a date for the funeral. More difficult were the neighbours, acquaintances who felt obliged to express extreme shock and sorrow, as if doing all this on my behalf. They were perhaps disconcerted by my apparent lack of emotion and strove to compensate for my deficiency. Mrs Crook in particular seemed eager to keep me company, now that we were both widows, and I was obliged to listen to her own reminiscences for one whole afternoon, a helpless prisoner in my own flat. As soon as I felt able to do so I mimed exhaustion and excused myself, saw her back to her door, washed the teacups, ate a banana, and prepared for the main business of the day, which was to walk. This I could only do at night or in the very early morning, when there were no witnesses and pure anonymity could be taken for granted.

I discovered this resource on the night after Digby's death. I may have had a genuine physical longing for fresh air, but what I really wanted was an illusion of liberty, of freedom from the immense amount of labour that confronted me, not in learning to live without Digby, for that I knew I could manage, but in composing a life in which there would be no limits, no demands on my time or my attention, no duties from which I could make a legitimate escape. This was easier to contemplate in the dark than in ordinary daylight, and besides, I was no longer tired. My walks were long but uninteresting. One night I walked in a straight line along Old Brompton Road to Knightsbridge, to Hyde Park Corner, along Piccadilly, through St James's, and back along the Mall, Ebury Street, Pimlico, Royal Hospital Road, and then, in a taxi, to Melton Court. Another night took me along the river, though I was careful to go nowhere near the Fairlies' house. I had put their names on the list I gave to Miss Thompson; they would be informed along with all the others. I had no wish to see them, to see anyone. When Betsy telephoned about our proposed lunch I told her the news briefly, and heard her faltering expressions of sadness for me with gratitude, but without much sadness in my response. My own sadness was not an issue. I had told so many people that I was able to manage that I felt obliged to be tougher than I was expected to be. My own expectations were as shadowy as those obscure silent wanderings, passing from the light of one lamppost to the next, barely aware of other wanderers, who I assumed to have much the same preoccupations as myself, grateful to be among strangers.

For it was not quite grief, this feeling of displacement. It was rather more like a period of transition, an initiation into a different life, one without instructions. I should have to invent a life that others would see as normal, but which would in fact be profoundly, essentially different. If I thought of Edmund, as I did, it was because I knew that sex is the antidote to death, and also because I was newly aware of the domesticity of others now that my own had disappeared. In the early morning, almost before daylight, I peered into the windows of basement kitchens, saw tables with checked tablecloths, place settings, or, alternatively, blinds and shutters which excluded me and my kind. I was not yet ready to confront the knowledge that Edmund, in his household, was catered for as easily as I had perhaps catered for my husband, that his life was normal, more normal perhaps than his indulgences. My stolen glances into other people's houses, sometimes symbolically frustrated by curtains, could not help but encounter the solidarity of those not yet obliged to confront my solitude.

I saw Edmund now as he was, a family man, to use the quaint expression, a man supported by all the systems that have to be in place if life is to proceed normally. A knowledge of the rules to be obeyed, together with a consciousness of having in due course obeyed them, had brought about a sense of safety from which it might become necessary to escape. That was where I fitted in, and I saw my tenure as limited. Perhaps I was unduly pessimistic, perhaps I had a general sense of endings, but now I also saw how little emotion this sort of affair could contain if it had to remain pleasurable. Hence no empathy, no curiosity, none of the conversations I was able to fantasize on my own and which had no place in Britten

Street. No place anywhere, for intimacy would be reserved for home. A sort of loyalty would thus be maintained which would give a man like Edmund a consciousness of behaving correctly, for any real infidelity would involve an exchange of feeling. If no feeling other than the purely creaturely were experienced then no real transgression could be seen to have occurred. It came to me, in the course of one early morning walk, that only worldly respectability, of the sort enjoyed by Edmund and his kind, could act as a bulwark against the qualms of conscience and the reproaches of the just.

It was perhaps an added unfairness – a purely social un-fairness – that it was my position that was impossible rather than his. I should be conspicuous now, no longer shielded by my husband. I should be subjected to scrutiny, as the lonely always are, a subject of speculation for those very people who had expressed sympathy on my behalf. I no longer thought of disappearing to Paris; the thought of greater isolation intimi-dated me. The only protection would be another man, not the kind of man to whom my thoughts all too naturally turned, but someone mild, respectable, well thought of – rather like my husband, in fact. I should be warmly accepted back into the mainstream so long as the idea of passion were rigorously absent. What I desired would not be relevant. I should be re-admitted if I exhibited all those marls of benign normality – holidays, dinner parties – that are the province of the main-tained and the protected, of whom no questions are asked. If I were to exhibit an unseemly solitariness I should fail a number of tests and be condemned to perpetual marginality. On my own I should have to live without a mask. Men would leave me alone, for any appeal to them would be ambiguous. Even Edmund would find me awkward, as if he feared encroachment, as if I were making some kind of appeal. We were not friends, as I now saw. We had no common ground, and apart from what took place in the flat in Britten Street, no real intimacy. From his own intimacy I could expect nothing; Constance had disliked me even before she had any reason to do so, and I had always been a little frightened of her without quite knowing why. Now every kind of custom or politeness barred me from her presence. It was not the company of women that I craved; I needed something stronger, more cynical, more brutal. Only a sustained scrutiny of the facts would help me to ignore those glimpses of other lives afforded me on my dawn walks, of a table set for more than one place, of a vase of flowers on a windowsill, of a child's toy abandoned by a chair.

'How will you live now?' asked my mother on the telephone from Spain. We had agreed that she would not attend the funeral but would come later, for a proper visit, as she put it. 'Of course, you'll have the flat,' she went on, without waiting for an answer. 'And enough to live on, I presume. Did Digby leave much?'

'I have no idea.' This was true. 'I haven't seen a lawyer yet. I suppose that takes place after the funeral.'

'It's not easy,' she said. 'Even with money, although money helps. When your father and I split up I felt a certain relief. And of course it wasn't a sudden decision. We'd been back and forth for years. And we weren't happy. Were you happy, would you say?' Again she did not wait for an answer. 'Happy enough, I suppose. And we'd always looked after you. A charmed life, really.'

'Yes, I was lucky.'

'Yet when the relief wore off I felt rather exposed. That's why I went away so much. It took courage, I can tell you, but I managed it. I met new people, although I never got to know them. That was how I met Judy, the girl I share with. I call her a girl but we're really two old women. When I look at her I see myself, and I don't like it. Oh, we get on all right, I suppose, but I can't help feeling that women aren't meant to live together. But what can I do? I'm no good on my own; I need company. You're not like me. You were always happy enough on your own, even as a little girl. Of course you'll feel it now. I should marry again, if you get the chance. Even today, in this liberated age, married women have more prestige. Or you could always take a lodger.'

At first I thought she meant a lover, until I realized that there was no love left in her make-up either for herself or for anyone else. This demonstrated to me the extreme dislocation of my own family life. I did not wish my parents back – my fear was that my mother would suggest moving in with me – but I should have welcomed the opportunity of moving in with someone else's family. There was no family I knew who could perform this function for me. Nor was I willing to take on my mother. My father had sent a letter, to which I should eventually have to reply. I had no wish to see him either. Nor had his present wife any wish to see me. My mother's disaffection had apparently been handed on to her. Either that, or he had the knack of marrying the wrong sort of woman. I felt immensely distanced from both of them. What I did notice, unwillingly, was my mother's increasing solipsism. She seemed more anxious to talk about her own plight than of mine. I took this to be emblematic of my new reduced status. Either that or she was succumbing to the distress of advancing age, which was not yet my affair.

'So look after yourself,' I heard her say. 'Don't neglect your appearance. Take care of your teeth. Nobody could say I've let myself go. Not that there's anyone here to take a blind bit of notice. Still, I have my pride, or what's left of it. Best foot forward, and all that. Lots of love, and I'll see you soon.'

This was Wednesday. I had somehow to get myself through to Friday, the day of the funeral. I had never been to a funeral before: at my age, still young by any reasonable standard, I did not know anyone who had died. I assumed that after the brief ceremony people would come back to the flat, that I should have to acknowledge their good wishes and express a gratitude which would put the final seal on Digby's death. In the mirror I looked haggard and unkempt, the result not only of my vagrancy but of my recent obsession. I felt genuine shame on my own behalf, as if I had woken up after a period of madness. I saw that I had behaved badly, and also that I had behaved out of character. For surely I was not a bad person? I had accepted what had been offered; now I saw that what had been offered had been insufficient, and worse, that I had over-invested in something that was intrinsically worthless, or at best of no consequence.

My feeling of shame extended even to Edmund, who had no use for it. The excuses I had made for him were, I saw, unnecessary, for I had no way of knowing how he felt. His initial enthusiasm, born of speculation, was now exhausted, and my all too eager response was, for the moment, extinguished. I viewed my behaviour with horror, a horror that extended to my nightly wanderings. In truth these had only occupied the few days when nothing appeared to be happening, but they had felt enormous, as if establishing a pattern that I should be obliged to follow for the rest of my life. Now, in this brief interlude of lucidity, I saw that I must behave differently, that my safety, and indeed my sanity, depended on a change of course. I should have to obey the rules, observe the social norms, not those whose pleasure it was to defy them. I saw the rules as safeguards. If one obeyed them one would be entitled to ask for help; if not, not. I even saw that Edmund should obey the rules, that he was a fortunate man who had never doubted his good fortune. There was no need for me to make allowances, either for Edmund or for myself. I thought in terms of transgression, an idea I had not previously entertained. Self-indulgence, such as we both had felt, was perhaps a weakness, and not, as I had thought, a strength. A distant contempt was beginning to make itself felt. I went into the bedroom, put clean linen on the bed, removed Digby's glasses from his bedside table and took them into the study. His place was there now. He would not haunt me, but I had learned about goodness from him, and that, I hoped, would be his legacy to me. The memory of his benevolence would surely protect me in the days to come.

I tidied the flat, prepared it to receive visitors, checked to see whether I had enough coffee, sherry, funeral baked meats. What were these exactly? I resolved to do some shopping, issue into the streets at a normal hour, behave like a woman of my class and type, almost old enough to conform to the pattern set for me. I had grown thin and pale, strange considering all the fresh air I had had. But the air of those nights had seemed mephitic compared with the light of this new day. The sun that bathed the restored prospect was beneficent, as beneficent as the new order I was meant to observe. The only aberrant thought that occurred to me was that Edmund might be at the funeral, might even come back to the flat. He had been associated with Digby's business, which would now, I supposed, have to be sold. He knew the extent of Digby's investments, held his portfolio, if that was what stockbrokers did. I supposed I might be quite comfortably off, another legacy from Digby. All this could be dealt with by a solicitor.

Nevertheless I did not want to be seen in my present distressed state. I made an appointment with the hairdresser, took my keys, and with a feeling almost of curiosity went out into the normal day.

It was a radiant autumn, one that inspired kind thoughts, I am sure, certainly kind smiles on the faces I encountered. The early mists that had shrouded me on recent mornings had dispersed; the sun now had a certain warmth. There was abundant colour, in the trees, in the dahlias and asters at the corner flower stall, yet one knew that all this was brief, subject to the iron rule of the coming winter. These now were my surroundings, and I should never leave them. I was light-headed, with hunger, I supposed, yet I did not like to stop at a café, was in fact not quite ready to do so. I was enveloped in something like modesty, viewed my notion of going back to Paris with trepidation, almost with alarm. Such adventures were appropriate to the very young, just as my love affair, I supposed, was appropriate to early middle age. I was after all no longer a girl, and the day would come when I might be glad not to have to be subjected to strenuous activities such as those which had taken place in Britten Street. I felt that I had suffered two losses, that of Digby and that of Edmund, for I did not see how the example of the one could fail to affect my opinion of the other. Digby had always obeyed the rules, and I saw the virtue of this. Integrity, consistency – qualities I had once doubted – were now uppermost in my mind. I had thought the pagan gods of antiquity were protecting me: I should have remembered their carelessness, their fecklessness. While still untouched by any alternative mythology I was obliged to rethink my earlier attempt to be worthy of those careless feckless deities. I was human, fallible, yet I did not intend to do penance. The memory of my emancipation was still too vivid in my mind for me to disallow it. The memory might fade, had, perhaps, already faded, but it would not disappear. These two ideologies, goodness and freedom, were difficult to reconcile. The conundrum had never been resolved. Certainly I could not resolve it. Yet, strangely, both imposed a loyalty, an obligation. It would be difficult to see how such an obligation could be met.

At the hairdressers women nodded and smiled at me, as if re-admitting me to the company of the righteous. Sylvia, the receptionist, came out from behind her desk, clasped my hand, and murmured, 'I'm so sorry.' This, from a virtual stranger, was so affecting that tears filled my eyes, the first since Digby's death. 'I'll bring you a cup of coffee,' she said. 'I know how you like it.' She was a woman of about my own age, unmarried, to judge from her ringless finger, and yet in comparison with myself she seemed mature, dedicated to her sexless profession, for no man ever came here, unless to collect his wife. I did not want to be drawn into any female conspiracy of the sort I had often witnessed in this place, women discussing minor ailments or telling of laughable mishaps which were somehow reassuring. For this was an establishment not favoured by the young; I liked it because it was so close to home, and because Alex, who did my hair, was so soothing and deferential. In my normal state of mind I found this irksome; in my reduced condition it felt like balm.

'Even when you expect it it's a shock,' he said, smoothing the hair back from my face.

'I didn't expect it,' I said. 'I thought he was perfectly well.'

This was so sad that I felt the tears threaten again. A glass of water was tactfully placed at my elbow. 'It's just that I'm rather tired,' I tried to explain. It was true that the exertions of the last few days were beginning to tell on me. The thought that I could sleep in my bed again comforted me. A long night, one in which I would remain safely indoors, looked like normality restored. I could hardly believe that I had felt so little, wandering in the dark. With the threatened return of sorrow, and with that other less legitimate sense of loss, I would be obliged to conceal myself at home until I had shaped the new character I should be obliged to inhabit.

These kind people had done something to reconcile me to the daytime world, which was now my world. I thought with distaste, even bewilderment, of my recent nights and early mornings, in which I had fancied myself as some sort of exile, or a character in one of those foreign films I used to devour when on my own in Paris. And those glimpses of other lives that I had imagined . . . These daytime streets, through which I moved almost naturally, impressed me by their very neutrality; there was no danger, no sense of exile, rather an impressive ordinariness in which I might attempt to immerse myself. Life must now be invented, with no nostalgia for a past which at last seemed truly past. Almost without emotion I went to the shops, bought the sort of provisions that would be appropriate, acceptable to the unnatural gathering that would take place after the funeral. I would make tiny sandwiches, like the ones my mother used to serve to her guests after their afternoon bridge game. I never went back in my mind to those early days, as I dare say most people do: they had been so uncomfortable that I had been glad to exchange them for everything that came later, though that too had been uncomfortable. I should spend days in my flat, comfortable at last, but comfortable only in the sense that there would be nothing further to disturb my peace.

The worst had happened, or had it? Apart from the almost welcome blankness of the future, I did not foresee any incident that would bring back the memory of those night walks. Of my other life, the life that had almost threatened my real life, I thought less. My main feeling was one of gratitude that Digby had known nothing of it, and that I had been with him at the end. For that reason some fragment of decency had been maintained. It was that fragment, minimal though it might have been, to which I clung. It would have to sustain me through the days to come.

In the flat the mild sun bathed the unobtrusive chairs, tables, lamps that appeared newly dear to me. I sat down and wondered how to fill the rest of the day. I could read, of course, but I realized, with a further sense of loss, that I no longer wanted to, and, worse, that I might have no further use for those romances that had so absorbed me in the past. For surely they were romances? My definition of a romance was a story that proceeded to a satisfactory conclusion. This, rather than a happy end, was what made literature so compulsive. Those heroes, those heroines, even the most benighted, had weathered the storm and had been brought safely home. Novels, the sort of nineteenth-century novels I had loved, had conferred a sense of order, of justice, that was surely a moral gift. Jane Eyre, David Copperfield, had survived their time of trial, and even if that time had been grievous their authors had seen fit to reward them. Therefore one participated in that reward, since it seemed so natural, so merited. Now it seemed to me that such endings were fanciful, that in fact there were no endings to human affairs, particularly not to affairs of the heart. One's sad longings might be, and usually were, unsatisfied, so that if one were lucky they merely receded, but remained subject to conjecture. One returned time and again to memories, or fantasized alternative endings, in which the triumph of the moralist, or of the novelist, prevailed. But I had been expelled from that sequence and should now have to live with doubt. I did not wish to read novels that drove this message home. Therefore I might not be able to read at all, or not until a time when I could draw the line under my own life with a feeling of gratitude that I had done no real harm. This might be the most conclusive loss of all. I put the books back tidily on the shelves. *Madame Bovary* was the last to be cancelled in this way.

If I felt unhappiness on the day preceding the funeral it showed itself in symptoms which I recognized for what they were: fear, above all fear, and a sort of childish distress. The headaches, the nausea I was able to overcome because their origins were so obvious. The greatest dread was of the ceremony itself, when I should have to show a courage I no longer possessed. I saw, in a detached sort of way, that mild illness could provide an alibi for a day that was bound to be dreadful, that one could treat oneself gently, take remedies, abandon any kind of initiative, even sleep. In the end I went to bed and did indeed sleep. But it was a sleep from which I woke with the feeling of dread intensified, as if only now coming into its own. The ordeal ahead of me seemed impossible for one of my meagre accomplishments. I willed myself to imagine the time when it would all be over, and saw, with a flash of something like hope, that there might yet be room for the sort of energy that must have left a trace, and even for pleasure. This did not strike me as disloyal. I too should have to die, and it was incumbent on me to live for as long as I could, in the circumstances that the gods had devised for me. I reminded myself that these gods were not jealous, like the fearful God of the Old Testament. They were indifferent, malicious, even, but their concerns mirrored one's own. With such an arrangement one could come to terms, however hard the process might be.

As it happened I was hardly conscious of the actual funeral. I was aware of Betsy's hand under my elbow, but I felt so faint that I had to close my eyes; had it not been for Betsy I might have fallen. My strength returned as soon as the doors of the small chapel were opened and the light flooded in. In the flat I was glad of the company of about thirty people, few of whom I knew. I thanked everyone profusely, urged them to eat, to drink. I did not look forward to being alone again. I saw Edmund, standing in a corner, saw him detach himself from the wall against which he had been leaning as Betsy approached with a plate of smoked salmon sandwiches. I saw his polite smile warm into something more appreciative; I saw Betsy's eyes widen, a slight flush spread over her cheeks. I was distracted by the guests who were leaving. When I searched for them again it was too late. They were already gone.

The following morning I went to Britten Street, let myself into the flat, and left my key on the table. In that way there would be no need for explanations on either side.

9

'You got home all right?' I asked, in as neutral a tone as possible.

'Oh, yes. That nice Mr Fairlie gave me a lift.'

I felt there was nothing else I needed to know. What was to follow I knew already. Besides, I was finding it difficult to maintain my side of the conversation. I felt curiously abstracted, as if I were taking in too little oxygen. I was sitting in Betsy's flat, without altogether remembering how I had got there. She had invited me for coffee, and I had gone, though I had had a strong impulse to refuse her invitation. Yet I had no reason for doing so. What I really wanted was to stay at home, in bed, if possible. I wanted the coming winter to enclose me, so that I could not be seen. That was my instinctive wish: that no one should see me.

'He's very nice, isn't he?' said Betsy. 'Very easy to talk to.'

I had never found him easy to talk to. To listen to, perhaps, or rather to tease out what he was not saying, matters I could supply for myself, in the shape of those domestic details for which I was hungry. It was those basement kitchens which now formed naturally in my mind, those imagined lives which were, I was sure, rich in the kind of detail I had previously found in books, and which I embraced in a way that seemed to have persisted for a long time and to have survived my own routine attempts, some of them successful, to create a domesticity for Digby and myself. Those other lives seemed more fulfilling than my own, as if they had been composed in another dimension to which I had only intermediate access.

'What did you talk about?' I said idly.

'Well, he asked me how I knew you, and I told him we had been at school together. Then he asked me what I had done since, and we got on to Paris.'

'Did you tell him about Daniel?'

'No, no, I didn't.' She looked puzzled. 'Do you think I should have done?'

'No, of course not.'

'It's just that the whole episode seems slightly unreal now. As if it happened a very long time ago. As if we were both children. I felt rather badly about that. And I don't fully understand how I could have let myself in for that sort of . . . adventure. I'm not really a romantic. I think I always wanted to settle down. Yet sometimes I should like to discuss this with a man. To get a man's point of view, you know?'

I did not at that moment see that I was in any danger from Betsy. Someone so artless, so sincere, could not possibly appeal to a man like Edmund, who was surely expert at deflecting that sort of desire for full disclosure. There had certainly been true feeling between Daniel and herself, but it would have been the feeling between two adolescents, children, even. In that sense it would have been authentic, but in that sense only.

'He asked me what my plans were,' she went on happily. 'I told him I was looking for a part-time job, even something voluntary, and he said he might be able to help me. Apparently his wife is looking for an assistant.'

Like many women of her type Constance Fairlie ran a small charity that had to do with aid to the homeless and was based in some aristocratic religious organization to which, surprisingly, she gave her adherence. This had been mentioned at those far-off dinner parties that Digby and I had attended, and in those days I had been full of respect. Her part in this endeavour, as I came to see, was to extract money from her wealthy friends, and this she did by hosting or sponsoring various functions – dinners, receptions – at which some relatively prominent speaker would give a brief address. This efficient but painless way of doing good was completely in tune with Constance Fairlie's strange and to me unknown loyalties. I could see how her acid humour, which might well co-exist with religious leanings, would make her a more than proficient worker in this field. I doubt if she ever got very close to her homeless beneficiaries: that task would be left to others. But as worldly patron she would have been quite an asset. She had the status necessary for such work, and she had the attributes, the fine house suitable for such gatherings, and the genial husband who gained additional respect from his wife's gratifying activities.

'What would you be doing?' I asked Betsy.

'I've no idea. But it might be quite nice to work in a private house. I mean, she works from home. I shouldn't have to go to an office, or anything. It would be voluntary, of course. And it would get me out of the flat.' She grimaced. 'It's definitely a flat you'd want to get out of, isn't it? I said as much to Edmund, to Mr Fairlie.' She blushed slightly. 'He said I must call him Edmund.'

'Why not?' I said. 'And when do you start this job?'

'Well, apparently there might be a slight delay, because they're going to move. They're looking for a house, something slightly smaller, I understand. So he said he'd let me know. I gave him my telephone number.'

I could not help but salute the ease with which this had been engineered. At that moment I had warnings of what I might be called upon to witness, for I had no doubt that the

Fairlie household would be the target for all Betsy's ardour, the loyalty that should have made her the ideal partner, and indeed had already done so. I also knew that both Edmund and Constance would be expert at deflecting that ardour, or rather those elements of it for which they would have no use. I knew something of their cast of mind: they were in control, and determined to remain so. I understood this because I had tried to be the same, and for a time had appeared to succeed. But I had never succeeded as well as Edmund, whose will had always been superior to my own. And as for Constance, whom I hardly knew but whose cruelty had always seemed to proceed from supreme confidence, I now saw that Constance might even be superior to her husband in this respect. Would she not have had enough practice over the years at discouraging other women, women who might have been drawn to her so attractive husband, and would she not have been expert at this task, putting paid to some misplaced enthusiasm with a light but stinging remark? Might not Edmund rely on her to do this for him? Such collusion between partners, or indeed associates, could, to the outsider, appear revolting, or enviable, depending on how that outsider was placed. I hated to think of the defeats thus inflicted, and endured. Some life-saving instinct had prompted me to divorce myself from this situation before such a defeat, which I might have sensed in the abstract. Edmund was protected by his own immunity – to remorse, though that was too simple: to sorrow. He and Constance were monstrous in so far as their emotions were rudimentary, confined to self-satisfaction and self-preservation. I could see why Constance might have had religious leanings. She might, over a period of time, have become aware of her own coldness, might have sought to put this out of reach, as if true warmth were the gift of another, or rather Another. And having discharged a passing distress in this manner, and made it the province of that Other, she would return briskly to her various obligations, one of which was to maintain marital equilibrium in the way that both she and her husband understood.

I did not care to see Betsy go down that road, nor did I care for the part I should have to play in this. Far better that I should pursue a dull existence, without memories of my own former addiction. Yet what I knew of Edmund was, though reprehensible, ultimately reassuring. He was too practised to get himself involved with a woman of Betsy's type. It was even likely that he was unacquainted with Betsy's type, that he thought all women able to take care of themselves, as the feminists of the time were so loudly proclaiming. He would have admired such women, seen them as equal partners in the sex war. That sex might be a metaphor for love might have occurred to him as a young man, when those matters were less clear, was a possibility, yet very little sentiment had been carried over into his adult life. A woman like Betsy, with her desire to become part of a family, would strike him simply as odd. Were women in the 1980s not pursuing their own ends, eager to get ahead with plans to conquer territory formerly the province of men? Was there not something Napoleonic about the new woman, something titillating as well as provocative? Whereas Betsy, who asked only to lay her life at some man's feet, would be regarded as quaint, anomalous, by Edmund, by any man prepared to make war, not love.

Yet I had to admit there was an aura about her. Though I knew it was an aura of goodness others might see it as desire, as passion in its most restricted sense, whereas it was destined to be unlimited. That wide-eyed sympathy, that need to go too far, that potential realm of excess, with which I had had little sympathy in the past, when her avidity had seemed irksome, had been slightly tempered by her experiences in Paris, so that she no longer overwhelmed one with her enthusiasm, but was able to listen, to comment, like any other sensible grown-up person. And yet threatening to break through, to break out, was the girl who had proclaimed tragic soliloquies as if they alone could express the weight and pressure of her longing. What mysterious deprivation had occurred, before I knew her, perhaps even before she knew herself? The data were explanatory but insufficient: the slightly discredited father, the spinster aunt whose self-abnegation was mirrored in the pale lips and the discreet garments that had evoked my mother's pity and derision . . . The most crucial figure – the mother – was entirely absent. Nor did Betsy ever refer to her, either because the subject was too painful, or because a veil of silence seemed to have descended on that household. More likely the latter, I reckoned. Thus the awkwardness of an unexplained absence, almost a social solecism, had been maintained, and it had been entirely due to Betsy's loyalty that her reduced family had enjoyed anything approaching normality. Yet perhaps there had been some flaw, some taint, in the mother to make her die so young, of 'complications' which were also mysterious and to which Betsy could only refer vaguely and with a sense of embarrassment. Perhaps the mother had been eclipsed in other ways, mentally, emotionally; perhaps – a dreadful supposition, this – she had also been the victim of her husband's diagnostic inadequacy. None of this could be known, but it was surely relevant. Betsy's desire to be part of a viable family would have been her most primal need. This had been obscured by her determined blitheness, as she shouldered the task of being a credit to her aunt and appeared to look forward to a future of work and effort without the advantage of any sort of encouragement. No doubt Miss Milsom had done her best, but Miss Milsom had been defeated from the start by a sense of duty she had not entirely chosen. She may have been aware of her own inadequacies: her legacy, not entirely financial, might have been an unspoken message to Betsy that there were choices to be made, though she had known few herself.

And then that fortuitous concatenation of high and low drama, of Racine and Hollywood, the lines learned and declaimed to indifferent friends and classmates, and the cinema on Saturday nights, and the mystifying behaviour of those who obeyed different codes, who knew about calculation, and delay and how to defeat rivals! The one must have warred with the other, yet the message of both was that love was the true business of men and women, particularly of women. She would have rejected the amorous sleight-of-hand deployed by the stars and allied herself with the tragic sincerity of those other actors, those heroic players in the eternal game of love and loss. '*Dans un mois, dans un an, comment souffrirons-nous / Que tant de mers me séparent de vous / Que le jour recommence et que le jour finisse / Sans que jamais Titus puisse voir Bérénice . . .*' She had adopted such behaviour as her standard, not knowing or not caring that it was obsolete. Her belief, and it was almost a religious belief, that such virtue as those prototypes represented must find its equivalent in human affections, and that she need only maintain that belief for the ideal conclusion to be reached, was what gave her fine eyes that strange starry light, as if at any moment her very own hero might materialize and escort her to a future which would unite them both.

It was true that her looks had benefited from that idealism. Her air of expectancy would appeal to some, though it might be misconstrued by others. Edmund no doubt had been amused and touched. His prudence would protect him from a false step until he was sure that she understood what was at stake and even then might hold him back. At that stage he would hand her over to Constance whom Betsy, if still unaffected, would embrace with equal fervour. If she responded like a normal woman she might, by the same token, prove onerous, in which case Constance would perform her usual function and Betsy would be carefully or not so carefully dismissed. I saw as if for the first time the dreadful dynamics of this couple, saw too that I had had a lucky escape. But was it so lucky? I had volunteered to leave, and in so doing had deprived myself of a source of pleasure of which I was now more in need than ever. I felt drab, drowsy, as if some life-giving supply had been switched off, leaving me almost comatose. I had nothing better to do than to sit in this room bearing witness to another woman's dawning excitement, for we were separated by something more than experience, even experience of the same man. Some lingering decency kept me silent, though it would have served my purpose to have uttered a warning. But whereas I had never doubted Edmund's duplicity, and had schooled myself to understand it, even to accommodate it, I knew that Betsy was entirely unacquainted with this particular quality. Her loyalty to Daniel had no doubt been prompted by the same idealism, whereas a normal woman would have summed him up as a fantasist and given him a wide berth. Therefore I must respect what was in the kindest interpretation a form of innocence that was unusual, indeed rare, in a grown woman. The sad act of growing up is that this quality is lost, worse, that it can lead one astray, and worse even than that, be derided, even be seen as a fault. Being good has no virtue if it is grounded in ignorance, and I could see from Betsy's apparent conversion (or was it real?) to

Edmund's passing favour that she was ready to place her entire time at his disposal, and to accept his overtures in the hope that they might lead to the sort of inclusiveness that she had always craved.

He might have seen something different in her response to his offer, might have intuited a fervour which it could be in his interest to explore. He would have no truck with her ideals, but was astute enough to be able to bypass them. My worst thought was that he might even have been wryly impressed, might indulge himself by feeling more than he should, might even fall a little in love with her. But here, at this critical point, my own hardheadedness prompted me to reflect that he would know the risks involved. That was the difference between Betsy and myself: I preferred to know the truth, however bleak, and what strength of character I had impelled me to look these facts in the face, whereas Betsy might have been created by Dickens. She was Little Dorrit, whose goodness, even on the page, grows a little tiresome.

There were unusual intervals of silence in our conversation, of which I think only I was aware. Betsy had retrieved some kind of authority from her recent turn of fortune, and I could see that in some mysterious way our positions had become reversed. Not that there was anything more than coincidence at work here: I was quite sure that she had formed no comparison, or no conscious comparison, between the possibilities open to us. Yet I made no attempt to hide from her, or from myself, that I had reached the end of one particular road: I was a widow, and it was proper to assume that my emotional life was over. This was so true that I saw no sense in disputing the fact. Whatever I might have wanted from the future was now eclipsed by the very obvious fact of my solitariness. I did not have the courage to undertake new initiatives. My recent decision to return to Paris was not after all a decision, for I was incapable of putting it into action, and in any event what would I do there? If I were to live the life of an exile I could do so much more comfortably by remaining where I was, surrounded by familiar possessions, my position unambiguous. I had undergone some further rite of passage, from the experiences that pertain to youth to the anticipation of ageing, when one becomes fearful of having one's habits and customs disturbed. This new vulnerability was brought about not only by Digby's death but by the removal of pleasure. I was able to mourn both Digby and Edmund in equal measure, disloyal as this might seem. One huge loss, which encompassed them both, seemed to be my lot, and I could see that unless I were very careful I might end up mourning for myself.

For I had certainly been reduced, as I had never thought I should be. Even in Paris I had maintained a certain inviolability. In London, at home, I might unthinkingly conform, as my mother had done, despite her frustrations. And I should have to assume a dignity which would be porous, made worse by the more successful lives of others. I should be useful as a confidant, an invidious position which I had no means of avoiding. For I could never recapture the kind of eagerness with which Betsy had outlined her useful future, the one now being devised for her. I could see only idleness for myself. No plans had been made for me; whatever I did or did not do was entirely in my gift. Yet the courage it would take to remove myself from this position was for the time being beyond me. I was only partly restored by the look of sympathy in Betsy's eyes. Sympathy was the last thing I wanted.

'You've let your hair grow,' I said quickly, to furnish one of those silences which we had occupied by carefully drinking coffee and eating biscuits.

'Oh, I couldn't be bothered with it. Does it look all right?'

'It suits you. In fact it suits you rather better.'

She had tied it back with a black ribbon, and the new nakedness of her face added to its appeal. She still had an air of having recently returned from abroad, in her deft movements, in her new confidence. I could see that she was very attractive, that the latency from which she had previously suffered was at an end.

'It was really a bit of luck, our meeting like that. Though of course it was a very sad occasion.'

'Meeting Edmund, you mean?'

'Yes. Did you know him well?'

'He was a friend of Digby's.' I got up from one of her uncomfortable chairs. 'I must go.'

'I'll walk with you a bit. I want to know how you really are. I can't believe I've been talking so much about myself.' She gave a little laugh, as if better to convey her disbelief. 'I do so want us to keep in touch. After all we've been friends for most of our lives. And now that I'm so near . . . You must let me help in any way I can. If you feel . . . you know. If you want to talk.'

It was kindly meant, I am sure. Yet once again a discrepancy had made itself felt. I belonged to the past. Suddenly, and quite fiercely, I wanted Edmund back for myself. In the next moment I saw that I had ruined my chances, and, worse, given up without a struggle.

We left the flat, with its witheringly subdued light, and issued out into another beautiful morning. So far this had been a poignant autumn, a gift to the more poetic kind of journalist. I had taken to reading the newspapers very carefully, addressing myself to the facts, and I had been surprised by the unexpected soulfulness displayed in this matter. This gave me a moment of pleasure every day, for the weather is a democratic institution in which everyone has a vote, and in any case it made a change from the Business News, which I also read carefully in an effort to understand my financial position. This, as far as I could make out, was comfortable. I could, if I cared to, distribute largesse on my own account rather than respect those who were able to do so in a frivolous manner which, finally, had nothing to do with me. I had no desire to acquire property or to own anything that was not legitimately mine. I did not intend to keep different houses for different purposes. Of the whole affair this was what most offended me. The flat in Britten Street was a symbol of calculation that perhaps only a man could make. I could see now how perverse its appeal had been. More than the flat I regretted the garden and the afternoons I had spent sitting there. That was a pleasure of which I need not feel ashamed. I did not think I should ever go there again.

This particular morning seemed more significant than most, as if it marked the decline of one life and the resurgence of another, as if in fact I was sending Betsy off to a brighter future than any she could have designed for herself. I took careful note – of that sunlit patch of brick, of those late roses in a bucket outside the greengrocer's, of that damp butt of a cigar lying on the pavement. This was now the currency I might exchange with others, free from ulterior motive, free from personal concerns. I was aware of Betsy walking beside me in equable silence, as if she too were under the spell of the beneficent weather, but when I stole a glance I could see that her colour was still high. A kind of mutism prevented me from talking confidently or persuasively, although it might have been in both our interests if I had done so. I did not do this because although we were both silent, and although there was matter there that might have been discussed, she had not quite intuited what that matter was. If she suspected prior knowledge between Edmund and myself it was knowledge of a purely social nature: I had known him in my capacity as a married woman, and was thus disbarred from intimacy. She was disposed to pity me for what were certainly legitimate reasons, but I was not inclined to receive the sympathy she so obviously felt.

If Edmund had appeared before me at that moment I should have sent him away, as I had never been able to do. I should have consigned him to whatever complexities of feeling he might have entertained when sitting in Betsy's flat after the funeral of an old friend. Indeed the emotions aroused by a funeral might have had their effect. His own mother had recently died; he might have been touched by a sense of mortality. If he thought of me it would have been with the same unwelcome aura. But I was convinced that he no longer thought of me, nor was I able to derive any pride from the way I had avoided tedious discussion. What reasons could I have given for ending the affair? None that he had not known, and ignored. My own actions now appeared to me severely delimited, as if a natural conclusion had been agreed by both of us. He would have had a brief nod of recognition at the elegance of my gesture in leaving the key, and then have given the matter no further thought.

'You will let me know if there's anything you want?' Betsy said. 'I mean, you must be pretty worn out. Let me know if you don't feel like shopping . . .'

'I'm not an invalid,' I said.

'Of course you're not. But I know how these things take their toll. Are you eating properly? I'd suggest lunch, only I've got to be back for the central heating man. You probably noted how cold it was in there.'

I sent her on her way, knowing that that was what she wanted. I had a feeling that the central heating man had been an excuse. Yet when I turned at the end of the street I saw that she had done the same. As we both waved, with unmistakable yet surprising fervour, I saw in that precise moment that we were still friends, and that it was precisely our friendship, odd though it was, that would save us both.

IO

Seated in the restaurant at Peter Jones, after a fruitless morning spent comparing prices and disputing the advantages of this sofa over that, and ending up defeated by the spirit of the place which appeared to address itself to women who knew what they wanted, I saw that Betsy had accepted my invitation as if she were conferring a favour, whereas I had thought to do the same. I had a sense of obligation towards agreements which had been bred in me since childhood, and I knew that in a burst of fellow feeling I had suggested this excursion in an effort to make Betsy feel more comfortable in an uncomfortable world. Now I saw that I need not have troubled, for Betsy smilingly deflected my suggestions, which I urged on her as if I were her absent mother or some other elderly relative. It was I who selected the items I thought she needed, the chairs, the table, the lamps which she, still with a smile, admired but turned down, saying that she still had plenty of furniture in store and was in no hurry to replace it until someone was willing to advise her on this matter, or, alternatively, to take it away.

The restaurant did not restore my temper, since it was populated precisely by the sort of women I was coming to resemble. I wondered why we had not gone to a place frequented by men, in Covent Garden, say, until I reflected that we might not be very welcome or feel at ease there. Even in a feminist age the restaurant barrier is the last to fall. Kind waitresses, safe food seemed to be our lot, but at least no one pointed the finger of scorn, which was a considerable comfort when one had been reduced to the sexless protection afforded by a department store at twelve noon on a weekday morning, when all the serious people were at their work, speaking to each other in the kind of code employed by colleagues, enjoying a more natural form of protection than ours, although we had the freedom of our own decisions. This freedom only Betsy seemed disposed to exert as she gazed out of the window, paying little attention to her surroundings, as if marking a distance between herself and the other women, whom, as someone with a full timetable, she was inclined to pity. For this was her day off, and she was keeping me company, since her day off, in a sense, was time of no consequence, in which nothing much would happen, unlike the days she spent in the Fairlie establishment which were filled with incident and matters for reflection.

It was more than a few weeks since I had seen her, and to my alarm she seemed fully integrated into their household. I could understand this: I had craved such closeness myself but had had the wisdom to remain on the sidelines. My sceptical temperament saddened me but perhaps gave me an outsider's advantage. Betsy, however, would seek such closeness wherever she went and would no doubt persuade herself that she had found it, as she always had done. This seemed to me extremely dangerous, although I could see that this disposition was so entrenched that there must be some degree of satisfaction in indulging it. Besides, I was coming more and more to doubt my own judgement. Although I had behaved with a modicum of face-saving decency I did not care for where this had landed me. I was alone, without consolation, and growing more unwillingly independent by the day. Even I could see the advantages that Betsy now seemed to be enjoying, the chatter, the flux of family life, the more spacious vista than that afforded by her own cramped flat. And she had taken on some of that air of possession that is consciously or unconsciously enjoyed by those who have come into an endowment, either by inheritance or by association. She looked happily bemused, as if attending an entertainment that I had arranged for her. It was I who was disadvantaged now.

I was resolute in not asking her questions. Indeed what I most wanted was some sort of abstract discussion such as I craved and one I found extremely difficult to come by. Whether the constant evasiveness and jokiness were a particularly English feature I could not decide, but I did miss the sort of overheard remark I had so relished in Paris, the willingness to discuss first principles and to invest passion in one's own arguments. For instance, I very much wanted to debate the matter of right and wrong, or whatever terms were now relevant, though Peter Jones was hardly an appropriate setting for this. Why is the Bible so unreliable on this matter, I wanted to know? We are told that the wicked flee where no man pursueth, and then, in another context, that they flourish like the green bay tree. It was only too easy to imagine them, having flourished, fleeing to the kind of resort – Capri, or Cannes – where they would be adequately catered for. This was contingent on my old obsession that time passed doing one's duty was time wasted, or if not wasted, then not fully enjoyed, but who to discuss this with? Certainly not with Betsy, who could only recognize and embrace goodness, and whose acquaintance with evil was so rudimentary as to be useless as a guide. Even in circumstances of the utmost ambiguity, into which I was determined not to enquire, she would maintain a disastrous innocence, crediting everyone with superior and altruistic motives, herself included.

I could not help but notice an overall glossiness which made her stand out in this bourgeois setting, and something of that imperviousness to temperature which is the province of the happy and successful. The weather had declined into day-long cloud and mist and I was already shivering. Betsy, however, wore one of her Parisian suits and seemed not to feel the cold. Several women had appraised her as we had taken our seats, but had, presumably, been disarmed by her unassuming smile. For Betsy, with her excess of good will, was everybody's friend, or was prepared to be. I thought that such obvious virtue, if not its own reward, was certainly its own armour, affording a protection available in all circumstances. Predators would not prevail, for their intentions would not be understood. She was destined to be rewarded by a man of equally spotless disposition, the legendary knight in shining armour in whom she no doubt firmly believed, despite what experience had taught her. And if this person did not exist she would invent one in his place, as she no doubt had done with Daniel. As for the further disillusionment when it came (and there was no doubt that it would come), she would have to rally as best she could. In that way she was no more protected than any other woman, perhaps less so. And I did not see that I had any part to play in that débâcle. I had my own sadness to contend with; my sympathy would be limited by that very fact. And if the reasons for that sadness remained undisclosed, so much the better. One's dignity is a poor thing at the best of times. All the more reason to safeguard it from further attrition.

'What do you do in this job of yours?' I asked. 'I mean, what is there to do?'

'It's the lists, you see. Keeping them up to date.'

'Lists?'

'Lists of donors, actual and potential. There are so many

other charities, all fighting for funding, that it's important to get ahead of them. Fortunately Constance is well placed. She knows so many people. And she has the experience. Of course she does the actual asking.'

'Begging.'

'I don't think it feels like begging if it's in a good cause.'

'And where do you do this?'

'Well, there's a proper office, with a secretary, on the third floor. I sit in a little room she calls her boudoir. Fortunately there's masses of space.'

'You make it sound like Versailles. I do know the house. It's just a large house.'

Privately I was willing to concede that this was not a house like the houses most people lived in. Both Betsy and I had been brought up in houses of fairly generous proportions, but our instincts had remained suburban, as if fashioned by an older mind set. Besides, Betsy's living quarters were reduced to the two floors above her father's surgery, and thus of limited access. Now our homes were even more reduced, and our status had declined proportionately. The Fairlie establishment was palatial, in a prime position overlooking the river, and in the way of these things it conferred a certain splendour on its owners. And there was the mother's house in Scotland, which might be sold, the house in Hampshire, and the house in the Alpilles to which they also had some kind of entitlement, although it belonged to friends who merely lent it to them for the children's holidays. Even friends like these were not within everyone's scope. I thought of the secretary on the third floor, which must be the storey with the dormer windows which I had admired when Digby and I first went there. Even then I was attracted to windows. Now my windows looked out on to an ordinary street and a garage, and although the flat was pleasant enough it was also tame. Betsy's flat was even worse, a pit-stop for transients, overloaded with the furniture which she refused to replace. We had seen, or rather I had pointed out, some pleasant pieces which would have made it more habitable, but by now she was imprinted with the grandeur of the Fairlies' place and had metaphorically thrown in her hand, as if anything that did not rise to their standards was not worth bothering about.

She would never move now, that was clear, as long as she had this adopted home. That was the position: she considered herself to have been adopted. Whereas I was perfectly free to move, and at that moment I could see the advantages in doing so. But that would mean breaking off all attachments, and I was not quite brave enough to do that. Though I knew remarkably few people I could rely on the kindness of familiars, neighbours who had offered their condolences after Digby's funeral, the caretaker, the tradesmen, and my particular friend the dignified Indian who supplied my many newspapers. Though I longed for wider vistas and cleaner air I could not see myself in the country or even in a small town. There were possibilities in my present situation, as those neighbours were keen to remind me. I could visit exhibitions, the theatre, without worrying how to get home late at night. I had done none of this, but the possibilities were there should I choose to take advantage of them. Or I could take up some sort of study, a degree course at Birkbeck, or lectures at the City Literary Institute. I was free to do all or any of these things, and though I might not the choice was mine. The memory of those fictitious evening classes which had been my alibi clouded my mental horizon and might affect any reality I could hope to embrace. This was dangerous territory; such subterfuge, though no longer necessary, was something that troubled me. I was marked for life, whatever my own wishes in the matter. A stronger will than mine had ordained what had taken place, and although I had chosen to cancel it it still had the power of a broken contract which had left me mentally as well as physically impoverished.

'Do you go there every day?' I said quickly, while signalling for the bill.

'Most days, yes.'

'Not the weekends, surely?'

'Well, sometimes, if Constance has something for me to do I quite often help out in the house, or go to the shops, although of course there's a housekeeper.'

'You're not a domestic, Betsy,' I said, sincerely shocked.

'I enjoy it. What else would I do? Besides they're so nice. Constance says I'm such a help. And Edmund says she's grateful to have more time to herself.'

'When did he say this?'

'He sometimes gives me a lift home.' Her helpless smile, the unguarded look of reminiscence in her eyes, which she sought to disguise by looking out of the window, were eloquent in a way no words could convey. Nor were words needed to complete the picture. The picture was already complete.

I felt a sadness which had nothing to do with jealousy but was both more intimate and more universal. It was the same sadness I had felt when I had finally packed my books away, as if henceforth I should be excluded from their stories of trials endured and sometimes overcome. Endurance I knew about but I could see no victory at the end, merely an unwanted stasis. We were in the triumphalist 1980s, when it was almost indecent for a woman to be bereft and to yearn. I felt at one with all those people on the sidelines of life, forced to contemplate the successful manoeuvres in which others were engaged, obliged to listen politely and to refrain from comment. There were no surprises here: this situation had been adumbrated from the start. Indeed I felt as though I had almost willed it, though in fact I had always been an observer. Now, if I were not very careful, I should be called upon to observe another woman's love affair, and worse, to hear every word I spoke to be an agent of compromise, as if I welcomed this development which estranged me even further from a role I had once occupied, as if I were something neutral and colourless and well-meaning that could be called upon for protection and approval.

Nothing was left of the tactician I had once been, offering manufactured excuses, getting away, as I now saw it, with murder. The sun had seemed to shine on my adventure, not only metaphorically but physically, as I sat in that garden that was now only a memory. It had been spring, summer, but now the sky was grey, the mornings dark. I was dominated by the pathetic fallacy; the declining year mirrored my situation. And all I could count on was the night, on which I had come to rely. I yearned for those night hours at low points during the day, went to bed earlier and earlier, making an unnecessary ritual of bathing, comforted myself with a tisane, listened respectfully to the news in an attempt to connect myself with the outside world, in much the same spirit as I read the newspapers in the morning, eager for facts which did not on the whole concern me much. My safety was assured for as long as I did nothing, behaved discreetly, kept my remarks anodyne. The reward for all this was sleep. If I were not careful I should dematerialize. In comparison with this prospect Paris seemed once more a viable alternative.

I saw Betsy looking at me with concern, and I rearranged

my features into the sort of pleasant smile that was obviously required of me. Our positions had been reversed, as was all too plain, but she was too innocent to know the reasons for this. She must be kept in that state, if necessary at my expense, for I had been sufficiently imbued with the spirit of the times to believe in sisterly solidarity, although I knew this to be a fiction in the face of rivalry. But I had retired from this particular conflict, or been retired from it. I viewed my immense courage with astonishment, but in truth I was no fighter, and had always found my best protection to be my independence. Now I was not so sure, but to manage things differently was beyond my powers. I saw the logical outcome of my history to be a form of exile, both figurative and actually available if I had the further courage to put this into effect. And I need not confine myself to Paris; if I chose I could go anywhere, absent myself for good. On my honeymoon in Venice I had sat on the steps of the Redentore, and thought, 'Is this all?' This was not so much incapacity as a longing for further fullness, for completion. I was sufficiently clearsighted to know that I had experienced that completion only briefly, and that memory is no substitute for permanence. Now my place had been taken by another, whose blithe smile had reflected only confidence throughout her life and to whom I could not refuse a favourable outcome. That that was unlikely only added an extra poignancy to a situation which seemed to have come about at the behest of a dramatist of the old school. I was determined to behave well, for that was what I should be called upon to do. I no longer had any choice in this matter, and there was no one to blame.

'Are you all right?' I heard, as if from a distance.

'Me? Fine.'

'Only you're so quiet, not like you somehow. Of course

you've had a rough time.' Her face twisted into a sympathy which was clearly genuine. 'You need cheering up.'

I could not quarrel with that. 'What do you suggest?'

'Something new to wear, perhaps? I always think that helps. Let's see what they've got here.'

'I hardly think . . .'

'While we're here. You're not in a hurry, are you?'

No, I was not in a hurry, was even averse to going home, to an afternoon that would end only when darkness fell. Meekly I followed a now masterful Betsy down the stairs, and with a sinking heart submitted my almost extinct will to that of another. There followed the hell of changing-rooms, as I tried on one unbecoming garment after another, standing obediently as a seamstress pinched a too large skirt tightly at my waist. In a last bid for freedom I almost shouted, 'No, I'm sorry, I've changed my mind,' and had time to regret my rudeness as a disgruntled assistant removed the offending skirt. 'I've got plenty of clothes,' I pleaded. 'I really don't need any more. Besides, I'm not going anywhere.'

'That may be the problem,' Betsy said. 'You ought to find something to do. Mount a plan of attack.'

'I'm actually rather tired,' I said. 'And it's stuffy in here. Shall we go? We could walk a bit.'

I longed for air, for ease of movement. The horror of being penned in a small space with two women who saw me as a child waiting to have decisions made for her was still with me. And I had been rude, and was ashamed of myself. This was being a terrible day, and it was probably my fault. I had thought to offer my patronage in the matter of providing Betsy's flat with a few amenities, but this offer had been turned aside, disregarded, as if it were now beside the point. Favour had been found from another quarter; there was no longer any need to set a trap. Not all the re-arrangement in the world could compare with what had already been enacted.

Out in the air I breathed more easily, although a feeling of suffocation persisted, as if I were being swathed in fabric. This was intensified by the damp mist which pressed against my lips, as if willing me to silence. Such weather was hard to tolerate in the light of previous experiences, yet only yesterday, a day like today, a veiled orange sun of considerable immanence had manifested itself behind the greyness. The effect, however, had been far from reassuring, apocalyptic, rather, as if it might rain blood, or symbolize a warning, like the geese in ancient Rome. Yet nothing terrible had happened; slowly the sun was eclipsed, or perhaps eclipsed itself, and the shadows drew on more decisively in its absence. This was an hour when melancholy was pervasive. But it is true that at such times one calculates how many days, weeks, months will have to pass before summer, calculates how to outwit Christmas, the year's midnight. In the summer one feels younger, less burdened; it is easier to be tolerant, accommodating. I measured the distance between myself and a putative summer with dread, knowing that it would put all my powers of endurance to the test. It was the purest bravado that made me move to embrace Betsy, as we prepared to go our separate ways.

'I'll walk with you a bit,' she said. 'I'm not in a hurry.'

'You're not seeing Edmund this evening, then?' I asked, tired of my own delicacy.

She blushed. 'Well, of course not. He'd only come if . . .' I had to smile at this confusion. 'If he had a message from Constance,' she wound up unconvincingly. 'I wouldn't know if he were coming or not. In any case it would be up to him . . .'

Yes, I might have said. That is the prerogative of errant lovers, those who trade on a woman's mistaken patience. How unlike marriage, I could have told her, when the presence of the other can be taken for granted, so much so that one has time and opportunity to devise one's own escape. The benefits of adultery are not unlike those of marriage, the greatest of which is the knowledge that there is someone to come home to. This advantage, completely unearned, is likely to give offence to those of a narrower outlook. In this there could be a large element of envy.

'Are you all right?' I asked kindly, seeing the blush fade. I should not go down this route again but for the moment I had succeeded in restoring my composure.

'Of course I'm all right. It was you I was worried about. You hardly ate a thing at lunch.'

'It was my way of protesting against the sort of food that women are supposed to like. I should have preferred something coarse, sausages, baked beans on white toast. Tea in a mug. A slice of Dundee cake wrapped in cellophane. An unfiltered cigarette.'

'Well, you could have had the cigarette.'

'I don't smoke,' I said sadly. 'Though I suppose I could always take it up.'

'There are places where you can eat that sort of food all day, if you really want to. I don't suppose you're serious. Are you trying to shock me?'

'Possibly, although there's no reason why I should want to. Anyway, you're far too easily shocked. You always were.'

This made it easy for one or other of us to hark back to the old days, to ask, 'Do you remember So-and-So?' or 'What happened to Such-and-Such?' Here I should be handing the advantage back to Betsy, who had faithfully kept in touch with our old friends. They might now have to go, as she isolated herself in the interest of maximum availability. She too would in time discover the limits of this exclusivity, and for a moment I felt genuine indignation on her behalf.

'I think it's I who have shocked you,' she said.

'Not really.' This was true, though it is sometimes difficult to measure the extent of shock. 'Just be sure to look after yourself, your own part in this, I mean. However it turns out. Don't let yourself be monopolized by the Fairlies. They're a brutal couple.'

'Yes,' she said. 'I know.'

After that we smiled at each other, and embraced in good faith.

'Come to me next time. For lunch, I mean. Come any time. I'm always at home, for the time being, anyway. Until Christmas. After that I don't know.'

'I'd love to. It made a difference your being there. After Daniel, I mean, and my moving into the flat. Sometimes I wake up and wonder where I am.'

'Everybody does that.'

'Do they?' She looked surprised. 'And I do get frightened sometimes. That's why I've always been so grateful for company.'

That night I had a dream so vivid that when I woke I wondered whether or not a real event had taken place, or if it was not a dream but a memory that I had somehow mislaid. It took place in a dingy deserted restaurant, and I assumed it was too early for other patrons to have arrived. Edmund was seated at the only occupied table, and he was as I remembered him, in an open-necked shirt, a discarded newspaper beside him. As I approached he looked up, his expression abstracted. I knew, even in the dream, that any hesitation in a greeting was significant, that it might have meant inattention, even reluctance. So clear was this that I could even see the level of coffee in his cup, see the pattern on the cup itself. He looked at me, puzzled, then said, 'We make a great couple.' In a second his face exploded into joy as he saw Betsy approaching behind me. She was dressed in a loose grey sweater and trousers, the sort of clothes she never wore. He got up to welcome her, and as he did so her upper lip lifted into an answering smile that hinted at intimacy. This dream had no sequel: the moment remained frozen, as did their smiles, his joyous, hers open but with a hint of excuse, as if seeking my indulgence. I was simply an observer, and with some remaining instinct of self-preservation I walked past them and sat down at another table. My instinct was to be angry, at their discourtesy if nothing else, and this I managed for the second that my dreaming mind had decreed. Then, still in the dream, my anger gave way to a terrible dismay as I perceived the truth of their involvement, the joy on Edmund's face, the shy disclosure on hers. 'We make a great couple,' he had said, and this remark stayed with me. There was no turning back from this knowledge, which I had produced for my own enlightenment. I had witnessed a love affair, which had perhaps been going on for some time, and of which I had had no warning until it had been demonstrated, made manifest to my unsuspecting but so irrelevant self.

The horror of this dream was still with me when I woke, and it was only gradually, in the course of a normal morning, that I managed to persuade myself that it was in fact only a dream and not a real encounter. It seemed a matter of my continued existence, of life itself, that I survey what I knew of Betsy and discount the phantoms with which the dream had presented me. That there was a connection between them I already knew: Betsy had confessed as much. That there might be true feeling involved was something I had contrived to ignore. As the cold grey day wore on I persuaded myself that what I knew of both of them was my only guarantee of sanity. Edmund's curiosity, Betsy's sincerity could only result in a mismatch which would bring one or the other of them to grief. I willed on him the kind of punishment he had shown no signs of receiving: the wicked again, flourishing like the green bay tree. I urged on him baldness, impotence, gout, also absent, or at least not yet present. He would extricate himself the moment he felt endangered: that I also knew. It was difficult to imagine Betsy's reaction when that happened. No doubt she would blame herself. And my role was simply to watch, as I had done in the dream, seated alone at another table, my ruffled feelings giving way to the purest despair.

II

While I might have predicted that Betsy would fall under Edmund's spell, or even that she would devote herself to Constance, I was not prepared for her love for their children, which was absolutely genuine and not troubled by conflicting loyalties. 'They're so beautiful,' she said on the telephone when she called to wish me a happy Christmas. Though I thought the word unnecessarily emotive, I had to concede that they were indeed beautiful. This I had been able to see for myself when Digby and I had visited their house: shouts and protestations had issued from behind a closed door, to materialize into three ethereal presences when they were summoned to greet the guests. The girls had been fair, like Edmund, while the boy was dark, like his mother, and with a hint of her wolfish grin. I had seen that in time the boy, David, would eclipse his father and I was sorry that I should not be able to witness the process, for even at the time I read volumes into Edmund's pride and exasperation as he reproached the boy for some undisclosed misdemeanour, one that had preceded our appearance on the scene. In his eyes I saw a wonder, almost an admiration for the boy's loose limbs, his unfettered movements. In that glance, to which the boy did not respond, keeping his head obstinately lowered, Edmund seemed to perceive that at some point he would grow old, be replaced, and that his famed sexual potency would pass to the boy, with his mother's approval.

Constance, in fact, had given every sign that she would

welcome this moment, had treated the boy as an adult, had given full approval to his latent anarchy, and had dismissed him lightly after hearing his plans for the evening. They were all on their way out, the girls to one party, the boy to another. Privileged children, they were never at a loss for company or entertainment. Though the girls were beautiful, with their long fair hair and narrow features, it was the boy who captured the attention. Edmund's eyes had followed him as he left the room. Constance, whose victory was so clearly in sight, merely smiled pleasantly, savouring the moment of her ascendancy. 'Don't be late,' called Edmund, unwilling to see them go. But they had gone, nudging each other exuberantly, all movement suddenly restored.

They had been young then, the girls fifteen, the boy nearly twelve. Now they would all be adolescents, with even more exciting prospects. Betsy herself, in that same telephone call, seemed excited herself, at this new sign that the Fairlies had in their gift even more rewarding companionship than that which she already took for granted. For she had, as it were, renewed her lease with the Fairlies by making herself useful in the matter of the children, performing with alacrity those small tasks which might otherwise have fallen to the house-keeper, the renewal of their school clothes, the occasional visit to the dentist, the purchase of birthday presents for their friends, and perhaps most of all the confidences of the two girls, Julia and Isabella, who appeared to regard her as their governess. On holiday from their prestigious schools, they were, to her fond eyes, already more emancipated than she had thought permissible. Both girls had boyfriends, whom they discussed without for a moment doubting their own appeal, both could drive and had been promised cars, both were already familiar with fashionable bars and restaurants.

On the strength of her long sojourn in Paris Betsy's stock was high. Although with unwavering instinct they perceived her to be quite naïve, they were willing to give her credit in the matter of personal appearance, and listened avidly to her largely irrelevant advice. For a time they accepted her as part of the household, and, she said, felt genuine affection for her to which she had the wit to respond with moderation. She seemed happy, and I could only hope that her hero-worship of Edmund and Constance, differentiated but ardent in both cases, would cool and be replaced by a quite different and more justified love for their children.

This was apparent in her happy voice on the telephone, as she told me that she had been invited to the Fairlies on Christmas Day for lunch, or was it dinner? whatever that punitive meal was called, and that she would contact me after the holidays when we must catch up on one another's news. When I put down the receiver, my own holidays obstinately not taking shape, I wondered if this late avatar of family happiness were not feeding Betsy's particular addiction. I could see only too clearly that both Edmund and Constance had found an acceptable way of emphasizing her status as an acolyte. This may have served Constance's purposes, for Constance had always considered Betsy a subordinate who had been drafted into her home by a process which it would not have taken her long to understand. Edmund, whose feelings in the matter were unknown to me, apart from the evidence of that horrifying dream, the details of which were still vivid in my mind, might regard Betsy's position as the least worst thing to come out of their adventure. He may have had genuine feeling for her, but, seeing her with his children, had painlessly removed her to the background. This may have been inadvertent. Unlike his other loves Edmund's love for his children was fierce; not only were they miraculous, unique, they did not appear to find him wanting. And, less fortunately for Betsy, the beauty of the girls put her own looks into perspective. She had always been a pretty girl, but she was no longer a girl. We were both approaching the age at which a woman knows she will never have a child. The implications of this were, I thought, more apparent in Betsy's case than in mine. My small closed face had undoubtedly not benefited from the passage of time, but I could detect no major changes, perhaps because I was not looking for any. Whereas Betsy's fairness compared unfavourably with that of the girls, which was flawless. Despite her eagerness on the telephone she complained of tiredness, and the effects of fatigue on a fair complexion are well known. I urged her to reserve some time for herself, but she protested that there would be no opportunity to do so, as she had promised to help with various arrangements: the party on Christmas Eve, the open house on Boxing Day, and then seeing Constance and the children off to Scotland for the rest of the holiday, after which she promised to be in touch.

There was something vaguely worrying in all this zeal. I could imagine, though she did not appear to do so, that she had been relegated in some way. Why else did they consent to her continued presence unless it had become completely anodyne, without greater significance? And although she played her part with enthusiasm it worried me that she had failed to perceive the mechanism at play. Again, I had no means of knowing Edmund's feelings, nor did I intend to give her the opportunity of confiding in me. I was still sore at what I saw as his rejection, for he had not sought so much as a conversation with me, such as I took for granted before, during, and, perhaps more significantly, after any love affair.

He had not even indicated that he would be absent, nor for how long: his absence alone spoke for him. Though I was willing to accept that he had been touched by Betsy's naïveté, and perhaps more, it did not take me long to work out that Constance's will would prevail in this matter, that it was her own fine instinct that had engineered an outcome to a situation perhaps more threatening than most, and that by the terms of their contract he would be honour bound to observe it. Nor need it constrain him unduly: he was still free to visit Betsy, though perhaps by now he was able to cast a more critical eye on her surroundings. Infinitely more practised than she could ever be, he would wonder why she had not intuited change, would decide that at some point he would explain himself to her, but that before that point was reached he might as well take advantage of a not unsatisfactory arrangement. And she loved his children: he gave her credit for that. He may even have thought in terms of the end of the holidays, when family intimacy would return to normal, either with or without additions. When the children went back to school changes would take place naturally; there would be no need for explanations. And in any event he knew where she was, should he ever feel the need to see her.

All this was supposition on my part, but I thought I knew him well enough to work out what might have been on his mind. There was always the terrifying possibility that his feeling for her was genuine, but I had almost managed to convince myself that I had no real evidence for this. It was painful for me to deny myself information that I could have come by had I had the intelligence to question Betsy without revealing anything of my recent history. But I was not clever enough to be able to do that, and besides it seemed to me a morally distasteful thing to do. Why I was so scrupulous when so many other barriers had fallen I did not quite know. What I did know was that a relatively clear conscience, such as I was able to admit to now, gave me a better night's sleep. Although a part of me sought to gain eager admittance to what was after all a private affair I could not trust myself to withstand certain revelations, certain details that might have tormented me through untold quiet nights. All women compare themselves, in this situation, as I dare say men do: one longs to know how others behave, yet at the same time one evades the knowledge. Besides, I had no doubt that Betsy would be happy to unburden herself. It was only with the greatest difficulty that she had refrained so far, and I put down to the fact that we had been children together that we had never exchanged the dreadful confidences that women are supposed, indeed entitled, to share. We understood that we were bound to remain on the right side of defensible behaviour, whether it suited us to do so or not.

Besides, I had no desire for further contact with Edmund, either directly or by proxy. A kind of distaste had intervened, not primarily over my own behaviour but over his. I reminded myself that it was not his character that had attracted me: now I saw this as mildly meretricious. But to apply moral considerations to someone so profoundly and so gracefully amoral was misconceived. Nevertheless I took care never to be in his orbit, even by accident. That meant avoiding his street or the flat where we used to meet, until I reflected that he might have no use for this since he had a reason for going straight home with Betsy and thus economizing on both time and effort. I did not gloss over my own bad behaviour, but I viewed it more calmly. I had not been seduced against my will, but had been genuinely happy with what had been offered. This had been a rapture rather than a simple love affair, as I had known at the time: the gods, perhaps, reminding humans that it was they who were in control. Or maybe I was not made for moderate friendships. I even wondered whether I had not retrieved a kind of authenticity with Edmund that I had been in danger of losing. My marriage was by all accounts successful, but it was largely an affair of affection and good manners. I was bound by those standards out of a loyalty to Digby, but I remembered all too clearly the sheer excitement of leaving such constraints behind. Infatuation seemed to me a perfectly reasonable condition. Yet I knew it was no longer something I need consider, that it had passed to others, or rather to another, and that I must avoid all knowledge of it if I were not to succumb, perhaps more fatally, another time.

My own holiday plans had taken an unexpected turn. In one of the weekly journals to which I had graduated from the newspapers – I was a subscriber to everything, no matter how arcane: the facts! the facts! – I had seen an advertisement for a Christmas walk, or rather Walk, and a telephone number which, after some thought, I rang. This was desperation: I could not face the long empty day, the silent streets, and the ever present spectre of families enjoying themselves. In this I was more like Betsy than I had allowed myself to suppose. My telephone call was answered by a sombre male voice, to which I bravely announced that I was interested in his advertisement, but would like to hear a little more. Was this a sponsored walk? Was he an organization? Was it for charity? Not that I cared much. I did not intend to join anything.

'I am not an organization,' said the voice. 'At least, not in the accepted sense. My name is Nigel Ward. I'm the warden of a Hall of Residence for foreign students. Many of these can't get home for Christmas. We have a large contingent from

Japan. I thought this would get them out, give them something to do.'

'Is it only open to students?'

'Not at all. Anyone can come. I have found that quite a few people are interested. A small fee will be charged. The money will go towards buying a new coffee machine for the students' Common Room. As you can imagine the old one has had a lot of use. It won't last much longer.'

His voice died away. He seemed exhausted at the prospect of spending a day with his charges. But resolute. I liked that.

'Where would we be going?'

'I thought round Hyde Park, then down to Green Park, and on to St James's Park, finishing up at Victoria Station, where, if we're lucky, we may find a cup of coffee, even something to eat. That would be the end of it; people will find their own way home from there. Nothing too taxing, you see. Just a pleasant walk in the fresh air.'

'It sounds a very good idea. I'd like to come.' There was silence at the other end. 'My name is Wetherall. Elizabeth Wetherall. How do I find you?'

'Departure from Knightsbridge Tube Station at 10 a.m. Are you a good walker?'

'Oh, yes, I'm a good walker,' I said, thinking back to my night walks in the phantasmagorical interval between Digby's death and his funeral. These now seemed furtive, shameful, even illicit, as if I had hoped to surprise other lives, to take them unaware, steal their secrets. The prospect of something so honourable by comparison had a pleasing effect on me, as if I were being given a chance to expunge my former aberrations, now obvious in all their bleak opportunism, and I was almost eager in my acceptance of this prospect.

'Wear comfortable shoes,' said the voice. 'Is it Miss or Mrs Wetherall?'

'Mrs. How will I know you?'

'You won't. You'll see a group of people to which you will attach yourself. Or not, if you think better of it. Identities will emerge in the course of the morning, by an entirely natural process. You are free to be as private as you wish.'

'I will of course recognize the Japanese. Are there many of them?'

'Quite a few. Until Christmas Day at ten o'clock, then. Goodbye, Mrs Wetherall.'

I replaced the receiver with a small feeling of triumph. I had done something positive, as everyone had urged me to do. And it need not commit me to anything. If I liked I could silently steal away, into the depths of one or other of the parks; no one would hold me to account. And I should be mercifully free of all the wassailing and its attendant discontents, the noise, the headaches. This would also provide me with an alibi. Doing something for charity was unassailable, the ideal excuse to offer those kind neighbours who had enquired about my plans. And I had no plans, which might have been obvious. Young people were their own source of interest and amusement, and I rather liked the prospect of observing them. Just as I had admired the children on their way to school (and still did, timing my outings to the supermarket to encounter them on their way home) I was willing to enjoy, at a distance, the requisite emotional distance, the young and their conviviality, which might even be extended to myself. My only concern was that it might rain and the whole thing be called off. But the weather forecast was simply for low cloud and fog patches. These did not deter me. I had been used to seeing this weather through the windows of my flat for some days now, and I was more than ready to confront it.

In fact the day was almost enjoyable. The sombre Mr Ward, easily detectable because of his extreme height, was tactful enough not to insist on introductions, leaving our group, which consisted of about ten adults and perhaps a dozen Japanese, to make their own alliances. I did not see anyone I wanted to accompany, and struck off on my own. The other walkers were either elderly women or elderly men, some in pairs, all obviously willing to put a brave face on what might otherwise have been a day of acute loneliness. At one point Mr Ward loomed up beside me but was called away to answer a stout woman's enquiry. I was beguiled by the tiny Japanese figures threading their way along the misty paths, stopping to admire the Serpentine, which was glaucous on this dull morning, without movement or reflections, and chattering to each other in bird-like voices. They had all made an effort, were neatly dressed, polite to the old people, successful at concealing any boredom they might have felt. Although my legs were aching by the time we reached Victoria I was reluctant to see them go, and stood with them for some few minutes, my farewells more cordial, less guarded than my greetings had been. I thanked Mr Ward for his excellent initiative, and said I should be interested in any further activities he cared to organize. I left my telephone number and trudged the rest of the way home, my mind's eye still occupied by the sight of those small figures dispersed among the leafless trees, and their smiles as they shook hands on parting, their delicacy such a welcome contrast to our bulk.

At home melancholy overtook me once more in the dull silence, but the day had not been wasted. I would have liked to tell someone about it, but all doors were shut against strangers, and the telephone was mute. I was aware of Digby's absence, since the flat still seemed to be his by right. I had merely been drafted into it when I married him. I reflected that it was precisely an equable disposition like his that had enabled our marriage to run so smoothly, that I had been unworthy in treating it so lightly. And yet my infidelity had felt so natural, or had been made to seem so natural, Edmund's fatal gift being a laughing acceptance of things as they were, or as they presented themselves, with conscience a tiresome and unattractive irrelevance, so old-fashioned as to provoke scepticism, if not scorn. The ethos of the day was that one should claim one's freedom and enjoy it, and the claim must have had some validity because it has persisted and has now taken over the whole of human behaviour. There seemed to be no danger in obeying one's impulses; there was certainly no blame. What scruples that were left were unevenly shared, so that one never knew what reservations might have persisted in any one individual. But gradually the old taboos were being discounted, seen for what they were: prohibitions imposed on instinct, and therefore against nature. Everything else was a learned response and could therefore be unlearned. Some managed this more easily than others. And yet no one respects an adulterous wife.

In the days that followed I found it more difficult to maintain my equanimity. I was unwilling to face up to the implications of the coming year, when I should once again find myself on the sidelines. If there were any satisfaction in my position it consisted in the fact that I had not imposed my company on Edmund once I had outstayed my welcome. For this is always apparent. And it is not easy to depart gracefully. I thought with some exasperation of Betsy's enslavement to the Fairlie household. One attachment I could understand, but not the confusion between passion and friendship which she had persuaded herself that she could accommodate. When I judged that sufficient time had elapsed and that she was temporarily relieved of her duties, I telephoned her and invited her to lunch. 'We might go to the V & A afterwards,' I suggested. 'There's always something precious to look at.' And, I reckoned privately, but again instinctively, a public place, and one as dignified as the sculpture galleries at the V & A, would preclude the sort of confidences that I now dreaded to hear. In that way I was able to greet her with composure and affection. We were after all old friends.

My quiche lorraine was thoughtfully and sincerely praised. 'I wish I knew how to make this,' said Betsy.

'I'll show you. It's not difficult.'

'Actually, I think it is. I tried to make one the other night – Edmund came to dinner – but I had to throw it away. We had an omelette instead.'

'Edmund came to dinner?'

'Well, he's on his own, with the family away. Actually I've been seeing quite a lot of him.'

'Seeing' in this context is used as a metaphor. Yet her expression was more ambivalent than assured. She seemed confident, certainly, even brisk, but not particularly comfortable in the role I had once enjoyed. She was also a little untidy, which was out of character. One of the lapels of her jacket was slightly crumpled, and the jacket itself was beginning to show its age.

'You want to steam that,' I told her. 'Or I'll do it for you.'

'No, no,' she said. 'I'll do it when I get home.'

'Take it off,' I ordered, and was sorry I did so, when I saw the jacket's torn lining.

She smiled faintly. 'Yes, I know. Unfortunately Edmund noticed it. He asked me if I were short of money.'

'Are you?'

'No, of course not.' She blushed hotly, annoyed with us both.

'If you gave up working for nothing you could get a proper job and earn real money. You're bilingual. It shouldn't be difficult to find something.'

'Oh, I will. It's just that I promised Constance that I'd help them with the move.'

'How long will that take?'

'No idea. In fact it's all a bit undecided. Constance hates the new house, but then she doesn't much like the old one. She complains of the noise, which I can't say I've noticed. Anyway it's sold.'

'Where's the new one?'

'I don't like it much either.' (I had not asked her that. She seemed to consider herself entitled to a view on the matter. Rather as if she might at some point consider taking up residence.) 'Oh, off Oakley Street. You know, that rather bleak little square.'

I made a mental note to cross this particular area off my itinerary. It was an act of faith, as well as a matter of principle, never to encounter the Fairlies again. That way we could consider ourselves to be strangers, with no history behind us.

I tried to divert her by telling her about my Christmas walk, but she was less equable than usual and let her lack of interest show. Whatever the reason for this it could only be a sign of deep preoccupation. And it too was uncharacteristic, as was the proud brooding expression of which she was not conscious. She had a slightly unreliable authority, which would have been welcome were it not for the evidence of negligence that accompanied it. She looked as if she had slipped down a social notch or two, and was determined not to regret it. The torn lining of her jacket was merely the outward and visible sign of this. Yet it seemed that love no longer made her happy, from which I deduced that it was the real thing.

'I shall be glad to see the children again,' she said.

'They must be growing up,' I pointed out.

'Oh, yes.' She sighed, 'All too quickly. Even David.'

Her tone was proprietorial, as if she owned a part of them.

'How do you see your role there?'

'Part of the family, I suppose. An expendable part, but I know how to fit in.'

Always the family cited as protection, as if once admitted one need never fear expropriation.

This illusion was rudely shattered at the V & A, as soon as we had climbed the steps and were in the entrance. To my horror I saw Constance, in the company of an older woman exactly like her – a sister, I supposed – approaching from the direction of the shop. I took Betsy's arm to propel her away, but 'Constance!' she said delightedly. 'When did you get back?'

Constance considered her. 'My sister,' she explained, but did not introduce us. 'A couple of days ago. We should have stayed longer, but there's this wretched move.'

'You know I'll help all I can,' said Betsy.

'In fact we may not stay in that house. We're thinking of moving on. What have you been doing with yourself?' she asked me.

I made noncommittal sounds. 'Sorry to hear about your husband.' There was a pause. 'Happy New Year,' she added.

'I'll come tomorrow, shall I?'

'What? Oh, Betsy. Yes, come tomorrow, why don't you? I may not be there, but someone will let you in.'

Again there was a pause. The sister's impassive expression indicated that she was aware of the situation.

'It was kind of you to entertain my husband,' said Constance. Betsy's tell-tale colour flared in her cheeks. 'And I insist on seeing that you're not out of pocket.'

'There's no need . . .' said Betsy.

'Oh, I think I'd feel better if I knew you were paid something.'

The insult hung in the air, until, smiling, Constance and her sister moved on. My hand tightened on Betsy's arm. 'Come,' I urged. 'Let's go home.'

We wandered out in silence. 'You won't go, will you?' I said.

'Of course I'll go. I want to see the children before they go their separate ways.'

'Constance is no friend to women,' I warned her. 'Do you know what you're in for?'

'Don't worry,' she said. 'She can be a bit edgy sometimes. I'm used to it.'

But when I saw her walk down the road she did not turn and wave. This was a sign to me: the fault was mine, because I had witnessed her humiliation.

12

It promised to be an early spring. When I went out soon after dawn for my papers it was still dark, but the darkness was slightly leavened, not so much by a change in the sky as by a hint of luminosity to come. This transformed the coming day into something more bearable, although the promise was rarely kept. It seemed that we must endure the long passage of time before the sun broke through as best we could, and that, as always, was proving difficult. I was tired, with the tiredness of one who has too little rather than too much to do, and longed for the night when I could sleep again. Yet I seemed to be functioning normally, or so I believed: I had no notion of how others were managing. I ate conscientiously, although I no longer cooked proper meals, dressed, as I thought, appropriately, but sometimes I had to remind myself that I was not an old woman whose life was virtually over. I behaved as I was expected to behave, though there were few witnesses. 'You're looking better,' said my hairdresser. 'We were quite worried about you.' Again this kindness was proof that my progress was being monitored and was thought to be satisfactory.

I was more than grateful for this since I seemed to be entirely alone. This was not as threatening as it had been after Digby's death, though I was aware that I was not fully alive, or even fully awake. I spent as much time as I could away from the flat, even telephoned one or two old friends to arrange to meet for lunch. But these friends, most of whom dated from before my marriage, were so much more confident than I could ever be. They had jobs, which I envied, and I felt like a humble petitioner, seeking an hour of their time, in wine bars and restaurants near their places of work. Their conversation was full of allusions that were foreign to me and names I only half recognized. They viewed my empty days, which I could not hope to disguise, with open disapproval. 'What do you do with yourself all day?' was their most predictable question. What did I do with myself? I was not entirely inactive, or so I persuaded myself, for the time seemed to pass, as it does for everyone. But it was not the sort of time by which others reckoned. It was ruminative, attentive to change, to those alterations in the light, to tiny inconsequential happenings and accidents: that dead pigeon, a mess of dirty feathers, lying in the gutter, the warmer wind, a familiar shop being refurbished by its new owner, the smell of coffee from the open door of a café. I often wished that I could do something with these impressions, that I were a writer of some sort and could form them into a pattern, though there was no narrative thread that I could invent. I felt, mysteriously, that there was some virtue attached to being a witness. My walks afforded me a mild contemplative pleasure. At the same time I knew that I had no valid excuse to offer my busy friends, and that my efforts to renew contact with them were proving something of a failure.

I telephoned Betsy once or twice but got no answer. I assumed her to be out of reach, either at the Fairlies, or transporting their effects to their new house, and in any event not anxious to hear from me. A breach had opened in our friendship: the simple fact of my having been present at an awkward moment, even a critical moment, had served to turn me into a hostile witness, someone to be avoided. She was the sort of eager vulnerable woman who saw the mildest hesitation as a withdrawal of favour. I regretted her apparent absence, but was not anxious to enter into that world again, that worship of all the Fairlies, or worse, that intimation of darker confidences that I had no wish to hear. It seemed monstrous that Edmund's last gift to me was to deprive me of a friend, equally monstrous that Betsy would accept this, with perhaps a suspicion that it might be prudent to do so. She would by now be awake to jealousy, and to the sort of calculation that was not normally in her character. She had, as far back as I could remember, looked to me for a sort of legitimacy. I was the one with the correct attributes, a mother, a father, eventually a husband, and the sort of home that was open to visitors, whereas her homes had always been makeshift, unpeopled. Even her present flat, in which Edmund was the only guest, had resisted my efforts to turn it into something else, something more open to the public gaze, and was now reduced to its humblest elements, a hiding place for a more or less clandestine arrangement, and thus disbarred from the public gaze.

I had no way of knowing this for certain, but her very silence spoke for itself. I dismissed the crises of conscience she might have endured with a shrug: if she chose to behave in this or any other way that was strictly her affair. She was no longer the innocent she had been in Paris, in the rue Cler; she was embroiled not only with a married lover but with his wife, whom she continued to attend out of a sort of fear. So long as she proclaimed affection for Constance (and she may even have felt this) she could persuade herself that her crime was not great, that it was hardly a crime at all, but an extension of a love that encompassed the whole family. I doubted whether the Fairlies saw this in the same way. They may have been convinced by her sheer artlessness that she was no threat to their stability. They may have conceded her entirely genuine love for their children. They may even have laughed at her. Some quality of hers, that obstinate aura of goodness, might have prevailed against their cynicism. Quite possibly they had never encountered this before.

For I thought them demonic in a way that Betsy could not hope to understand, collusive, without shame. Their characters, in hindsight, seemed to blend together, so that their alliance was one of true equals. I had encountered this before only in books, and even between the pages of a book such evidence was frightening. And I had not entirely avoided the Fairlie influence, though some sense had prompted me to turn my back on it. The true danger had lain in my possible conversion to their way of thinking. I could have persuaded myself that there was no real harm in my, or even in their, behaviour, that such a descent was even an enviable path to maturity, that experience was valuable however it was procured. Even my own bad faith had seemed to me amusing: was I not a more interesting person because of it? That there were others more experienced in this field had never crossed my mind; in any event one does not quarrel with physical satisfaction. My buoyancy at the time had stemmed from the illusion that I had nothing to fear; now I saw that I should have been terrified. One fears for the loss of one's innocence, even when that innocence is little more than ignorance. And also the blamelessness that blinds one to the superior sophistication of others, and makes of that very sophistication a mystery which might reveal itself to have some value, even some merit, a capacity which one had been denied but which it might have been in one's interest to have acquired.

For this reason, if for no other, I was bound to question my own solitude, and to look back with genuine bewilderment to my former misdemeanours. I had been given the opportunity to measure the distance I had had to travel to reach my present position of relative safety. Betsy, I could see, would not have that consolation or that assurance. Always dependent on the good opinion of others, she would consider any failure to qualify for this to be a reflection on her own character. Her need to please, and to go too far in her desire to please, had been seen, in those distant schooldays, as something laughable; naturally, at that age, we did not perceive the tragedy implicit in such striving. And now her position would be even more precarious: how to please the person to whom she was doing an injury? Only, I saw, by increased devotion, usefulness, a humble acceptance of tasks which she knew to be beneath her. Her promised reward would be no more than a brief encounter with her lover, if he were that still. Even so she would have lost caste, as she seemed to have been doing all her life. I should have preferred her to remain the girl who had returned from Paris to be a guest at my wedding, her appearance immaculate, her confidence intact. I tried to believe that the torn lining of her jacket was of no consequence, but without success. The discomfort that this had afforded me was surely of some significance. She may have been short of money: I had no way of knowing. It may even have been Edmund's prompting that lay behind Constance's hateful remark. And if she had been forced to accept their money her obligation to them would be unending.

Therefore when the telephone rang it was something of a relief, as well as a disappointment, that it was not Betsy's voice, for which I must have been unconsciously waiting, but that of Nigel Ward, proposing another excursion, this time to Regent's Park and Primrose Hill, on the following Sunday. 'We shan't be quite so numerous,' he said. 'Just a few stragglers. It's a dull time of the year for them.' There was a pause. 'If you're interested,' he said. 'Baker Street Station. Ten o'clock. No need to let me know.'

'I shall look forward to it,' I told him.

But in fact it was to prove a disappointment. The weather had deteriorated sharply: there was a scudding wind – our version of the *tramontane*, the *föhn* – the wind that sets the teeth on edge and inclines one to murder. By the time I reached Baker Street Station my eyes were watering and my hair unkempt. The students, two Indians, two Japanese, and a Nigerian, seemed disenchanted, as I was, by the peculiar pall that hangs over a London Sunday. The streets looked tarnished in a light which promised rain. Mr Ward, his evident good intentions surrounding him like the attributes of sainthood, was engaging them politely in the sort of conversation they were in no mood to appreciate. When we set off we must have resembled a couple of dutiful parents with a family of disgruntled teenagers. Our semi-rural surroundings failed to enchant. The students wanted, as I did, some sign of urban excitement, and this was sadly lacking. The green of the grass looked crude and cold; the very real cold made one yearn for a different climate, different colours. Before we were out of the park I made an excuse, in fact a series of excuses, designed to make my departure less offensive, but Mr Ward was patiently amenable in a way which underlined his unusual good nature. This man, I reflected, must have been appointed to his job by someone exceptionally far-seeing. Unfortunately his obvious good nature made him seem merely dull, even subservient, a schoolmaster out of some improving nineteenth-century novel, one of those undervalued heroes despised even by the reader.

His equally unpopular attribute was to make our little party seem cheap and churlish, myself included. I wanted more creature comforts than a walk in the park could provide, as did the students who stayed obstinately together, unappreciative of their surroundings. Mr Ward, no fool, could see that this particular endeavour was proving a failure but had the good manners to give no sign of this, and went on talking pleasantly in a voice almost carried away by gusts of wind. He appeared entirely impervious to the occasional harshness of fortune, heroic, and sexless. I was impatiently aware of all this but unsympathetic. I was also tired of walking in a disaffected group. What was more significant was my realization that I fared better without company. Solitude was obviously my destiny. I regretted this, but I was not much discomposed by the discovery. If I desired company it was for the company of one other person, intimate colloquy, a form of nurture that I could certainly embrace. The whole idea of friendship would have to be recast if it were to mean anything. I must in future, I thought, set standards of my own. What was called for was not compliance but its opposite, the more extreme forms of exigence.

I missed my husband, whom Mr Ward strangely resembled. Not in physical terms: he was extremely tall and thin, whereas Digby had been of moderate height and bulk. The likeness was one of disposition. Both were courteous to women, a fairly unusual characteristic, and therefore gentlemanly. There was no need for me to know Mr Ward for any greater length of time to be entirely convinced of this. I felt safe in his company and endured the subsequent feeling of boredom with something like the familiarity of long association. Even after two meetings, the present one unsatisfactory, I knew that he would be a good friend if he would allow himself a little more freedom of behaviour and of inclination, but unfortunately there was no sign of his capacity to develop either. I wondered briefly about his marital, even his sexual status, but only because I had been spoiled in this respect, and had acquiesced all too eagerly in the sort of plans no gentleman would make. But this was forbidden territory, which I was not permitted to revisit, and I suggested to Mr Ward that he might like to come for a drink one evening. 'Do ring me when you're free,' I urged, my enthusiasm fuelled by the providential sight of a taxi. 'I'm always at home by five.' He bowed his head, as if accepting yet another challenge, which firmness of purpose would enable him to carry out. The whole group watched as the taxi carried me away. I felt ashamed, as if I had let them down, but in fact they were merely envious. My action in leaving was, if anything, applauded. Yet Mr Ward's noble nature had had this effect on me: he had made me want to do better.

Back in the flat I felt violently relieved, as if I had resisted a brainwashing. What had briefly been on offer was a succession of anodyne pastimes in the circumscribed company of an utterly respectable man. It would have been in my interest to bow my head and acquiesce in a process that might extend far into the future: I put it no higher than that. And yet this prospect roused me to a kind of anger. I wanted to remain in character, low spirited, but with a fund of unexpended bad behaviour. I knew that I should respond without hesitation to the right kind of stimulus, but that I could not be satisfied with the merely mild and useful. Even Betsy's behaviour struck me as more natural, more understandable, even more sympathetic than the entirely upright stance of those whose conduct was open to inspection. I was no longer willing to pass this test. I welcomed anarchy and had proved myself capable of sustaining it. At the same time I longed for company, as only a lonely person could. The problem was that the company I might be offered was not to my taste, was too peaceful to invite my interest. The conundrum resisted my efforts to solve it. I spent most of that Sunday afternoon asleep, and the evening watching television. By the time I went to bed I felt a paradoxical pride in having merely pleased myself.

These various considerations foundered, or were swept aside two days later, when, returning from a routine shopping expedition, I became aware of a car drawing up beside me, and heard a voice saying, without preamble, 'Elizabeth. Have you got a minute?' I nodded, as if it were the most natural thing in the world that I should be reunited with Edmund at a traffic light in the King's Road. I slid into the car, aware only that this was the first time that I had seen him for many months, and strangely calm, as if I had known that we should meet again some day. I longed to question him, but in fact we were both silent and staring straight ahead, as if we were two ordinary passengers on an ordinary afternoon, proceeding westward, and too preoccupied with our own thoughts to engage in conversation. Out of the corner of my right eye I took in the salient features. He was older, or he looked older, his relaxed stomach slightly bulkier than I remembered it, his face more furrowed, his hair longer and streaked with more obvious grey. He seemed tired to death, assured but no longer triumphant as I had always remembered him. It was that confidence of his, that air of having outwitted the gods and their designs that was his most humbling feature. No one who came within the orbit of his intense scrutiny could dissemble; from that first confrontation all actions would be known. As they had been.

'Rather an awkward situation has arisen,' he said finally.

'Oh?'

'I don't know how much influence you have on your friend . . .'

'I take it you mean Betsy. No influence at all. Were you intending to take me into your confidence? If so, I should warn you . . .'

He ignored this. 'When did you last speak to her?'

'Not for quite a time. Whenever I telephone I get no answer. I don't know where she is.'

'I can tell you where she is. She is round at my house, on various pretexts which are in fact quite nebulous. Although I have to say that she was a great help when we moved.'

'How is that going? Are you pleased?'

He shook his head. 'A mistake.'

'Well, I can't help you there. What is the problem?' I asked. Since this conversation was to be about Betsy I felt coldly objective, any hope that I might have intruded into his consciousness quite gone, leaving an absence of calculation, or indeed forethought, behind.

'The problem is that Constance is getting upset. It's not that they've had a disagreement – in fact Constance takes care to be out when Betsy puts in an appearance. It's just that Constance has come to dislike her. Quite irrationally . . .'

'Not quite.'

'Well, perhaps not. But there's never been any threat to my marriage. Constance knows that. And Betsy knows that I'm a married man, always has known it. I was wondering if you could have a word . . .'

'Why can't you have a word?'

He stopped the car in a discreet side street somewhere in Kensington and sat looking resolutely forward, his hands loose on the wheel.

'I can't hurt her,' he said. 'And I can't stop her coming to the house. She turns up as if it's the most natural thing to do, as if she's a member of the family.'

I winced. 'You put it so tactfully. And yet you say you can't hurt her. Why can't you hurt her? Are you in love with her?' These words I ground out, knowing that at last the truth must be faced.

'There has been a degree of involvement,' he said.

'Oh, please.'

'Difficult for you to understand, perhaps. She's not at all my type. Nothing I can do will alter the fact that I was taken by surprise by all this.'

'Is it over, then?'

He raised his hands from the wheel in a helpless gesture and let them fall again.

'I think it had better be. I have Constance to consider. And the children.'

'I thought she loved the children.'

'So she does. Too much. Wants them to take her into their confidence, and so on. The girls, that is. David takes no notice of her.'

'That is fairly harmless, surely? Women with no children of their own frequently love the children of others.'

'I don't want them to come under her influence.'

'I'm sure she'd be very discreet.' In fact I was not so sure; Betsy had never been discreet with her affections and would now be even less so. In the circumstances I thought Edmund more likely to be discreet than Betsy. He would have the fierce protectiveness that a man of his type would feel towards his daughters, prone to hatred for any man likely to remove them from his sphere of influence. And the advice, the intimacy of an older woman who might urge them on to independence, to other affections, might be more than he could tolerate.

'What do you want me to do, Edmund? This is strictly none of my business. I never wanted to know about your marriage or your love affairs, let alone this one. I can't take sides in this matter. You must sort it out for yourselves. What is so difficult? I'm sure you must have done it before.'

'She trusts me, you see.' His voice was sad, as if he had no desire for this trust but accepted it as a fact. 'And she has so little in her life, that awful flat, no friends apart from you. No family.'

'That, of course, is how the whole trouble started. She always wanted a family, as I dare say she imagined herself one day with children of her own. You may have given her what she wanted in one sense, but you've also done a considerable amount of damage.'

I could feel my anger rising as I became eloquent on the subject of Betsy's wants and needs, which were also my own. There were more things I could have told him, but did not: how we were both at an age when our bodies might impart unwelcome information, indications of change with which it would be difficult to come to terms. I did not tell him this, not out of pity, but because I suspected that it might arouse his distaste. And I was aware that in all this discussion he had not made the slightest enquiry about myself.

He started the car again. 'Where shall I drop you?' he said. 'Where were you going?'

'I was going home. Take me home if you would. Or you could leave me here. I'll walk back. I think I need some air.' For the atmosphere in the car was heated, suddenly oppressive, and filled with our uneasiness. Edmund in particular seemed aware of this, and opened a window.

'I'll take you home, of course. Still in the same place?'

'Oh, yes. Yes, take me home.' It was the only place where I could feel safe, where there was no need for me to be tactful, diplomatic, to look after any interests but my own. Even the telephone might now prove an adversary. It was preferable that I keep away from Betsy. There was no problem about keeping away from Edmund, for I knew that I should never see him again.

'You must understand that my family is my first priority,' he was saying. 'And Constance. She is seriously upset.'

'There's an old saying about one's sins finding one out.'

'I don't see it that way.'

'Neither do I, really. But you must admit there's a certain irony here. Your asking me to intervene.'

He looked puzzled. 'But you're the only person I could ask,' he said. 'I didn't expect you to take it personally.'

'You must sort out your own affairs, Edmund. Or if you can't do it I'm sure Constance would.'

'I wouldn't put her in that position.'

There was no answer to this. We sat in the car, apparently unwilling to move. Then at last I was able to look at him, knowing it was for the last time. I saw, in his slumped shoulders, that he was as much a victim as I was, as Betsy was, even as Constance was. Some element of – what was it? Certainly not justice – had intervened to bring about thoughtfulness, and to bring it to a situation which had once seemed agreeably natural, immune from examination. Maybe it was the classical principle that decreed a suitable solution only in the form of a dénouement, whether one accepted it or not. 'Be good to your daughters,' I said. 'Set them free.'

'I couldn't live without them. They are all the world to me.'

'You must remember that. They matter more than

Constance does. Than your marriage, as you so pompously put it.'

'I know.'

It seemed that there was to be no parting, or at least not one camouflaged by vague assurances that we would meet again. I accepted this. Edmund was too sunk in his own reverie to register that I had opened the car door and was on the point of leaving him to his thoughts. I doubt if he knew the exact moment at which he was alone. I, on the other hand, registered my every footfall as I walked away. There was a finality here with which I could not argue. One always recognizes the irreparable, in whatever shape it takes. Though there were now pretexts on which I could act if I wanted to bring myself once more within his orbit I knew that they would not be employed. This was not a moral decision. It lay in the evidence of the sadness we had both felt, a sadness proportionately different in both cases, and yet a humbling mutual acceptance of inevitability. I still knew nothing about him, had not made appropriate light conversation, asked about the new house. None of that applied. Nor was Betsy uppermost in my mind. The working out of the plot, devised by the Fates or the Furies, would take place without our consent, as it always does. I did not even think of myself. I thought of Edmund, showing signs of age, and beginning to perceive that he was no longer the favourite of the gods. I found that I loved him all the more for this, and I mourned him as if he had recently died.

13

Since our lives are ruled by chance it came as no surprise to me to encounter Betsy outside Peter Jones shortly afterwards. Nevertheless I had not expected to see her, nor did I want to: I had decided, or it had been decided for me, to have nothing further to do with a situation which cast me in a role so marginal and so ambiguous that the outcome was somehow liberating. If I were to meet Edmund again I thought that my feeling would be one of cordial dislike, and I imagined that he would feel the same. As a child, long ago, I had had to be the peacemaker between disaffected parents. This I managed by dint of an uncritical muteness which they were forced to respect. As long as I was in the room, and apparently attributing no blame to either of them, they lowered their voices, assumed pacific expressions, and looked on me with favour. I knew no better at the time than to be grateful for this, and it was only much later, on my own in Paris, and chronically uncomfortable in my meagre surroundings, that I began to question not only their behaviour but my own. I was not, I realized, a naturally servile person, rather the opposite. Indeed it was that unexpended opposition to the role decreed for me that led indirectly to my brief period of lawlessness in later life. And though that had once seemed so natural I saw now, at the moment of that meeting with Betsy, on a humdrum morning, in fitful sunshine, that I need never again play either of these parts, that it was perhaps preferable to be free of them and to live the sort of life that involved no collusion with others, to become known for this, and to have it acknowledged, and thus for the first time in my life to achieve a sort of dignity.

Nevertheless, and again in that first sighting of Betsy, I regretted that I was not able to greet her more warmly, or with something of the spontaneity that I had misplaced. I missed a female friend, though I could no longer trust anyone, friend or lover. I remembered with a genuine sadness those early days, when we had known not only each other but each other's circumstances. I still had, in my sewing-box at home, a little empty perfume bottle that Betsy had given me for some forgotten birthday: we may have been thirteen or fourteen at the time. I had thought it naïve of her, sentimental, and yet I had cherished it. Now more than ever it had come to symbolize the sort of early friendship which is so difficult to recapture in more complex days, and I looked back on that period of my life, largely unsatisfactory in most respects, as emblematic of what I had lost. I wanted to pick up the telephone unthinkingly, as I had done then, to ask her some idle question, about homework, perhaps, and hear her reply in the same tone of voice, and ask me questions in return. There would be no art in this conversation, no contrivance: that would be the beauty of it. I wanted everything to be once more understood between us, as if we had never let each other down.

Instead, there must be a certain mistrust, a withholding, for there were secrets that were never to be mentioned, conversations with others in which we were implicated, whether we liked it or not. Betsy, despite her oddly immovable naïveté, would surely have realized that Edmund had played a part in my life, may even have questioned him about this, and would have reacted to the perhaps unwelcome knowledge in the only way she knew, with redoubled assurances of affection. This would be so different in quality from those uncensored conversations of younger days that I should feel a genuine nostalgia for that lost time. The friends of one's youth are perhaps the only people who know one properly, know the background and the context as well as the presenting characteristics. More than extravagant love my overwhelming wish now was to be known in that way once more, before it was too late. The intimate support – the nurture – that two such friends instinctively supply was now denied to me, to both of us. And the little scent bottle, almost hidden by the scissors and the needles in my sewing-box, would serve to remind me of a time before prudence, before artifice, had come to rule my life, and to a lesser degree that of my erstwhile friend.

For I had seen a slight shadow pass across her joyous expressions, the merest suggestion of reluctance. It would not take long for that reluctance to blossom into mistrust, yet she too wanted me for a friend, the friend I had once been. It would have taken one far less solitary than myself to ignore that very slight alteration in her sighting of me: it was my predilection for noting small everyday accidents that made me alive to that momentary clouding of her welcome. My face, habitually under control, gave no hint, I am persuaded, that this was anything more than an accidental meeting shorn of other associations. At one level we were genuinely pleased to see each other; at another we were calculating how much information could be disclosed, how much concealed. To do us some sort of credit we both knew this, and were determined to go about the matter as best we could. For those childhood codes still obtained. Once we would have taken up the conversation where we had last left it. Now we had to negotiate a way of dealing with a situation that neither of us wanted to acknowledge, aware that it might divide us, and determined to let none of this appear.

She made the adjustment quickly, although the process was apparent to me. She was both pleased and not pleased to see me; for once I was the more assiduous friend. Although I feared her revelations (for I did not doubt that at some point they would break through) I was willing to meet her in the spirit of our now lost friendship, was even looking for some sign of recognition of the person I was once, or perhaps as we both had been. As a girl she had made up for poor resources by an anxious attention to detail, her shining appearance more than compensating for undistinguished clothes and unfashionable shoes. Now, in that lightning first glance, I saw that this arrangement had been turned on its head. She was attractively dressed in a grey trouser suit, yet her hair was slightly disarranged, as if creeping out of her control. She looked like the other women going into the store, looked, I dare say, like myself, but with a difference. She seemed to have changed her status for one less modest than previously endured without complaint. Indeed she had the preoccupied, slightly important expression of a woman with a domestic burden to maintain, with appetites to satisfy, with a family to care for. I had often questioned this look on other women's faces, thinking them superior to myself, newly conscious of my lost culinary expertise, my idle ruminative hours. These women seemed to be characterized by a look of achievement, of accomplishment, as if they had passed some test of all-round competence. It was a competence that was somehow linked with a quality of desirability, and I knew myself unlikely to qualify ever again for such a badge of caste. Now I was convinced that Betsy was so qualified, knowing her as few others did. There was about her a trace of that complacent haste that was a more than adequate disguise for her true feelings, whatever these might have been, and which she seemed disposed to enjoy, even to cultivate.

'What a lovely surprise,' she said. 'We seem doomed to meet here, don't we? Have you time for coffee? You're looking well.'

I followed her meekly into the restaurant, where she now took her place as of right, summoning a waitress with an uplifted hand, a gesture she would not normally have permitted herself.

'Let me look at you,' she said, with the same proprietorial air. 'Yes, you do look well. What have you been doing with yourself?'

This was so like the questions I was used to being asked by my genuinely busy friends that I dealt with it in the way I had devised after several humiliating episodes: I ignored it.

'You're not working today, then?' I enquired, hoping to get on to firmer conversational ground. Only distaste for the artifice that had overtaken our relationship had made me venture such a question.

'No, they can do without me today,' she laughed. 'Actually Constance's car was gone when I got there. She must have left early.'

'Do you ever wonder whether she needs you there any more?'

'Oh, I think I've proved my usefulness. I may have to do so again, if they can't settle down. Constance has really taken against that house. Amazing how easily some people give up.'

'I should leave them to get on with it. Moving house can be very traumatic.'

'Well, of course. That's where I come in. Helping to get them settled.'

'Them?'

'Well, Constance. I'm worried about her. She seems quite neurotic.'

'Perhaps you've outstayed your welcome.'

Her face hardened. 'I like to see the girls,' she said. 'They're used to my being around.'

But in fact the girls were largely absent, as no doubt she knew and as I surmised. The reason for her assiduity was imperfectly disguised: she was in love with Edmund and was willing to court humiliation, if that were the price to be paid for those unedited glimpses of him in his domestic setting that would otherwise be denied to her. I was profoundly shocked. No woman of my generation is allowed to behave so slavishly. Women's liberation had surely been designed to free us from such masochistic impulses. But in Betsy's case such a liberation might not have taken place. She seemed to proclaim the sort of fidelity that most societies other than tribal have done their best to shed. I was in two minds about this, as, I dare say, are most women. I admired the ideal, but had observed that it could lead one into extravagances of behaviour no less deleterious than the wildest licence. Proof of this was being supplied by Betsy, whose unfortunate attachment might sooner or later achieve the hitherto unthinkable work of dismantling her character altogether. For I knew, or thought I knew, of Edmund's obsidian self-regard, so like his wife's. At some level they would unite in distaste for this eager acolyte, and though nothing might be acknowledged between them some attitude would result from their shared impatience, some manoeuvre be initiated that would safeguard their original alliance. This would not be easy; they might be brought face to face with an awkward need to avoid embarrassment in a situation that was already sufficiently embarrassing. And

Edmund was affected by her, may even have been in love with her. For Edmund love was about an initial attraction that might profit both partners. Nowhere did it imply duration. For duration, or durability, he could rely on his adamantine wife whose most notable attribute was a sort of inscrutability, so much more acceptable than the bizarre sincerity, the sheer incomprehension of a woman whom experience had taught so little as to make her seem anomalous, even threatening, like a dysfunctional infant who persists in courting one's approval.

Though animated she looked tired. She had that aura of contained excitement which is exhausting in the long run. Although deluded, her condition was enviable, enviable to me in my newly restored respectability, enviable perhaps to those other women in the restaurant, with their shopping bags at the side of their chairs. A woman senses the level of sexual activity in other women and instinctively resents it, particularly if she is bereft of male company. All thoughts of innocent long-ago friendship were erased from my mind as I was treated to a display, perhaps conscious, perhaps unconscious, of determined insouciance that failed to mask a single overriding preoccupation. I noticed new busy feminine gestures that sent out their own semaphore – a sweeping back of the hair, a turning of the cuff to check the time on her watch – and saw myself reduced to the level of an onlooker. Outwardly peaceable, I was engaged in a struggle to defeat my baser self. I may even have succeeded, but the struggle had left a victim, or perhaps two victims. We could no longer lay claim to the friendship which had survived earlier vicissitudes. Lucidity had brought in its train a revision of previous attitudes. Without examining these more closely – for what good would it have done? – I saw that she too had recognized the change that had taken place. The display, the determined gladness were no doubt consequent upon closer understanding of my relations with Edmund. There was no need to acknowledge this. It stood out a mile.

A sudden shower of rain peppered the windows; below us in the street umbrellas bloomed. 'Be careful,' I said quietly. 'They are much cleverer than you.'

She laughed angrily. 'I think I know that, thank you. I'm not completely stupid.'

'Then why persist? Surely it would be better to leave them to their own devices. Be discreet, retain some dignity. *Finir en beauté*. Such a useful phrase, I always thought, though there is nothing really fine about endings. They have to be managed as best one can. The saving grace is to be in control.'

As if I were spelling out her fate the bravado left her. 'I can't do it,' she said. 'They have become my family.'

'You mean he has.'

'Yes.'

'But what do you hope for? Even if he were in love with you . . .'

'He is.'

'Has he said so?'

'Oh, I don't need a declaration, if that is what you mean. I just know. And for the first time in my life I've something of my own. A secret. Something that excludes everyone else. Even you, though you think you know all about it.'

It was important to me not to join in this mutual confession. My one thought, and an imperative one, was that I must go away, away from the tedium of the English weather, away from the more menacing tedium of female soul-searching. I would go back to Venice, where the light was stronger; I would even go back to Paris, which haunted me, as a lost opportunity often does. With careful management I could be away for six months, or even longer. Digby had left me comfortably off; I should not even need to let the flat. There was in fact no reason why I should not spend the greater part of the year abroad, returning to London only in the brightest days of the summer, and then only briefly. I should be one of those odd Englishwomen who could be counted on to haunt the Riviera in the low season, taking advantage of reduced rates, not minding the discomfort of a small *pension*, and badly dressed in a way that would not be noticed at home. The vision appealed to me, its sheer sexlessness an added attraction. I should read novels over dinner in restaurants which would soon accept me as a regular patron, and wander back to bed along some notional promenade which I had not yet quite located. I was, I thought, entitled to spare myself any further involvement in this affair which might yet intensify on my part as it would on Betsy's. I was, it seemed, not quite free of it. That was not to say that I had to relive it by proxy. A long absence would also remove me from Betsy, who was now on the defensive, within a hair's breadth of disliking me. I busied myself in gathering up my purchases, preparatory to leaving. I was aware that she was looking at me fixedly, as if trying to read my thoughts. I should have to keep my Mediterranean fantasy to myself, leaving suddenly, without warning, after only the briefest of telephone calls. Acting out of character was permitted to a woman of my age, though I was probably being optimistic in imagining that this would arouse comment. I knew few people who would be interested. Betsy, oddly enough, was closest to me, by her reckoning, if not by mine. I saw her once more as someone in need of protection, even patronage, still longing to be sheltered, more perhaps now than ever before.

'You say you've never had anyone of your own,' I said, fishing in my handbag. 'But in fact it's folly to think you can lay claim to another person. I know how lonely it can be without someone close to you, but it becomes quite difficult to work out why. Probably status is involved. A woman with a partner feels superior to a woman who has none. But this is illusory. All one ever possesses is free will, and even that has to be safeguarded. Handing over one's life to another person is not really to be recommended.'

'You didn't love your husband, did you?' she said. 'If you had you wouldn't say what you've just said.'

I was deeply shocked. This seemed a far more dangerous intrusion than the one I had originally feared, the one I had done my utmost to deflect. It seemed to me that it was Digby who was under attack, and that he needed me to defend him. I would not dignify the conversation by responding, but I must have gone slightly pale, for she reached out a hand to grasp mine. 'I'm sorry, I'm sorry,' she said. 'That was not what I meant to say. What I meant to say was . . .'

'Shall we go?' I stood up, glanced out of the window on to the rain.

'Will you ring me?' she said, disconcerted, awkward. Unprotected, as I now saw all too clearly.

'Yes, I'll ring you.' This would be the telephone call that announced my imminent departure. This seemed to me satisfactory, though my heart was beating uncomfortably. She took my arm, and I made no attempt to remove it. Thus had we sometimes wandered home from school.

'What about the children?' she said, almost to herself. 'Surely one can lay claim to children?'

'Only when they are helpless,' I replied. 'They are programmed to seek their independence. That is their strength.

Goodbye, then. I'm going to grab that taxi.' I did not urge her to keep in touch. It was somehow beyond my reach to utter the simple formula. I knew she would be hurt by my failure to do so. Through the taxi window I saw her worried face. I lifted my hand briefly, and was thankfully removed from the scene. This now assumed the dimensions of a betrayal. On both sides. The fact that we were equally guilty did nothing to salvage my self-respect. Nor would she feel any better, rather worse, in fact. But I had no more sentiment to spare. I simply hoped that she would repair herself as best she could, without any help from me. Something awful had been uncovered. Reason demanded that the whole incident should be dismissed. An error, quite possibly indelible. It would be in no one's interest to compound it.

Back in the flat I accepted the slow grind of traffic outside the window as an appropriate accompaniment to even slower afternoons. It had the power to hypnotize me, even to re-concile me to what was by any standards a singularly dull life. With an effort I went into the bedroom, opened a cupboard, and dragged out a suitcase, as if my travel plans must be implemented without delay. I need not pack much; it would be sunny where I was going, as it is in all fantasies of displace-ment. Paris first, I thought, and then a slow train south. I would leave this train on an impulse, somewhere off the main line. I would walk, on a still afternoon, until I found a small hotel, where I would be immediately recognized as a traveller, rather than a tourist. My days would be entirely empty, entirely insignificant, giving me time to evaluate my life, and also to remove myself from the life I had already lived. My aim would be to detach the present completely from the past. If this process were successful I might never feel the need to come home.

But then I thought of my bed, of Digby's desk, of the chair in which I had once sat to read. These were now my attributes; it might be hard to leave them. I was not old, but widowhood must have incremented the ageing process, so that I was now a creature of settled habits when all around me women were having adventures, taking lovers, running corporations. It was my feeling of shame at this comparison that had prompted me to seek the only sort of freedom I could manage. I even congratulated myself on my lack of entanglements, of obligations. I saw exile – for now it was becoming that – as cleaner, nobler than love and its delusions. For surely all love contained an element of delusion? Though that delusion was empowering, enabling one to go beyond oneself, it was not to be encouraged. I looked back approvingly to the sobriety of my marriage, an honest affair from any point of view, utterly defensible. I had never had any desire to disguise it, accepting its dullness as a necessary virtue. That it had precipitated an equally necessary madness seemed to me to warrant no further consideration. I would never speak of this, though to do so would no doubt make me seem a more interesting figure. Interesting to women, rather. No man should hear of it, not that there was any man to enquire. The empty suitcase yawned. Anything would do to fill it, for I should be leaving most of myself behind.

At some point in my rather confused upbringing I had formed the notion that friendships should last for life, that an association once established could be relied upon not to change. Even in middle age I clung to this idea. I could see that what was in essence a conviction, an article of faith, might not always be shared, but this eventuality struck me as unlikely. I preferred the comforting illusion that I should always be known by someone to whom I did not need to explain myself.

Although aware that this condition pertained to love rather than to friendship I persisted in this way of thinking. That it had some validity was proved by the distress that a broken friendship signified, and I was in no doubt that Betsy no longer regarded me as a friend. She mistakenly saw me as a rival, albeit a rival whom she had managed to vanquish, whereas I was compromised in every way by what I had heard from both the protagonists. I had not wanted to be a party to her confessions, let alone to Edmund's moment of candour: both were incompatible with the friendships I had hoped to sustain. I now saw this as an illusion, and that one could expect to witness the defection of friends as well as lovers. This seemed to me incomparably sad. It was perhaps the last ideal I had managed to salvage, and I saw my proposed exile, for it would be nothing less, as a desire to obliterate the evidence of such unexpected disharmony, and to form myself anew, or perhaps to grow up a second time, in suitably desert surroundings, in that wilderness that awaits those who have broken all ties, or perhaps been abandoned by those whose affinity with oneself had not stood the test of time, with whom one can no longer share experiences in a way that adds to common knowledge, or ever again speak with the spontaneity, which is, I now saw, the climate of childhood rather than that of later life.

Evening might have found me there still, sitting on my heels in front of an empty suitcase, had the telephone not rung. I ignored it, thinking it might be Betsy, to whom I was not ready to speak. But it sounded authoritative, as unanswered telephones do, and it occurred to me that it might be my mother, that something might be wrong. (My father I kept in reserve; his health might concern me at a later date.) With a sigh I got to my feet, stumbled on cramped legs to the living-room. 'Elizabeth Wetherall,' I said. There was a sound of a throat being cleared, almost a sigh that responded to my own. 'Hello?'

'Nigel Ward here. You very kindly gave me your number.'

'Mr Ward. How nice to hear from you.'

'I am going to be in your neighbourhood this evening . . .'

'But you must come for a drink.' I looked at my watch. 'Any time from six, if you can manage it. I should be delighted to see you.'

Another sigh. 'Would six-thirty be convenient?'

'Of course. I look forward to it.'

I replaced the suitcase in the cupboard. Since I had all the time in the world to plan my journey I decided there was no rush. But I should leave, no matter who sought to detain me.

14

'You walked here, I imagine?'

'Oh, yes. I walk everywhere. I find it's the best way of ensuring a good night's sleep.'

'How far was that? Your walk, I mean.'

'My flat is in Bedford Way. Not that I spend much time there. My days are organized around the students. It's important to keep them occupied. Most of them are far from home, you see . . .'

'Yes, I remember you saying that.'

He looked far from home himself, lost, rather alarmed to find himself drinking a glass of white wine in a strange woman's house. I wanted to put him at his ease, but was aware that I must not alarm him further. What he might have wanted was not apparent. I did not entirely believe his explanation for his presence – that he was to be in the neighbourhood – but this may have been the truth. He did not look the sort of man given to lame excuses. A rather frightening rectitude emanated from what was an elegant if mournful appearance: even seated he seemed excessively tall, taking care to fold his long legs out of the range of any furniture they might encounter. I registered the fact that his head was well proportioned, that he might be considered good-looking. He had a stern nineteenth-century face that put one in mind of incorruptible officials in a world long since faded. I did not quite see how he fitted into our shabbier times. No doubt consorting with young people afforded him a certain amount of company, even of comfort. I thought him lonely. Certainly he seemed unattached. Why else was he here?

'Have you always done this kind of work?'

He smiled. At least he was not so inexperienced that he could not recognize a woman's curiosity. 'In a sense, though not in the way I intended. I find I am happiest in a student atmosphere, no doubt because I was so happy as a student myself. I am no doubt arrested at an early stage of my development. That's what Freud would say, anyway.'

'You seem quite normal to me. One imagines Freud dealing with something more dramatic.'

'Those were his women patients. Women had a hard time of it then.'

Still do, I thought. 'What arrested your development, then? Can I give you some more wine?'

'Thank you. Oh, I can time it pretty well. I was in my last year at Oxford. Magdalen. I was doing well; everyone seemed pleased with me. I was being encouraged to think of an academic career, a fellowship, even. And I had already met my future wife, a fellow student. We were unrealistically happy, in a way that never comes again.'

'Why do you say unrealistically?'

'Because we were escapists, or I was. I was warned about neglecting my work but took no notice of the warnings. We planned to marry as soon as the summer term ended. I had sailed through Finals, convinced that nothing could go wrong. I was in a sort of euphoria, madness, even.'

'What happened?'

'I got a Third, instead of the First everyone had so confidently predicted. My tutor was furious. It put an end to my proposed academic career. I had a wife, no job, no home of my own, and a mother whom my father had entrusted to my care before he died. We had no choice but to live with her, while we both looked around for work.'

'How did that work out?'

'Not well. Oh, everyone was very civilized, but my mother was more keen on a career for me than on my status as a new husband. Widowed mothers have a tendency to infantilize their sons. Not so my mother. She really wanted me to be her own age, or older, able to look after her, even to be a sort of consort. She regarded my wife rather as if she were someone I had brought home from school for tea, no more serious than a childhood friend whom I should now put away in the interests of my new seniority. Which she had imposed on me.'

'And your wife?'

'She was bewildered. We agreed that she should live with her parents until I got a proper job, when we'd start our life again. But it took too long, and she was lonely.'

'You, too, I imagine.'

'Yes.'

There was a silence. 'Forgive me,' I said. 'I'm asking too many questions.'

He smiled. 'There aren't many more that I can answer. I took various tedious courses, all very far removed from the classics I still longed to study, and eventually became the bursar of a college of higher education. I took early retirement – mistakenly – found I had too little to do and thought voluntary work might be the answer. That's what I do now.'

'And your wife?'

'We divorced. Or rather she divorced me. We stayed married but separate for a long time. Then she met someone else.'

'And you?'

'No. In a sense I remained true to her. To our early promise. It was hard to recover from that.'

'What a strange story.'

'It ruined my life, of course. My mother became ill and begged me not to leave her. My wife reproached me, quite justifiably. But really what had happened was that we had been forced to grow up, face reality.'

'Like Adam and Eve.'

'I've always been on their side.'

'At least you had your time in Eden.'

'Yes, I had that.'

Again, silence fell. I had not been prepared for this operatic confession. In fact I suspected I was being given an edited version of a much longer story, one that he thought he should offer as explanation for himself: his calling card, as it were. These were confessional times, all discretion gone. Also I suspected an analyst somewhere in the background, either in the past or perhaps still on the job. There was probably more: a breakdown at some point. I hope I gave no hint that I suspected this. My role seemed to be one of contained listener, like the presumed analyst, in fact. But the analyst always has the excuse of being allowed to indicate when the session is over. I had none. Besides, I was getting hungry. I had no food in the house. I had done no shopping. The whole day had been wasted, and as well as wasted, spoiled. I warned myself to stick to the present circumstance and not to drift off again into my own preoccupations.

'You must be hungry after your long walk,' I said. 'I'd love to offer you something to eat, but I've nothing suitable.'

I thought this would give him a chance to invite me out to dinner. Instead he got to his feet, thinking he was being dismissed.

'Please don't go,' I said. 'There's a small restaurant round the corner where my husband and I used to go. That might be the answer. I'm really ashamed of my lack of preparedness.'

'That would be very pleasant.'

'It's an Italian menu,' I said. 'I'm sure you'll find something you like.'

No further conversation was forthcoming on the short walk to the restaurant, for which I was grateful. The evening was so benign that it shed its aura in a way that was almost abstract. I had been too long deprived of normal conditions not to marvel at their apparent availability. In this early dusk, dissolving only gently into a night that promised restful sleep, it was easy to remain in the present, to accept this inconsequential companion as an appropriate traveller on the same route as I had long schooled myself to undertake, and which I now saw as one of intolerable loneliness. That acceptance of friends, of lovers, that burden of their subsequent loss, seemed to relegate me to a sub-species of those without either, although I knew that to acquaintances, to strangers, even to this particular stranger I appeared a competent, self-sufficient, even unsympathetic person who had no need of close attachments. I was, I saw, too proud, or too ashamed (they are the same thing) ever to have confided, to have confessed in any company. The strain was great, but I knew no other way of behaving. That was why the idea of flight had presented itself, and why flight seemed to be the next logical step. I envied the silent Mr Ward his young companions, most of all the trust he must inspire, for I could see that this was a man with elevated standards, however bleak these had proved to be. He would conduct himself well, that was clear. I envied him his discipline. At the same time these qualities seemed too harsh to offer any emotional or even spiritual relief. Virtue, being its own reward, rarely if ever compensates those who possess it.

The atmosphere eased slightly when we were seated in the restaurant, surrounded by the low murmur of discreet fellow diners. It was still too early for the young people who would surely arrive later. Our present companions were presumably on their way home, or perhaps going to see a film at one of the local cinemas. We surveyed the menu, although I knew it by heart.

'Are you brave enough to eat seafood?' I asked. 'I believe it's good here, although I've never liked it. I once had a bad experience with dressed crab.'

'Lasagne,' he said, laying the menu aside. 'I am not an adventurous eater.'

'I'll have the same.' Something simple seemed indicated, in deference to the tentative nature of our association.

'You came here with your husband,' he stated. It was not a question.

'He died.'

'I'm sorry.'

'I don't know how one deals with loss,' I said. 'I think I've made a poor job of it.'

'The ability to deal with loss is perhaps as important, or rather as significant, as the loss itself.'

There spoke the therapist, I thought, that figure in the background whose shadowy presence I had intuited.

'And yet my husband was too kind to leave me bereft. I miss him as a friend as much as anything. Just to know he was in the next room was enough.'

I did not tell him that it was the other one I missed, sometimes with an urgency that shocked me. I took a draught of wine, hoping that it would make me drunk. Sober, I did not think I could add much to this conversation.

'Some losses are in nature, of course,' I heard him say. 'Those are the ones from which one eventually recovers. Mine was not like that. Mine was entirely self-inflicted.'

'How do you live now?'

'Oh, quietly. I am a disgrace to everyone's concept of masculinity.'

I could hardly, on so short an acquaintance, ask him about sex. 'I do the same. I am a disgrace to my generation. But I think I was born a little too early to appreciate the fact that I was free to please myself.'

'That is the orthodoxy now, certainly. Though I think it has to be amended by wider considerations. One's own freedom is rarely absolute.'

'The idea is attractive.'

'Yes. And misleading.'

There was a silence after this, as if to mark the end of the matter. Silence did not seem to worry him, although I felt the need to furnish it. It struck me that his evenings might be spent in such a manner, perhaps without a companion. When I thought the silence unduly prolonged I asked him whether he would go away. What I wanted to know was what he did about holidays, apart from leading students on forced marches.

'I shall go somewhere, I suppose, I usually do a long walk in France. I have friends in the south. And you?'

'I had a journey in mind, yes. The details are yet to be confirmed.' This seemed to me both vague and respectable, as if I too had friends to whom I could go.

This journey now seemed to me phantasmagorical, though it remained a presence in my mind. There were in fact friends of Digby's, whom we had dined with and met at the theatre, who had pressed me most warmly to visit them, in the houses they seemed to possess in a variety of places. I had always thanked them but had managed to imply that other friends had offered similar invitations. The real reason, and I think the correct one, was that I knew that my silence, my solitude, acted as a deterrent on both sides, and that these kind people would do better without me. That they did not know the depths of that solitude seemed to me preferable. I knew it was not something that would yield easily to day-long company. My own company, unrelieved as it was, seemed to enfold me like a carapace; I doubted now if I could ever manage without it. Within its restrictions I knew what I could and could not do. This seemed to me a knowledge worth preserving, whatever the cost.

Yet at that moment I saw that the cost was great. In these pleasantly familiar surroundings it would be easy to let down my guard. But there was no reason for me to do so. I was with a stranger, whose conversation, interesting though it was, revealed a solitude as closely guarded as my own. It was not in my interest to dismantle it, nor indeed in his. He was luckier than I was in having activities that absorbed him. I was lucky only in being free of financial considerations, in being housed and independent, in not being a burden. I knew that my earlier thoughts would return when I was alone again. The despair, the shock, the thoughts of flight were part of a pattern which seemed to me fixed, not subject to alteration.

'Would you like to come home with me?' I heard myself saying. It was then I knew I was drunk.

When I could bear to look at him I saw that he was smiling, a rare smile that illuminated his austere face.

'Is that you speaking, or your generation?' he said.

'Women do this all the time. It seems there is nothing to it.'

'So you want to be part of the *Zeitgeist*?'

'Oh, yes. I never have been. I have been a fool. And now I dare say it is too late. Please don't look at me like that. You are supposed to acquiesce eagerly, no questions asked.'

'The questions may come later.'

'Not this time?'

'Later. Shall we go? I'll walk you home, of course. If you are not too tired.'

Outside the blue evening had deepened, darkened, giving promise of fine weather on the following day. Cars rushed by, their headlights cutting a swathe through the otherwise quiet street. I felt weary, ashamed, headachy, unequal to the task of rescuing this strange evening. I searched for anodyne subjects of conversation. Easter was early this year; surely that would do? Yet the thought of Easter, the first of the year's annual migrations, depressed me even further. Everyone had plans: it was a social duty to enquire what these were.

'I suppose you will take a break?' I said.

'Probably. Almost certainly. And you?'

'I'm not sure yet,' I said, maintaining the fiction of those friends vying with each other for my company. We walked on in silence.

'Did you really just happen to be in the neighbourhood this evening?' I asked.

'Yes. I had to see someone at Imperial College about finding a place for a homesick first-year Indian medical student.'

'And did you? Manage that, I mean.'

'Oh, yes.'

He was no more talkative than I was, as if the evening had made us equally exhausted.

At the entrance to Melton Court I resolutely held out my hand.

'Thank you for dinner.'

'It was my pleasure.'

It did not then seem as if it had been a pleasure. He had retreated into his earlier mournful self. What he had no doubt wanted was not something I could supply. The brief recitation of his emotional history had served some purpose, but I was not able to evaluate this. No doubt it had been defensive, even pre-emptive, in order to forestall any more leisurely enquiries. It now seemed entirely irrelevant, yet I knew that I should give it further thought. He seemed to regret it, but it was in keeping with his general stoicism not to offer excuses.

'I'll no doubt be in touch after the holiday.'

'I hope you will. Goodnight, Mr Ward.'

'Nigel.'

'Elizabeth.'

'Goodnight, Elizabeth.'

I turned away quickly, in case I should seem to be watching him stride off. He would of course walk home. It would be a relief to him to be on his own again, as it would be to me. I no longer had much taste for my own company, although alternative company usually left me unsettled. What I dreaded (but this was routine) was returning to my empty flat, in which I should not be disturbed. Tonight the rooms seemed airless, and more silent than usual. I was never glad to get home, though frequently reassured that I had managed it. It occurred to me that I was not bound to stay in this flat, could in fact move. I had a vision of a house, of a family kitchen, a back door opening on to a garden. I promised myself that I would explore the side streets that I usually ignored, and perhaps let myself plan an alternative future. The advantage of moving might in fact be even greater than the advantage of a long journey: no one could get in touch with me, and I need offer no explanations. And I need never come back to this place which I suddenly found inimical.

There was no trace of Nigel Ward's presence, apart from his empty glass. This I tidied away, together with my own and an untouched dish of olives. How bored he must have been! And yet I reminded myself that he had more or less arranged the meeting, had telephoned, and might telephone again. Unfortunately I lacked the stamina for an association in which I might be required to behave discreetly, circumspectly, as if everything might be reported back to the analyst, if he had one. I had to remind myself that the analyst was, until verified, merely a figment of my imagination: Mr Ward, whom it would be difficult to think of as Nigel, might be his own analyst. He certainly had penetrating insights, was certainly a better tactician than I had proved to be in the course of the evening. Yet the need for circumspection would remain, and I preferred other ways of behaving. I preferred, in fact, the absence of circumspection, as I believe most women do. In trying the direct approach I had made a serious mistake, though this struck me as laughable rather than tragic. I had been irked by his civilized restraint; I had not been prey to sudden urges. All my life, it seemed, I had longed for direct engagement, for total intimacy, and had encountered it only once, in the least poetic of settings, in a rented flat of no great amenity, which nevertheless held the secret which had at last been revealed to me. However shabby, however second-rate, however deplorable in the eyes of the world those encounters could, with hindsight, be seen to have been, they had answered my most profound need, and in themselves had proved sustaining enough to remain the standard by which all other attachments had to be measured.

It was perhaps strange that I, an ordinary woman of no great distinction or accomplishment, frequently overlooked by others, no longer studied by men, should have discovered this for myself and should cling to it as proof of my validity. It would, I knew, never be repeated. The best I could hope for – and this was a great deal to hope for – was that the memory of such pleasure might be shared, might bring a reminiscent smile to another's face. I lived on the possibility that this might be so, yet sometimes I found it hard to sustain that hope. Now it came back to me with a sort of anger, the anger I unjustly felt for Nigel Ward's punctilio. Behind that anger lay the trace of Betsy's bold claim that she had in some way succeeded where I had failed. I no longer saw her as touching and vulnerable; in the again unlikely setting of Peter Jones she had seemed confident, even over-confident. In my memory I invested her with a slight sneer, which I knew had not been there, but she had implied that my marriage had been faulty in some way, that I had not loved my husband, that her love affair was superior to any I might have known, and for that I should find it hard to forgive her. There was no way I could convince her, even persuade her, that I had emotional resources of my own, since she had decided that no trace of these remained. And behind even this, but stimu-lated by it, was the longing for a rash act, such as I was no longer permitted, after which I would truly vanish, with the satisfaction of having answered a need of which others had hitherto been unaware.

I was late getting to bed, and the usual soothing routines were not effective. I lay in the dark, trying to rid myself of the events of the day, which had been unusually disconcerting. Of the encounter with Betsy I preferred not to think, and so far the events of the evening were not quantifiable. My bold suggestion to Nigel Ward had been out of character; it was company rather than sex that I had wanted, although the body can often prove a traitor. What disturbed me was the thought that I had not been in good faith, and that I had no real interest in this man beyond his no doubt unusual story. It would have been one of those makeshift intimacies in which I too should have to furnish a history, something I was not willing to do. This particular man seemed to be proceeding on the same principle, yet I had to remember that he had turned me down. I had also been prompted by a certain shame at my own continence. This was no longer *de rigueur*, was almost suspect. My standards of behaviour were markedly out of keeping with the spirit of the times; they were standards remembered from the novels I used to read, in which there was no doubt that virtue and sexual fidelity went hand in hand. It was entirely possible that such standards could only be attained in fiction. At the same time there were disturbing echoes of the same belief in Nigel Ward, whose physical presence, though agreeable, was somehow hollow. I could see that he was imprinted with the memory of his early experiences; his standards had been set by a combination of Oxford, of love, of confidence, and of early promise, none of which had borne fruit. No doubt he had moments of lucidity, in which he saw himself as a hostage to the past, and by his own decree a hostage to a grim present. His flat in Bedford Way would be austere, a cell suitable for a latter-day penitent, and long walks his remedy for inconvenient physical promptings. He gave the impression of having made a good job of his life, of coming to terms with it by devoting his energies to young people with whom he sympathized largely by virtue of their youth. In his lost world he had been a participant; now he was merely an observer. Such confidence as he had enjoyed had proved fallacious, yet he still treated it as if it remained his sole capital. He had conveyed all this in very few words, yet left the impression that it remained an article of faith, likely to outlive whatever had come after. At some point there would have been a reckoning, an unwelcome realization of the truth, perhaps even a slow recovery. In that respect he was superior to myself. Yet I knew, by instinct, that we both preferred our failures to our relative successes. In that respect we were perhaps more alike than unalike. Perhaps friendship would be possible. Perhaps he saw that too.

15

The season changed, and I, reluctantly, changed with it. Though there was little raw nature in my immediate surroundings to inform me of this change I could not help but be aware of the lighter mornings and evenings, the longer days which faded slowly and almost imperceptibly into shadow. I regretted the dark that had previously enfolded me, permitting the voluptuous descent into welcome sleep. Now my sleep was fitful, so that the day never really ended, and I was awake before dawn at the beginning of another long day. It was also warm, so that it was a relief to throw back the bedclothes, to get up and take a shower. Thus my day began when other people were still asleep, and I found this unwelcome, revealing to me as it did my lack of occupation, or rather of direction.

Occupation of a sort was available, but the greater part of it took on the nature of displacement activity. My mother telephoned from Spain to ask if I would like to visit for a few days, but I knew that there was no room in the little house she shared with her friend, and that I should have to go to an hotel. I was not anxious for her company, nor she for mine. I knew that her days were filled with arguments, as they had been when she lived at home with my father; she accepted this as natural behaviour, as I dare say her friend did. Some women are contentious by nature, relieving their anger at the hand life has dealt them with a pointless stream of criticisms which they dare not direct against themselves. I no longer questioned my father's decision to leave, though I had thought him cruel to do so. I had become so used to my mother's dissatisfaction – in which I was aware that I played a part – that for many years I accepted her references to her unusual sensitivity, which were constant, without questioning her claims to her refined nature, her dislike of other people, particularly women, even of her closest friends.

I had come to a sterner assessment of these claims, but was uncomfortably aware that she was an unhappy woman. I thought that in her exile she had found some sort of solution to her various discontents, arguing, as she had always done, proclaiming the rightness of her decisions, animadverting freely against those whom she accused of letting her down. She had had the good fortune, if that was what it was, to find a companion similar to herself in outlook; no doubt they understood each other perfectly, and did not complain, or not more than was customary, about their routine disagreements. I viewed this arrangement as something unnatural which I did not care to witness at close quarters. The idea of a woman choosing to live not with a man but with another woman was unfamiliar to me, nor did my attitude ever change. Therefore sorrow for my mother, mixed with the difficult love we still felt for each other, kept me away from her. Nor did I have fantasies about an alternative mother whom I might fashion in my own image. No doubt childhood was something I was prepared to forgo. I do not remember at any time regretting this.

At Easter the streets had been deserted, and I had felt uneasy at the prospect of what seemed endless uninterrupted time. The unusual warmth had made me aware of the confines of the flat, pleasant enough in winter, but now inappropriately restricting. On Easter Sunday I walked round the park, but this inevitably brought to mind Nigel Ward and his student followers. I thought perhaps, as I had not thought at the time, that the students were indulging him, that they had no real interest in the long walks, and would rather be drinking coffee somewhere more convivial. I now saw his efforts on their behalf as noble but a little sad, and also rather impressive in their innocence. I imagined him on his holiday, walking purposefully through France, persuading himself that there was some satisfaction in carrying out a self-imposed task, and doing so successfully, so that when he eventually met up with his friends he would in fact have little to say to them, the mere enactment of the task being paramount.

His friends, in their turn, would welcome him warily, their affection tempered by his unwavering sternness. Yet there would be affection, I thought. One is touched, even moved, by a spectacle of such virtue; one is also made uncomfortable by it. I myself had felt shabby, flimsy, in his company, I had been impressed but also appalled by the vision he had given me of his life, the depth of disappointment that had spoilt his youth and contributed so unhappily to what should have been the years of his maturity. In many ways he had been frozen in time, and therefore exhibited a conduct of extreme ambiguity, although to him this may not have been apparent. An attractive man by any standards, he was paradoxically unapproachable. There had been no hint of a woman in the background, apart from the child-bride to whose memory he had remained faithful. He did not seem to know that such unclouded times, if one is fortunate enough to have experienced them, can never be replicated. He would conjure up their memory, and be eternally saddened by his inability to build on it. Yet he was intelligent, and seemed to need no consolation. He had made strenuous efforts, the sort of efforts beyond most of us, certainly beyond myself, and the result was a rigidity of behaviour that might alienate any possible company he might have wished.

There was a mismatch here between us which I regretted but could not ignore. Whereas he had been permitted to enjoy youth and its optimism I had been the opposite, restrained and expecting nothing. I now looked back in something like horror to my lonely days in Paris, and knew quite suddenly that I should not go back there. I was not keen to emulate the stoicism of which I could not help but be aware. Our approach to each other had been as tentative as that between automata, and I had been both impatient and embarrassed by my failure to intrigue him. I had never been a great success in this way; I was not confident enough to make claims on my own behalf. That was the great virtue of my husband, whose easy tolerance and good nature had appeased my sexual misgivings, no doubt the result of a homesickness for romance that I had felt in Paris and had not found with the few young men I had met and known there. I had owed him an immense debt that I continued to honour. It was entirely possible that Nigel Ward could provide the same sort of loyal companionship – anything less would be unthinkable – which would leave me comforted but unassuaged. I had never committed the indignity of blaming Digby for the passion I felt for Edmund, but no doubt it would serve as an explanation. I had been aware of checks and balances since my early adolescence: if I renounced this then I could have that. It had never occurred to me that I could have it all, as the feminists proclaimed. I saw this as impossible: how could one reconcile such diverging opposites?

The question that preoccupied me as I walked round the park was whether either of us was so tired of our lives as to seek out each other, and why this prospect should appeal to one so ferociously guarded as Nigel Ward. The advantage to myself would be obvious; no longer a careful widow I might enjoy more dignity than had recently been my lot. Indeed I was conscious, as I might otherwise not have been, of how drab a figure I must have appeared to anyone who had not known me in the days of my confidence as both wife and mistress. I could see why Betsy's hateful remarks had so offended me, stirring in me thoughts of flight, of exile: I appeared to her, and no doubt to others, as a polite relic, all fires put out. I had been so successful in my concealment that none thought to question it. In a sense this was appropriate: my secret was safe with me. Now I saw that it had not always been so, that it had been overlooked only by virtue of certain codes, a barrier which Betsy had knocked down. The defiant freedom I had once felt had been eclipsed and could never be re-invented. What I wanted now was something quite different, a sort of blamelessness such as adults rarely come by. I wanted, if anything, some of Nigel Ward's virtue. I wanted a good conscience, such as I had not enjoyed for a long time, perhaps never.

I viewed this matter almost in the abstract, since my feelings were not engaged. This fact did not disturb me unduly; rather it seemed a matter for congratulation. Fate had presented me with a possibility which I could hardly ignore. I was not old, but I was no longer young. Nor was I particularly worried that I was thinking these thoughts in isolation, without reference to the partner whom I was speedily taking for granted. Sex might be a problem, but I was prepared for that. His physical reluctance had been unmistakable, not merely in his smiling refusal of my invitation, but in his obvious avoidance of contact, even in the precipitate way he moved his legs when I approached with his glass of wine. Such conduct seemed to me pitiable, though it was obviously part of his life, and had no doubt been fashioned in rigorous circumstances. I doubted the existence of another woman, let alone other women, although other women must certainly have punctuated his austere existence. Flattered by his good manners such women, if they indeed existed, would have expected a favourable outcome, only to be puzzled and disappointed by his lack of desire. Thus each promising beginning would be followed by a period of such extreme caution that some would shrug their shoulders and move on. I had proof of this caution, for he had not left me his home telephone number. At first I had assumed that he had forgotten to do so; now I saw this as a tactical manoeuvre, leaving the entire undertaking in his own hands, to implement or to discard as he saw fit. This was a more formidable obstacle than whatever sexual naïveté I ascribed to him. And yet I remained convinced that he would find his way back to me, that he was lonely, and even ashamed of his loneliness, and that I represented something agreeable and approachable which he might find to his taste.

I hoped that he would not take too long to do this, as the warmer days presented me with a problem. There was no patch of grass that I could call my own, and I could not bear to sit in the flat entertaining busy and no doubt reckless calculations. My fantasy of a little house, with a kitchen table and a back door, soon faded; I did not have the money for such an enterprise. What I had was the flat, in which I was condemned to remain. Yet every morning I had an impulse to leave it, and as soon as I could I went round to a modest local café for breakfast. This place, thronged at that time of the morning with young men in tin hats and baggy shorts, took no notice of me: I could sit there for a couple of hours with a cup of coffee in front of me and read the paper. When the owner seemed to find this acceptable I had no further qualms about doing so, and would spend the morning being anonymous and untroubled. One good result of this regime was that I started reading again, with the hunger of one long deprived. I wondered how I could have borne to be without the printed page for so long, although what I read hardly corresponded to the thoughts chasing each other in my mind. I read *Villette*, and marvelled with something like despair at the noble heroine, yet I was convinced, as I once had been, of the superiority of such trusting behaviour. This opened up a whole range of role models, and they seemed so natural that I wondered how I could have left them behind. Dickens I would avoid; his characters were virtuous beyond my reach, perhaps beyond anybody's reach, and the archaic part of me was still trying to calculate what was and was not permitted. One comes back to nineteenth-century novels again and again, largely because of the sheer beauty of the reasoning: happiness at last, achieved through the exercise of faithfulness and right thinking. That this was still possible if one were a lesser, even a fallen being, I doubted; nevertheless it continued to make a forceful impression. And there was always a marriage, seen as the right true end, and this I did not doubt. The fragmentation of present-day society had meant a loss of hope, so that those who harboured traditional leanings were largely disappointed. My love affair, in which I still believed passionately, was in truth largely a matter of bad faith for all concerned, and its unexpected aftermath, in which I had become unwillingly involved, even worse.

In the café, among the young men in their work clothes, I felt temporarily restored to a mild version of hopefulness. No one knew where to find me, and I read on until an influx of people alerted me to the fact that it was nearly lunchtime. Then, reluctantly, I drained my third cup of coffee, waved to the proprietor, and made my way home. The afternoon would present a problem, as it usually did. I felt shy of imposing my presence on the café once again and tried to continue reading in the flat, until discontent or merely claustrophobia drove me out again. That was when I walked – anywhere, it hardly mattered – buying the food I should be obliged to eat alone, and returning to the flat only when this pretext seemed too futile. In any event I was not hungry; I had not experienced a keen appetite for a very long time. I suppose that I languished. That too seemed a consequence of poor behaviour; it was impossible to think of Lucy Snowe languishing. I concluded that I was simply not good enough to gain re-admission to the high standards of fiction and must make do with the sorry business of real life. There had been no telephone call from Nigel Ward, a fact which was becoming increasingly relevant.

After *Villette* I decided on *The Portrait of a Lady*, which I took with me when I joined the tin hats in the café on subsequent mornings. This was far more instructive, I found. It was a story I had once rejected, thinking it too sad for my purpose. I must have been very young when I first read it, and still hopeful, but the prospect of a woman living up to the task of being or becoming a lady had seemed onerous, too harsh to contemplate. Yes, there was a marriage, but when I was young I could not believe that a marriage could be so hateful, although I had the example of my parents to convince me. It was simply that I expected art to furnish me with better examples, as I suppose most people do, and I could not abandon my belief that in a certain favourable context one would behave as well as one had been programmed to do. One's subsequent behaviour was bound to represent a fall from grace, and this no doubt was the universal experience. Mine had not been an abrupt expulsion from Eden, rather a slow recognition that life is subject to accidents, that these are too beguiling to ignore, and that one was bound to make one's peace with them, if one could. Nevertheless Isabel Archer's choices filled me with sympathetic horror. Behaving well seemed to me too high a price to pay.

I was perhaps a third of the way through it, and sitting in the flat waiting for the afternoon to end, when the telephone at last rang. I no longer knew whether I had been waiting for this call or not; I had occupied a not altogether unpleasant limbo of reading and wandering, alternating between accept-ance and bewilderment. This, I dare say, is the essence of languor, if that was what I was suffering; I had lost my earlier purposefulness, and with it my decisive thoughts. I still knew what I should do to gain my chance of companionship but I wished the matter to be someone else's responsibility. The earlier scenario, in which I guided events to my satisfaction, now seemed to me utterly unconvincing; no doubt my read-ing, or rather the examples I had chosen, had undermined my resolve and revealed my thinking as erroneous. I wanted the impetus to be in other hands, though I saw this as unlikely. Indeed I felt it might be better to forgo the whole relationship rather than make a false move which might be fatal for both of us. Though the price might still be worth paying I doubted my expertise, as, strangely, I had not done previously. No doubt I was now nearer the truth of the matter, which no longer had anything to do with expertise, life once again revealing its ability to teach one unwelcome lessons. It took a certain amount of courage to answer the telephone, although I knew instinctively who was calling.

'Hello?' I said, my voice rusty, as if I had recently returned from afar.

A clearing of the throat. 'Nigel Ward here.'

'How nice to hear from you. Did you have a good holiday?'

'Very pleasant, thank you.'

I calculated that he had been silent for something like six weeks, and I felt a spurt of annoyance that he had not been more assiduous. It was already May; soon he might disappear again, probably when the students began to disperse for the summer, and I decided that matters must be moved on. Thus, without willing it, I reverted to my earlier resolution. This, after all, had initially felt appropriate. Now that my mind was made up I felt almost careless, the *belle indifférence* of the manic or the deluded.

'You must tell me all about it,' I said smoothly. 'Why don't you come to dinner? This evening, if you've nothing better to do.'

'That would be delightful.' After a few seconds' silence he rang off. From this I calculated that he may have been in the same state of mind, but with less conviction.

There was little food in the house, but I made a large salade niçoise; that, followed by cheese and fruit, would have to do. In any case I doubted that we should be spending the evening at the table. I showered hastily and dressed in a manner that would not frighten him. I wished that I had told him to take a cab; I was not up to a long wait. Evidently he had thought along the same lines, for within half an hour I heard the whine of the lift. I walked slowly to the door, opened it, and held out my hand.

'How nice to see you,' I said. 'Do come in. What a beautiful evening. A glass of wine?'

He settled himself cautiously in Digby's chair, and drank his wine with some speed, as I did.

'You had a good walk?' I said. 'Where were you? Did you visit your friends?'

'Well, no. They decided to go to Greece. I shall no doubt see them in the summer.'

'Where did you go, then?'

'The Loire Valley. I'm particularly fond of that part of France. Beautiful air. Pleasant towns. Tours. Angers. The châteaux, of course.'

'Digby and I did that, also at Easter. Blois. Amboise.'

'Yes.'

That seemed all there was to say about the Loire, since he was not willing to expand.

'Shall we eat?' I said. 'It's a very simple meal. I hope it will be enough for you.'

'It looks delicious.'

He was nervous. I was impatient. He applied himself to his food, though the hand that held his fork trembled slightly. He was aware of the rite of passage to come, and saw that escape was no longer an option.

'Are you busy?' I asked, to put him at his ease.

'Not very, no.'

'I suppose the students are preparing for their exams?'

'Yes.'

This was going to be more difficult than I expected.

'That was delightful,' he said, laying down his fork. Most of my meal was still on my plate. 'Can I help?'

I was exasperated. This was not how a man should behave. It seemed that I should have to take the initiative. With a sigh I stood up and collected the plates.

'Leave everything,' I said. 'Bring your wine.'

'Elizabeth, have you thought this through?'

'Oh, yes,' I said. My clothes were coming off even before we reached the bedroom.

I was kind and patient, as I might have known I should have

to be. He was clearly not a good judge of his own performance, for he appeared dazed with relief. Maybe that was what he felt, after a period of abstinence, but I also suspected gratitude, and I had little use for that. If anything I preferred him stern and judgmental, thinking this a proper basis for an honest evaluation of the facts. It is not true that one man drives out the memory of another, but it was good to recover that illusion of intimacy, and when I saw him in Digby's towelling bathrobe I was unexpectedly touched. This was a sign of the domesticity for which I still retained a longing. Without his clothes he had seemed infinitely more attractive, had made no attempt to cover his nakedness. In the bathrobe, which reached only to his calves, he was gaining authority by the minute.

'Did you know that that was going to happen?' he said.

'It is what most people do. It is even mandatory. You didn't object?'

'You are a very attractive woman.'

'I'll make some coffee. Or perhaps tea. Tea seems more appropriate. You sit down.'

Covered but not dressed, we drank the tea thirstily. I had no further fears for the summer. *The Portrait of a Lady* could be left for another day.

'Shall we watch the news?' I asked him.

With the benign accoutrements of the tea and the television we both relaxed in the almost normal atmosphere, almost normal apart from our disarray. Yet there was much that was still undecided. I could see that he was slightly disturbed by the rapidity with which events had taken place. There was no poetry in it; that was what disturbed him. In that he was more romantic than I had ever been. Yet I had willed this, had brought it about. I was no more sure of my own feelings than he was of his. With the television finally switched off an awkwardness, which had not been there at the beginning of the evening, descended on us both. He disappeared to dress, and I began to clear away the remnants of our supper. When he came back, once again restored to his formal persona, I could see that he was anxious to be gone. I did not attempt to delay his departure. Future arrangements were not discussed, such was the state of our separate preoccupations. He would be back, of that there was no doubt. But his overriding wish was to think things through, as he would have put it. There was no way in which I could enter into this process.

When the door closed behind him I found that I too was a little disturbed. The flat was redolent with the trace of another person. That was what disturbed me. I even regretted my normally inviolate bed. It was when I finally settled, in the dark, on my own again, that I allowed my mind to wander freely. And what came back to me, in that semi-conscious state, was nothing more significant than the memory of certain streets, or certain odd townscapes once visited, and, intermittently, the image of a bright garden to which I no longer had access.

16

Nigel overwhelmed me with kindly suggestions as to how I might improve my life, which he saw as lacking in one important dimension, that of duty, stern daughter of the voice of God. Not that God came into it, I was relieved to see: this was sheer conscience, an uneasy suspicion that I was lacking in moral purpose. This was entirely true, but I could not quite bring myself to acquaint him with my fundamental nature, let alone my history. He urged me to find work, although I did manage to convince him that I was completely unskilled. This, however, was no barrier to his ingenuity. I could do voluntary work, he suggested, at the local hospital's League of Friends. I responded that I should rather read than walk round with a tea trolley, cheering up patients with good-natured questions about their families. This, I could see, shocked him; had he been a woman of some means, as I was, this was the sort of thing he might have done himself. Or I could in some way interest myself in the lives of his students, with well-placed comments, or even invitations, on those Sunday walks which continued well into the summer. He saw us engaging in some form of supervision which would benefit both parties. I had been able to observe the benefit to him, but also to divine the students' unwillingness to participate in this form of missionary activity. He might have seen this for himself, for he made no further attempt to pursue this particular line of argument. Or I could hire out my culinary skills once again and provide dinner parties for the sort of people he was convinced I knew.

I pointed out that if I did this I could no longer cook dinner on the evenings when he indicated willingness to join me. Lunches, then, he said; there were, he was sure, firms who would be glad to have something served in the staff dining-room. I pointed out, as tactfully as I could, that he knew as little about this business world as I did. He at last conceded that this was an impractical suggestion, but did not entirely relinquish the idea. He seemed determined to launch me on a new way of life, one of service, though after a time he came to accept that it was perhaps preferable that I should always be on the end of a telephone should he want to reach me.

This he did fairly often, and then at last regularly. I came to rely on his telephone calls on the occasions when I did not see him. I sensed that he wished to be left entirely free, and that this freedom to do as he pleased was my only possible gift to him. I had always enjoyed the sensation of a man's freedom, as if it were appropriate that a woman should to a certain extent refrain from taking the initiative. This, of course, was not in keeping with the new raised consciousness of women, but I was correct in supposing that it suited him very well. He was an old-fashioned character, rather like one of those upright heroes in my favourite nineteenth-century novels, the ones whose virility resides in their strength of purpose. I had never stopped to wonder whether this was an adequate endowment: now I did. The better part of our relationship was one of solidarity; our affection was fraternal. It comforted me to be in bed at night, alone, and to know that he would telephone to assure himself that I was all right, that I was completely well, not wailing and gnashing my teeth, as he supposed I might be doing out of disappointment at his absence. His absence, in fact, caused me no great distress, although his company was pleasant and undemanding. It was too undemanding for my tastes, which remained lawless. I should have been happier if he had been more inventive, more singular, more urgent. I schooled myself to accept him as he was, always with the knowledge that I had known what I was doing when I had sought him out. For that was how I thought of it, although the facts were slightly different. The slight but persistent boredom that I felt in his presence was the price I had to pay, for those late-night telephone calls, for the knowledge that there was someone to whom I could apply in any difficulty. That was his gift to me, and that was the other part of the bargain.

My gift to him was slightly different. My house, though not my life, was open to him. He could choose to drop in, to visit, and not go home whenever he wanted to. When he sat in Digby's chair and recounted his day I could see that he was comfortable, even happy. His anecdotes were always about other people, whom I did not know; he was a solitary who had the grace to occupy himself with other lives. His brief burst of truth-telling, on the occasion of our first real encounter, had served the purpose he had intended for it: his life story, as it were, had been offered, had been accepted without criticism, and now need never be re-examined. I never found out whether he had been seeing an analyst, for the moment for that kind of explanation had passed, and I sensed that it was an immense relief to him not to have to discuss it. As far as he was concerned I was a friend, his friend, even his particular friend. My chief virtue was that I never queried the exact nature of this friendship.

To myself, of course, I did. Had I been brave enough to admit it I should have acknowledged the stupefying nature of such irreproachability. Yet, miraculously, I managed to keep my impatience in check. It was enough, or almost enough, to shop for food with some enthusiasm, to devise a meal that would tempt him, to make him welcome. For I too had been lonely, though well enough equipped to deal with loneliness. There was genuine pleasure in knowing that my evenings would be occupied, and by a man who was becoming less and less of a stranger, but that was how I had felt at the outset of my marriage. I did not, could not, envisage another marriage: the idea oppressed me, although an outside observer might have concluded that this stately friendship could end in nothing less than marriage. That was not within my sights, although on certain evenings it might seem as though it had already taken place. We ate, we cleared away – he now knew where everything was kept – we watched television together. Like the solitaries that we remained we were fascinated by the alliances, the domestic arrangements of the characters in the soap operas. His attitude towards these imaginary people was severely critical: they were stupid, or, more often, workshy. I could see that he was well on the way to becoming a testy old man, and I on the way to becoming one of those humorously tolerant women whose presence I had always found so soporific, largely on account of that very tolerance. Take a lover, I would urge silently, when stopped by one of these women in the shops or in the street (for now I seemed to know quite a few people, or perhaps they knew me), or, as one of my erstwhile Parisian acquaintances would recommend, in stronger terms, 'Faîtes de la gymnastique, ou faîtes-vous baiser.' There was a certain mean pleasure in knowing myself to be on the right side of orthodoxy, to be entitled to a certain smugness, to be able to accept as normal this strange entitlement to which I was still not accustomed. We understood enough about each other to enable us to avoid disharmony, and if this was not quite enough for me I could see that it pleased Nigel. Indeed his satisfaction at the way things had turned out was almost palpable. He seemed both younger and older than I was, younger in his lack of worldliness, older in his unvaryingly courteous demeanour in all circumstances. There were times when I longed to torment him, to goad him into some form of spontaneity, to inspire in him some rude initiative, but these times were becoming increasingly rare. I was almost a reformed character. Nigel, of course, had always been one.

When the telephone rang I said, 'That can't be you; you're already here.' He loved that kind of remark, with its implications of assurance, of continuity. We had been leaning on the window-sill, gazing out at the brilliant evening, struck by the beauty of the summer season. Reluctantly we turned back into the comparative dimness of the unlit room. 'You sit down,' I said. 'I'll tell them to ring back.'

'Hello,' said Betsy. 'How are you?'

I had forgotten all about her, willingly. I had thought it better to leave our fractured friendship alone rather than go through the tedious motions of reviving it.

'I'm fine,' I said. 'And you?'

'Well, not so good, actually.' Her tone was merry, but with an undertone of distraction.

Nigel mimed a query. He was not used to having his presence disturbed. My success in making him feel at home had, perhaps, been a little too complete. I put my hand over the mouthpiece. 'We're out of wine,' I said. 'Could you bear to go out and get a bottle? White. We're having fish.'

I heard his steps on the stairs and removed my hand. 'Betsy? What's wrong?'

'Oh, nothing really. It's just that I'm going into hospital tomorrow, and I thought I'd better let you know.'

'Are you ill?'

'No, I don't suppose I am. It's just for tests. Isn't that what they always say?'

The merriment had left her voice, in which I now detected tiredness.

'What's wrong?'

'I've been having a little discomfort. I expect it's nothing really. I'll only be in a few days.'

'I'll come and see you. Where will you be?'

She mentioned a name that meant nothing to me. 'It's a small private hospital somewhere across the river.'

'Why private? Wouldn't you be better off on the NHS? They have the resources . . .'

'Edmund insisted.' Her pride was unmistakable.

'So Edmund knows about this?'

'Naturally. The thing is, they want the name of my next of kin. Well, as you know, I have no next of kin.' She laughed. 'I wondered if you'd mind if I gave your name? I'm sure they won't bother you. As I say, it's only for a few days. And you can see that I can't give Edmund's name.'

'In your place I think I might have done.'

'Oh, no. And anyway I don't want him to think of me as ill. He hates illness. Even when one of the children is ill he's quite squeamish. So I probably shan't bother him until I'm home again. Of course if he turns up that's a different matter.'

'Quite. Give them my name by all means.' There was a pause which seemed to me significant. 'Are you sure it's nothing serious?'

'Well, I don't think so. As I say, discomfort, rather than anything else. A little pain, perhaps. I didn't know what to make of it. I've never been ill before. I'm quite healthy, really.'

'I'll be along to see you. When are you going in?'

'Tomorrow. Leave it for a day or two. They'll want to do these tests.' There was another pause. 'You will come, won't you?' This time the voice was wistful, as if she had shed all her irritating adult mannerisms and had reverted to being the girl not yet damaged by the ways of the world. That was my thought at the time: damage. And in a moment that summoned up our previous history I wished that we were both still our uncorrupted selves, before the onset of calculation. I too was damaged, if only by the decisions I had made. These decisions had not been fatal, but neither had they been innocent. I had always been conscious of the work that time, that enemy, can do, or rather undo. Now I had the sensation of being rather more implicated in its processes than I had previously recognized.

'Let me know if there's anything you want,' I said. 'I'll see you in a couple of days.'

Even a couple of days seemed a difficult prospect. I stood, with the now silent telephone in my hand, unwilling to move, wishing the previous untroubled hours back again, wanting to be on my own. When I heard Nigel's steps on the stairs I was conscious of the need to greet him in my familiar disguise, that of a person of good will whom he thought he knew, whose good faith he was beginning to trust. And really nothing had changed, apart from that seismic revelation that I was no longer secure, that there was no direct menace other than that provided by the unknown, the accidental, the change that must be investigated, subjected to 'tests'. In this process I was as vulnerable as Betsy, even though the hour had not yet struck.

A voice. Not Nigel's. Edmund's.

'Your door was open.'

'I'm expecting a friend. He should be back in a moment or two.'

'Very unwise, leaving your door open. I shan't keep you long.'

'You came about Betsy, of course.'

He looked tired, even haggard. 'I must get home. We're going out to dinner.'

'Ah, yes. How is Constance?'

'Don't look at me like that, Elizabeth.'

'What do you want from me, Edmund? I'll go and see Betsy, of course. I rather gather that you won't.'

He sat down heavily. 'This is a bad time for me.' I could see that it was. 'It has damaged my family for ever. I bear the burden.'

'So does everyone else, I rather imagine.'

'I thought it could be kept within limits.'

'Men always do.'

'Instead of which she has, deliberately or otherwise, not understood my situation.'

'She had her own to consider.'

'She rings up the girls. God knows what she says to them.'

'She is a decent woman. She would not do anything underhand.'

'Constance may not forgive me. I have to take notice of that.'

'What will you do?'

His hands, which I remembered acutely at that moment, went up to cover his face, to rub his eyes.

'I know what has to be done.'

'Can't you tell me?'

'No, I can't drag you into this. You're not involved.'

'I am, you know. Not just with Betsy. With you. I have never doubted it. I don't doubt it now.'

He stood up, shocked out of his misery. This scene of

tacit complicity was what greeted Nigel when he returned.

'Edmund is just leaving,' I said, but with a voice that hovered between terror and confidence. 'I'll see you out.' In that moment the future was banished. In the hallway we spoke in lowered voices, conspirators.

'You'll go and see her?'

'Not you?'

'I may have to go away on business. If there's any change, of course, you'll let me know.'

'Is she really ill?'

'I don't know. She looks pale, certainly.'

'You've just come from there?'

'Yes.'

He made the supreme mistake of handing me his card, which I thrust angrily into the nearest telephone directory, knowing that I should not bother to retrieve it. He went on to compound the mistake by laying a heavy hand on my shoulder, a gesture which he obviously thought appropriate to the circumstances. And yet there was intimacy there, as well as deliberation. Distantly I heard Nigel clearing his throat in the living-room. When Edmund was half-way down the stairs I shouted, 'Who's paying for this?' His upturned face was creased with sorrow. 'Provision has been made,' he said.

I stood in the hall until I heard the outer door close, then his steps on the pavement, then the car starting up. 'Provision has been made,' he said. To make provision: to provide for. So Edmund had been contributing to Betsy's life in more ways than one. I was profoundly shocked, as if giving money to a woman implied yet more intimate responsibility. I had not understood this, although I might have done. Money was not anything Betsy had earned or inherited. The strange equality that existed between us was not a matter of our respective resources. It was both deeper and more troubled than that. He had also said, 'I know what has to be done.' This was equally shocking, hinting at the stirrings of conscience. Did he mean to marry her, to escape from Constance and her dinner parties? To me he had merely given his card, as if I were a business acquaintance, or a client. I knew that I would never forgive him for that.

'Where are you?' said Nigel, coming out to find me. 'Why were you shouting?'

'I just remembered something I should have told him.'

'I have never heard you raise your voice before. Who was that?'

'Someone I used to know,' I said. When I looked up and saw his face I knew that I had made a mistake. 'Dinner is not ready, I'm afraid. Shall we go round to the restaurant?' For it was important to get us both out of the flat, to observe an interval that might otherwise be filled with questions.

Yet it was time for questions to be asked, if there were to be more honesty between us. I suspected that he had already come to his own drastic conclusions about my association with Edmund: that wordless confrontation, even more than my conspiratorial manners on the stairs, would have convinced him that I was concealing a liaison of which he had previously known nothing. In a sense he was correct, though all this was long in the past and of no immediate relevance. But he was the sort of man who expects and demands full disclosure, in the manner of the account of himself he had given me, obviously hoping to convince me that I need not fear further revelations. This had satisfied him, as he had supposed that it would satisfy me. But I knew that this was of no further interest, that I should have been rather more aware of him had there been signs of conflict in his account, and also in his present behaviour. He now appeared to me as a man of little emotional energy (though I had already been conscious of this) and I had to ask myself whether I could live the rest of my life with such latency. What brief signs of impatience and dissatisfaction he ever betrayed were confined to the dilemmas he saw portrayed on television. I had thought it curious that a man of such obvious strength of purpose should let himself be persuaded by such ersatz sensations.

I had not previously thought this anomalous, but now I did so. Perhaps it was not significant; what was significant was that I now knew that I could not tolerate this level of conversation and preoccupation as my staple evening diet. Of his virtues I remained convinced; what I now perceived was a certain determined superficiality. He had decided that I had no history that need concern him. He was less sure now. My stance, with my back to him as he came upon Edmund and myself, and, if he had caught it, Edmund's brief spark of appraisal, of involuntary memory, would have spelled out some kind of wordless knowledge that could only presuppose long acquaintance. And that was true; his conclusion was entirely correct. It would now fall to him to adjust all his attitudes, and if necessary to withdraw whatever favour he was granting me. Any explanation that I had to offer – that we were discussing the fate of a sick friend – would not excuse that stance, that look. He had further work to do on himself in the light of these new facts, work that might exclude me altogether.

This did not seem to be my problem, and yet it was. The sight of Edmund had revealed the different nature of the two men, and their different appeal. Edmund was essentially a transient, and I had always known that. Nigel was what would do duty as my next of kin. He would stand by me in all

circumstances, but only if I fulfilled certain moral requirements. I could see the advantages of such a settled arrangement, but I could no longer see the attraction. I might do
better on my own, with my own knowledge to guide me.

For I was still processing the past: it had not left me. In a
sense it had revived; my long dead feelings were once again
active, and I could no longer bear to let them go. And I should
have to do so if I were to have any sort of future with this
man. I foresaw with something like dread the day when we
would agree that he should move into the flat with me,
inaugurating a lifetime of domesticity in which our respective
roles would be decreed by immortal custom. I could see him
reading the evening paper, seated in Digby's chair, while I
busied myself in the kitchen. I could also see that in time I
might be tempted to attend fictitious evening classes, not
necessarily in order to meet a lover, but rather to escape the
dead weight of Nigel's presence.

We were silent on our walk to the restaurant, although the
beautiful evening was conducive to mild peaceable conversation. He did not touch my arm or take my hand, the sort of
gesture that endorses existing physical experience and awakens
the indulgence of passers-by. We were glad to sit down, to
unfurl napkins, to greet our usual waiter. Apparently there
was to be no pretence that nothing untoward had taken place,
yet neither of us knew how to broach the subject. At last I
broke the silence. 'There is nothing for you to be afraid of,' I
said. 'We were discussing a mutual friend, who may be rather
ill, and working out what was going to be needed.' ('I know
what has to be done,' Edmund had said.) 'I'm afraid I was
rather shocked; I had not realized that she was ill. I had not
seen her for some time.' Whether this explanation satisfied
him or not was irrelevant; it had the authority of truth. But

then the fact of Betsy and her illness surfaced and bid fair to overwhelm me. It was as if all my associations were in turmoil, and the past, that other enemy, coming back to haunt me. Our youth, Betsy's and mine, was once again threatened, and we must both now deal with the realities visited on adults, whether or not they are prepared. I felt an ache in my throat, laid down my fork. 'You must forgive me,' I said. 'This has been a shock.'

Then he did lay a hand on mine, and his touch comforted me. But he did not stay with me that night. It was easy to imagine him walking off, alone, into the night, his purpose, his life, even, subjected to careful revision.

17

What could have been a breach was repaired, and quite soon: we may have feared a return to an unregarded and unpartnered state. In retrospect we both, individually, and without discussing the matter, remembered those stretches of time which had been filled dutifully and without pleasure. For both of us it was a novelty to be connected. For that was the underlying message: connection. I doubt if it was ever more than that, though it was a relief to surrender our solipsism, to allow a more or less chosen companion into our lives, and to feel increasingly at ease in this new companionship, to pick up references, to reserve anecdotes, to accept as a given one's desire and indeed one's right to pleasure.

This was enough to override any residual misgivings and misunderstandings. But because we were aware that our association had so nearly been undermined by that glimpse of what was undoubtedly genuine and unrehearsed we were on our best behaviour, not only out of fear but out of a residual sense of honour. We were bound to do justice to the situation which we had both created, to value its merits, its sheer suitability. We were alike in so far as we approved of consistency. Nigel no doubt appreciated this more than I did. But I had only to imagine myself in a hospital bed, with no visitors, to cling more closely to what was in essence the simulacrum of an affair, a marriage, the benefits of which it was impossible to overlook, though the strains were now rather more pronounced. The incompatibility of our tastes and temperaments, both forged in more passionate circumstances, might have warned us of difficulties to come. Instead we averted our eyes, became more careful than was entirely comfortable. Nigel, of course, was blameless, but I could see quite clearly now a lurking censoriousness that placed me on probation. So far I had given no cause for undue suspicion. Suspicion, however, was what I now had to allay. Instead of making me indignant this made me cautious. I told myself that I was beyond the age of meaningful glances, of involuntary memories. I was a middle-aged woman and it was in my interest to rescue myself from what would almost certainly be that further age in which there are few compensations.

The image of the hospital bed, which had come out of nowhere, was impossible to dismiss. I knew that this applied to Betsy and yet I felt the anguish of the situation as though it were a very real threat to myself. I saw the dependency, the acceptance that illness brings with it, and the loneliness. I had always been perfectly healthy; there was no reason for me to experience this horror. It was a horror that I had first encountered as a child, when my grandfather was dying: I associated the figure in the bed with the miasma of sickness, the dense tainted atmosphere in the room, the impotent scrabbling of his weak hand. I had cried, protested, been sent out to play. But play was incompatible with what I had seen, although I could hardly have understood it. It was then that I understood the notion of damage, which persisted until I managed to give it a name. Naming it, however, merely increased its power.

It was perhaps significant, perhaps not, that I had another dream at this time, again connected with electricity. In the dream I had tried to switch on the light in the bathroom, only to see and to feel coils of wire dripping from the socket, down the walls to the floor. This was repeated in all the other rooms.

I told myself calmly that an electrician must be called, but before I could do so the door was pushed open to admit two women whom I did not know. They appeared to know me, very well, so well that they made themselves entirely at home, at one point lying down on my bed. They chatted between themselves as if they were in a public place. One produced a bottle of hand lotion which she passed to the other; they shared it carelessly, so that it spilled on to the coverlet, soiling it. I knew that I should find traces of this same glutinous substance on the chairs, the table, the carpets throughout the flat. The two women, absorbed in their conversation, paid no attention to me. And there was no help for it: that was the point. I struggled out of this dream, or nightmare, with a sense of horror so great that I did something I had never done before. I telephoned Nigel, who must have sensed my distress, for he promised to come over. It was five o'clock in the morning. By six he was with me.

He was of immense value to me at that moment, although he did not quite understand why I should be so frightened. My nightmare he was inclined to dismiss as a little woman's nervous imagination, but I think it pleased him to see me as timorous, fallible, anxious for his opinion and his reassurance. My woeful appearance seemed to have called forth some extinct manliness, so that he took charge, made tea, and informed me that we should spend the day in the park, Holland Park, and eat lunch there. I knew that we were both behaving out of character, he so strong, I so weak, and yet it was a relief to us both to indulge these alternative characteristics, to give in to a rarely glimpsed temptation to be other than we were. We both knew that a return to normal was inevitable, that it was necessary but not entirely welcome. I pleased him further by worrying that I was taking him away from his work, and it was at this point that normality began once more to intrude, for he confessed that there was little work for him to do, that perhaps there never had been, at which point his bleakness threatened to overtake my own. I was not willing to pity either of us – pity was too dangerous – so I showered and dressed and made breakfast, relying on these reassuring activities to put us both to rights. The sun was already at full strength: we had passed the longest day. The fear of summer's decline convinced us that we must take advantage of this light, this heat. We set out for the park before nine.

There, sitting on a bench, we had our first real conversation. He wondered why I had been so frightened by what was only a dream, and I tried to explain my concept of damage, and how it had been revived by news of Betsy's illness. Were we very close, he asked. No, but we had grown up together, I replied, and then began to do what I had not intended to do, to reminisce about the past. It all came out: Bourne Street, Pimlico Road, our earliest urban landscape, then school, and our easy unthinking association which ended when I went to Paris, leaving Betsy to deal with her aunt's demise on her own. When she succeeded me in Paris we lost touch, until she appeared at my wedding, hopeful, even joyous, as I had not been. I broke off my account at this point: I still wanted to prolong the ceremony of innocence. But I could hardly convey what this meant to me, and how sadly I had grown away from it. He questioned me astutely as we sat there in the sun, but there was nothing more I was able or willing to add. My feeling that a part of life had already come to an end was too strong, and the knowledge that I had not particularly valued that part too sad.

'And this is the friend you are worried about?' he said.

'Yes,' I replied. I then surprised myself by saying, 'I suppose we have been shadowing each other all our lives. And now she is ill and I must face up to all the implications. I think she must want me with her at this time.' I managed not to say, 'Despite our knowledge of each other.'

Then he said a kind thing. 'Do you want me to come with you?' To the hospital, to the bedside, to the duties that devolve on a person designated as the next of kin.

He prevailed upon me to eat lunch, on a day that seemed stranger than any other. Then he put me in a taxi and stood waving until I was out of sight.

But as the taxi sped away my mood of grateful appreciation declined, and I became hard again, as I knew I might have to be. Tearful empathy was not what would be needed, nor were misgivings and reminiscences. Also I perceived the gratification that my momentary weakness had bestowed on Nigel, for whose conscientious support I now felt a certain impatience. It would seem that in the absence of passion I could feel little except fear. That was the singular gift of passion: it eradicated fear. Now I felt fear, but only for myself: the real thing. I feared the night to come and the dreams it might bring. I feared what I had already perceived, my transformation into the kind of feeble needy woman whom a man like Nigel might think appropriate. I feared a collapse of the nerves that might precipitate me into troubles I had so far only glimpsed. I feared a loss of authenticity which would leave me at the mercy of others, my own vestigial strengths quite gone. Therefore I willed myself to think of Edmund and how I might get in touch with him again.

Yet I was forced to acknowledge that my brief foray into the unconscious, or wherever it was that dreams were manufactured, had done me a disservice, turning me into a younger frightened person, or worse, an older sicker one, and that

Nigel was somehow associated with this process, through no fault of his own, and possibly none of mine. He had been competent, considerate, yet there had been something in his behaviour that distanced me from the man whose measure I thought I had taken. There had been a touch of complacency as he had sought to calm my fears, and the arm that he had laid on my shoulders had been that of a nurse or a guardian, or even a parent: sexless. As we had walked through the summer flowerbeds the arm had grown heavier and I had wanted to shrug it off, but could not do so without causing offence. If we were to continue together I should have to get used to this uxorious possessiveness, and yet his kind action was that of a clumsy man whom I knew I could never meet on his own terms. His gesture – the arm around my shoulders – went with a certain elaborate patience as he listened to my account of that dream of intrusion, of soiling, as if such matters were unknown to him. I had done my best to turn him into a sort of companion with whom I might spend a major part of my life, yet always with an unacknowledged reservation, namely that he was a stranger and likely to remain one. This at last was the breakthrough into an unwelcome truth: I could no longer tolerate him, any more than I could feel comfortable with his heavy arm shackling me to his side. I had done my best to turn myself into another person, the sort of woman who would not puzzle him, who would be anxious for his welfare, good-tempered in all circumstances, content with what he chose to tell me about himself, and keeping mute about my own true nature. And I had done this quite successfully, leading him perhaps towards a conclusion which he accepted too readily. I had not been aware of the strain, yet now I felt fatigue at the prospect of continuing along this road. Edmund's reappearance had done much to accelerate this process, yet Edmund was not to blame. It was Nigel who was to blame, for his very virtues of leniency and conformity – conformity to a stereotype which was perhaps inauthentic in both our cases, out of character. I knew nothing about him except what he chose to tell me. The same was true in my case. The inevitability of marriage loomed frighteningly large. I had had one such marriage, and had known the restrictions it had placed on me, but my true nature had won out, and I could not risk this happening again. For I remained convinced that Nigel was a good man, as Digby had been, and that with him I might lead a dull life and a more or less contented one. He would be proof against further bad dreams, and yet to indulge in the very indulgence I might call forth would seem a sin against all forms of creative energy. For a woman to put such primitive forces aside meant, I knew, a diminution of all her faculties, so that a dryness would ensue, a loss of some sort, a complaisant and complacent acceptance of what had been more or less willingly entered into but should have been seen from the outset as the danger it was.

All this I registered as the taxi proceeded through a landscape that was unfamiliar to me; once past Lambeth Palace I had no idea where I was, or how I should get back. My unease increased with the knowledge that I should shortly have to confront a situation even more unpleasant than my own. And then, in a wide calm street, I came to the heart of the matter. I knew, without needing to be told, what was wrong with Betsy, what those tests would disclose. I knew this, and I imagined that she did. For I think one always knows when one is threatened. That she was no stranger to this feeling, from as far back as she could remember, might, if she, or nature were benignly inclined, make acceptance easier. I saw now, in that blank street, how valiantly she had opposed her fate, which was essentially that of someone denied the protection that enables one to confront the inordinate difficulties that must be confronted if one is ever to achieve a fugitive maturity. Without it one is an orphan, as Betsy had been in reality. I thought back painfully to the ease with which I had taken this for granted, as a given: I had parents – most people had parents – but she had only her faded aunt with whom she lived in a house too big for them, a substantial property which even in those early days was being eyed by speculators. I remembered the evenings the two of them had spent at the cinema, and the epics and extravaganzas they were both perhaps too innocent fully to understand. I saw her in Paris, in Mme Lemonnier's awful kitchen, still making the best of things. I saw the extent of her love affairs, and their all too obvious limitations: as far as I knew there had been only two, both of which had succeeded in denying her essential nature, that of a loving simple girl, an all too willing victim. The absurd Daniel de Saint-Jorre, to whose assumed name she still obstinately clung, had perhaps done no lasting damage; at least she no longer mentioned him. Edmund was another matter. He had become vulnerable to her orphaned state, and though this had made her happy, or at least triumphant, it had turned him against himself, against his own instincts, had created an unwelcome disturbance in his life, gone to the very roots of his family. I could see, with dread, that he was ready to consign her to her fate, and that if ever I were to see him again we should both know the extent of our defection, his and mine. Recovery from this situation, if it ever came about, was less than assured. One came back to the same conclusion: damage. This aura was as palpable as whatever the doctors might uncover. When the taxi drew up I realized that all three of us knew this. With these considerations in mind Nigel receded into the background, dwindled, was almost forgotten.

What united us, Betsy and I, in this strangest of pairings, was the fact that neither of us had children, and that we had therefore failed the one essential test that all women feel obliged to pass. Even celibates measure their success or failure by this standard, and those who remain childless throughout their lives wonder what faculty has been lacking to bring this about. Yet neither of us had been maternal in our outlook, although Betsy gazed fondly on any children she encountered. She was, perhaps, too busy being her own child, the child she had to nurture in the absence of anyone else able or willing to do so. As for myself, I saw any potential children as an impediment to my freedom, for at the back of my mind I kept in readiness a plan of flight from circumstances I could no longer tolerate. (This I might need to activate again.) Now I saw our childlessness as an indictment, a reproach to what had been our folly. In this assumption I included us both; we had seen ourselves always as lovers, whereas sensible persons, or perhaps those with a greater understanding of the world, make their peace with existing circumstances, and know joy and pleasure with the sort of acceptance afforded by a settled state, in which there is no need of concealment. For that concealment I now felt an immense distaste. Only very young romantic girls thrill to the idea of a secret lover. And we had chosen, she and I, to stay within the limits of this exalted and fragile condition. While there might have been a son, a daughter, at Betsy's bedside, there would now only be myself, a poor substitute. That agreement between us never to discuss this matter, or even to think of it, was yet another indication of our lack of true progress. Quite simply, we had not grown up; worse, we had not perhaps known this until now. For nature is insidious and undeniable, and in the presence of a threat, as we now were, makes evident what may have been clear to others, if not to ourselves.

And yet there was no sense of tragedy discernible in the hospital, which was light, bright, and surprisingly quiet, the patients neatly stowed away behind their private doors. I found Betsy sitting up in bed, her eyes expectant. 'I knew you'd come,' she said. She was noticeably thinner in the face than when I had last seen her, but otherwise there was little change, although her elaborate nightdress registered the beating of her heart against its thin folds. I realized with some embarrassment that I had come empty-handed, and resolved in that instant to do all I could to make her comfortable. Neither of us had much taste for the roles we had to play; all the more reason, therefore, to play them to perfection.

'I didn't bring anything,' I said. 'I didn't know what you would want.'

'Nothing, really. A spare nightdress, if you have one. It seems I have to be in here longer than I thought. I'm to have an operation.'

'When?'

'I don't know. Perhaps you could find out. By the way I'm Miss Newton here.' She smiled faintly. 'Stripped of my title.'

'I'll sort it out.' There was a brief silence. 'When is this operation to take place?'

'I don't know. They say they want to feed me up first. I don't like the sound of that.'

'I think it's rather encouraging, their wanting to build you up.'

'Yes.' Again a brief pause. 'What's it like out?'

'Well, it was a beautiful morning. Real summer. Now it's clouding over a bit.'

'Is it hot? I feel hot.'

'It's warm, certainly. There may be rain later. I had lunch in Holland Park. It was pleasant. We'll go there if you like. When you're better.'

'Yes.'

'Real summer,' I persisted. 'And still plenty of it left.'

She lay back on the pillows. 'I don't know why I'm so tired,' she said.

'You have a rest. Sleep if you can. I'll come back tomorrow. I know the way now. It's no problem.' Her eyelids drooped. 'I'll see what I can find out,' I said. 'Leave it to me.'

In the corridor I saw the brief flash of a nurse's uniform as she turned the corner.

'Excuse me,' I called. 'Could I have a word? Are you looking after my friend?'

'Betsy? That's what she told us to call her. I'm afraid I can't tell you anything. To begin with I'm not authorized, and to go on with I don't know. If you'd like to ask at the desk they may be able to tell you.'

'She's to have an operation, I gather. Do you know what it's for?'

'You'd have to speak to Mr Harvey. The surgeon. He won't be in until Friday. That's when he operates. As I say, if you'd like to speak to them at the desk they may be able to tell you more.'

I followed her to a sort of waiting area which was empty. Just as I was resigning myself to one of the seats a plump dark woman appeared from a doorway I had not noticed. I knew that I must ask questions, knew that I did not want to hear the answers. 'Wetherall,' I said. 'Elizabeth Wetherall. I'd like to know more about Betsy Newton. I'm her next of kin.'

'You'd have to ask Mr Harvey. She's scheduled for Friday. Visit whenever you want to, of course. There are no restrictions.'

'You have my telephone number? You can call me at any time.'

She scanned a list. 'Wetherall. Here it is; I have it. Of course you can ring here. My name is Purslow. If you ask for me . . .'

'Yes, thank you. Actually I'll probably be here every day.'

'That's fine. Oh, just one question. To whom should the account be sent?'

'I'll take care of that. You have my address.'

'Thank you. I think that's all for the moment. If you'd like to check with me? I'm here every weekday. There'll be somebody else over the weekend. Just as good.' She smiled firmly. I was dismissed.

As the doors slid closed behind me I felt a huge relief, almost gratitude. After the sanitized coolness of the hospital the murky air of the street struck me as beautiful. I had no desire to go home, only to escape. I walked in the direction of what I thought must be the centre of town: eventually, after passing buildings which seemed devoid of people or activity, I found a bus stop, boarded a bus with an unfamiliar number, and was eventually carried back to recognizable surroundings. Only then did I feel delivered from the threat that had enveloped myself as well as Betsy. Yet I knew that I should have to return on the following day, and on the days after that, to join the nervous visitors with their flowers and their small treats, although I had not been aware of any. The hospital seemed to enclose only Betsy and myself: even the nurse, even Mrs Purslow, seemed like actors, supporting characters, while the shadowy Mr Harvey was merely a menace on the horizon.

Once inside the flat the feeling of menace increased, became so strong that I knew that no subterfuge would be possible. The cheerfulness, even the false cheer that was to be recommended in these circumstances, would, I suspected, be beyond me. The irritable sympathy for Betsy that had accompanied me all my life had been changed, by a process which it did not occur to me to question, into a gravity which imposed its own laws of behaviour.

When Nigel telephoned, as I had expected he would, I knew instinctively that this gravity did not encompass him. That too was a lesson I had learned from these events. Besides, I knew that out of principle, he entertained only robust convictions: one got ill, then one got better. Doctors were there to help. All of this spoke of a man who had never been ill in his life, although I knew that he had a severe regard for his nerves and his digestion. It occurred to me to wonder how I was to balance these two modes, until I realized that I should not need to. My time would be taken up with Betsy and the hospital, and in comparison with this and what it would involve Nigel's company would of necessity be restricted to the small amount of attention I could spare him. He would do occasional duty as a distraction, rather like a play or a film, an artifice the purpose of which was to disguise those life events which could not otherwise be disguised.

'Do you want me to come over?' he said.

'No, no. I'll probably have an early night. I'm rather tired.'

'How did you find your friend?'

'She is rather ill, I'm afraid.'

'I'm sorry. The important thing in these cases is to be positive. Mind over matter.'

'Of course.'

'Have you got enough food in the house?'

'Food? Oh, yes.' There was a pause. 'Thank you for lunch. Forgive me if I ring off. I really am rather tired.'

'I'll be in touch tomorrow.'

'Goodnight, Nigel.'

Though the sun was still on the walls of the adjacent buildings I undressed, took a bath, and lay down in the bed which had seemed so damaged and corrupted by my dream of the previous night. The dream had been prophetic, not in its specificity or its details, but in the fact that it had frightened me so. My own life now seemed fragile, subject to the same processes which only a determined opacity entitles one to ignore. I moved my arms and legs tentatively, experimentally, to assure myself that I was still intact. Intact, certainly, but perhaps no longer whole. The work that had begun in the dream – the spoiling – would now continue.

18

We have it on the highest authority that the meek shall inherit the earth. But if the meek don't want it? Betsy, opened up and then closed again, with a regretful shake of the head by the surgeon, wanted most definitely to remain *in situ*, though she did not know the extent to which she had been invaded and overtaken. In fact, when I first visited her, fearfully, after the operation, she was quite cheerful. 'I must be getting better,' she said. 'I managed to eat my supper.' This seemed so unlikely to me that I asked to see her doctor. Mrs Purslow, with whom I had managed to negotiate a fairly confrontational relationship, sighed, as if this were an unusual request. But the young doctor, for whom I was allowed to wait in yet another small empty room, was more explicit.

'There was nothing we could do,' he said. 'Why did she leave it so long? She must have known that something was wrong. Who was her GP?'

I said that I had no idea, that we had not been in touch before this had happened. There was no point in telling him, young and smiling as he was, that women living on their own are obliged to be stoical, or to assume a stoicism that will do duty in unalterable circumstances. How could this young man, who may, for all I knew, have been a husband, even a father, understand the terror that may prevail at night, or the despair in the face of another day? Betsy's life, as far as I knew, depended on Edmund's visits, but these could not always be relied upon. He would not, I knew from my own experience, make plans in advance, would simply ring up from his car to say that he was on his way. And I could all too easily imagine her, sitting in her flat, having reserved her evening for his visit, and then slowly coming to terms with the fact that she would have to wait another day, or even several days, before she saw him again.

And the next day she would resign herself to the same painful routine of waiting, with little to distract her. In fact distractions were to be avoided, her love affair demanding an exclusivity that anyone not affected by this particular madness could hardly comprehend. Easy enough, therefore, in these circumstances, to ignore any intimations that all was not well. It was essential only that she should appear presentable, the outer envelope untouched, all her resources employed in the task of maintaining an intimacy which took precedence over meaner considerations.

I did not attempt to explain that Betsy's illness was of a quite different order of magnitude, that it was in a direct line of descent from those tragic heroines whom she had so admired in a youth now disappearing into the shadows. *'Que le jour recommence, et que le jour finisse/Sans que jamais Titus puisse voir Bérénice/Sans que de tout le jour . . .'* For she would have overlooked his occasional impatience to be gone, to get home, to rejoin familiar surroundings, perhaps been unaware of his distaste for her flat, to which she clung as the place where he knew how to find her. And perhaps – though this was difficult to imagine – he felt something of her exaltation, recognized the unusual nature of her feeling for him, however exasperating he may have found it, or, quite simply, felt a pity that opened up a part of his character of which he had not previously been aware, and which revealed him to himself as vulnerable, as helpless, as he had managed not to be for all his adult life. 'I know what has to be done,' he had said, but whatever had to be done would be tantamount to a decision the gravity of which only he could assess, and which, characteristically, he intended to keep to himself.

'How long must she stay here?' I asked the doctor. 'She could come home with me . . .'

'I'm afraid that would be impractical. She will need some nursing. And of course we shall sedate her. I can recommend a hospice, if that is what you would prefer . . .'

'No. How much does she know?'

'We have said nothing. Eventually she will ask. But in many ways it is better if she does not know.'

'Can she stay here?'

'Yes, of course.'

'How long?'

'I can't tell you that.'

I could see that in his way he felt badly, rather on account of his own performance than for any other reason. He had been assigned an impossible task and had done his best to carry it out. Despite myself I felt sorry for him. 'Don't worry,' I heard myself say. 'We shall manage.'

Walking along the neon-lit corridor to Betsy's room my one feeling was a great longing for the outer air, with its pollution, its gases, its microbes, and its other less visible dangers. I was aware, by the fact of its very absence, of the heat of the summer's day, of the sun which only that morning had shone through my windows, of appetites which could still be satisfied. In this place the line of distinction between sickness and health was sharply drawn, not in any symbolic or minatory way, but in the distant laughter of young nurses contrasted with the heavy closed doors behind which their patients waited. I was not exempt from their necessary feelings of detachment. I dreaded the time I had to spend sitting by Betsy's bed, all too conscious of the glorious day from which we were both excluded. There was little to say. We were both intent on behaving well, which meant that our conversation was largely meaningless. We instinctively avoided the moment when a painful truth might emerge and alert us to imminent change. Therefore Edmund's name was never mentioned. Instead we looked to the past to furnish us with subjects for discussion. Do you ever hear from so-and-so? What was the name of that girl whose parents emigrated to Canada, taking her with them? Do you remember how sorry we felt for her, thinking Canada a far cry from swinging London? Do you remember the Sixties? You haven't changed. You were just as serious then. And just as pretty.

There was no point in telling Betsy that she had not changed. What was unchanged was her determined cheerfulness: she was valiant. I could not bear to imagine what this cost her, but maybe it was innate, a genuine virtue, one that qualified her to inherit the earth. The same went for her attempts to present a decent appearance, though this was becoming difficult; her hair was now lank and thin, and the colours she obstinately applied to her face looked harsh and irregular. I dared not deter her from making these efforts, lest she take that as a sign. She had always been so meticulous that her physical envelope represented yet another sign of her stoicism. As my admiration for her grew I found her situation, and I have to say, her company, less and less tolerable. When at last she showed signs of fatigue I got up to leave, and asked her my usual question: 'Is there anything you want?'

She turned her eyes away from the window, and I saw how large they had become.

'If you could get a message to the girls?'

'The girls?'

'Edmund's girls. They will wonder why I haven't been in touch. They may not know where I am. Could you bear to go round to my flat? The number is on the pad by the phone. I should love to see the girls. And David.' This last was an exhalation of pure longing.

'I'll see what I can do. Is there anything else you want from the flat?'

'If you could water the plants. And ring the girls. Tell them . . . Don't tell them anything. Just give them my love.'

Her face was turned once more to the window. My departure was awkward, as it always was. It was assumed between us that she wanted to sleep, was in fact on the verge of sleep. This tactic averted the need for encouraging words, reassurances, references to the future. For it had been observed between us that such references were out of place: the past was such inasmuch as it was over, whereas too many queries hovered over the present. My departure was an ungainly scramble, or so it seemed to me. Only when I was out in the corridor did it occur to me to wonder if I looked as mad and dishevelled as I felt, but when I consulted my mirror I saw that I was much the same as I had been when I left home, as reluctant then as now, the sun indifferent, but now even more splendid. Again as the doors slid closed behind me I breathed in the normal air as if my life depended on it, as perhaps it did.

The contrast between the brilliant streets and the darkness of Betsy's flat was eloquent. I could not see anyone wanting to return to this place. To its habitual air of desolation was now added a film of neglect: dust nestled in the curlicued legs of her nest of tables, while the parchment shade of her over-large lamp looked unequal to the task of filtering light. A faint stale smell of scent I traced to a bottle of room freshener which was abandoned on the side of the sink, together with a cup and saucer which had been washed but not put away. The plants were quite dead. I took a duster and wiped various surfaces, but I was unequal to the task of hoovering. This I would leave for another day. My dusting seemed to have effected no great difference to the place, from which I was anxious to be gone. I dialled the number on the pad by the telephone and was not surprised when it was not answered. I went into the bedroom and took a couple of nightdresses from the bulbous mahogany chest of drawers. Then I threw away the air freshener, which would no longer be needed. My conscience instructed me to try the telephone again. Again there was no answer.

My own telephone was ringing when I got home, but stopped as I went to pick it up. I thought of making tea, and even got as far as filling the kettle, when the telephone rang again.

'Where have you been?' said Nigel. 'I've tried you two or three times. I tried you ten minutes ago.'

'I've just come in. I was making tea.'

'Tea? It's six-thirty.'

'As I said, I've just come in.'

'Well, never mind that now. There's something I want to discuss with you. I'll be there in half an hour.'

'I haven't done much shopping. Will an omelette be enough for you?'

I did not want to see him. That was all I knew. I wanted to go out, into the still beautiful air, to walk, to be alone. To go to bed alone.

'Yes, of course.'

'Come when you're ready.'

He came almost at once, or so it seemed to me. He settled

himself in Digby's chair, watched approvingly as I poured him a glass of wine. I suppressed a sigh. Clearly I was meant to be at his disposal.

'Have you thought about a holiday?' he said.

'No, no, I haven't. I rarely take holidays.'

'Well, I think you will this year. My friends in France have invited me for the second half of August. I mentioned that I might bring a friend. They were delighted. Very hospitable people; I've known them for years. So what do you say? They couldn't have been more accommodating. They would be there when we arrived, and again before we left. In between they will be visiting friends in Italy. They don't like to leave the house empty, so our visit would serve a double purpose.'

'I don't think I can get away this year.'

'Gordes,' he went on. 'Beautiful place. Some excellent walks. An easy journey, and no need to pack much. Needless to say, it was a gracious gesture on their part.'

Except that they needed someone to look after the house, I thought. That would be my job. Then I saw his face, slightly flushed, expectant. This would be his experiment in domesticity, playing at house, being a couple. More important, this was his initiative, his attempt to arrange my comings and goings in a setting which he knew and to which he would make me welcome. It would be like playing house, perhaps something nearer the real thing. Yet the real thing was unthinkable: he had his occasional place in my flat, but I had no wish for his exclusive company, in a place of his choosing, with no regard to my own independence. And his friends would no doubt be intrigued, approving, having given him up as a lost cause many years ago, perhaps for as long as they had known him. Maybe they had known his wife, and were privy to the same sort of information as I was. Maybe they were his surrogate family, with only his wellbeing at heart. Their encouragement would be tacit, and it would weigh on me, particularly at a time when I should be noticeably distracted, the past and the present uncomfortably close. And he would want me to give a good account of myself, to play my part, to give satisfaction all round. I saw that it could not be done.

And yet the image of the south, the image that all northerners have, was irresistible. All the clichés came into play: markets, cafés, a more relaxed and indulgent way of life. And the sun, the sun! There was sun outside my window now, but for how much longer? We were in July, late July, and already there was an almost imperceptible alteration in the light, not in the daytime, but at night, a dulling of the atmosphere, a quietness, a sense of endings. Most people were away: the streets were almost empty. It was this emptiness to which I now held; this, I felt vaguely, was appropriate. My purpose was not to escape but to carry out the task which had been assigned to me. I had no right to pretend that it did not exist.

'I don't think I can leave,' I said. 'Not at the moment.'

He stared. I was not paying due regard to his invitation. I knew this; I was not happy about it. And I knew that he would not easily forgive me for the way in which I dismissed his exceptional offer. He had come to this conclusion as rapidly as I had, and it might well prove to be irreparable. 'Does your friend – I assume you are thinking of your friend – need you as much as all that? As much as I . . . might?' The confession had turned his face brick red.

'Yes. I think she does. Let me give you some more wine. Forgive me if I disappear into the kitchen. You must be hungry.'

He was not a man to take a rebuff lightly. His discomfiture was manifest in the way he took his second glass of wine, without thanking me. Our friendship had been revealed as less than exclusive: while he had introduced a thoroughly worthy audience into this delicate plot, I had merely responded with that less than satisfactory excuse, a sick friend. He saw this friend as an ailing and tiresome impediment to his plans, which he must have elaborated with much excitement. It was, no doubt, a handsome gesture on his part, and it would have cost him something to introduce the subject to a couple whom at last he was managing to amuse, to intrigue. And they too would have played their part, leaving us alone in a house full of provisions, as if we might not want to go out . . . There was, he had told me, a table in the garden, and most meals were taken there. The light was golden, unfailing. In such a setting one could be happy. His nostalgia for happiness was perhaps simpler than my own. It had to do with an appropriate setting, in which longing could be more easily brought to fruition. He genuinely could not understand my refusal. Nor could I. But I accepted it, with some sadness, not merely for my own sake but for his. His largesse had been spurned, and this was something that few men will overlook. I knew, or rather I apprehended, that the incident had been fatal, and I was sadly aware of the likely consequences.

We ate in silence. We were both mortified by a crisis which seemed to have arisen from nothing. It was clear that this particular evening would not be prolonged, as was by now our invariable custom. As soon as he had drunk his coffee he got up to leave. 'Perhaps you'd like to think about it,' he said. His tone was not entirely friendly. I promised to do so. I could do no less.

If, I thought, I could provide a substitute for myself at the hospital, if, in fact, I could persuade the girls, as Betsy called them, to take on my duties, then I might be able to free myself for a couple of weeks. I knew this was unlikely, but it was worth a try. I cursed myself for not retaining the telephone number on the pad in Betsy's flat, but was too tired to go back there. The ploy thus took on the dimensions of a fantasy: I should somehow contact the girls (Julia and Isabella, as I remembered they were called), who would gladly consent, or could be persuaded, to visit Betsy every day, leaving me free to enjoy the delights of the south of France. That this was unlikely did not bother me, so eager was I to believe it. The added advantage of such a plan was that it would give such pleasure to Betsy, so much more than my inadequate company. I could leave instructions with doctors and nurses before I left, maybe leave a telephone number in France. If I were summoned home I should respond immediately, and so no doubt would Nigel, who would be excellent in a crisis. The more I thought about this the more practicable it began to seem. But first I had to sleep, for I was suddenly mortally tired. In the morning I should make more detailed plans. This now seemed to me the thing to do.

'Hot enough for you?' was the greeting offered on all sides when I went out, to which the approved response was, 'We're not used to it,' accompanied by a shake of the head. Even so early the sun was an undeniable presence, bringing to mind a dominance which we had no power to evade. I revelled in this, recognizing it as my natural climate, to which the dark days were merely an unavoidable prologue. The idea of prolonging the summer in idyllic surroundings – that table in the garden – was overwhelmingly attractive, and I was already regretting my refusal of Nigel's invitation. There were two possibilities open to me, as I saw it. The first was to repair the breach with Nigel: this would be a clumsy manoeuvre, but I thought I could manage it. The other was to persuade the girls, and if possible Edmund, to visit Betsy: that was what she wanted, and if I could bring it about honour would be saved. Confidence in my ability to do this made me careless; it was possible that at that moment, powered by the sun, I did not fully understand the difficulties involved. I resolved to go to the hospital as usual, but only for a brief visit, then return to Betsy's flat and ring the Fairlie household until I got an answer. Then I realized that this might not be necessary. Edmund had given me his card which I had thrust into the nearest telephone directory, out of sight, as the hated object that it was. But I was now out on the street and unwilling to return home. I would buy food hastily on my way; Nigel too must be telephoned and invited for a meal – but not perhaps this evening. To act too precipitately was to put myself in the wrong. In any event I decided to postpone this decision; the other now had precedence. I would go straight to the hospital, and then, if possible, return to perfect my plans.

But as soon as I entered Betsy's room I saw that a change had taken place. She lay still, her eyes closed. I went out to find a nurse, but the corridor was empty. Mrs Purslow was evidently about her own affairs; in any event she was not there. I returned to the room, sat down quietly by the bed. I was aware of a hot stillness, of a silence I must not break. I took her hand and held it lightly, and then at last she opened her eyes and saw me. 'Beth,' she said. It was the name I had had as a child, vouchsafed only to a few chosen friends. Then her eyes closed again. I sat with her for an hour, her hand in mine. Eventually she sighed and said, 'Thank you.'

When I saw that she was asleep I tiptoed out, but without the usual feeling of deliverance. Instead I felt anger, even fury. The groaning bus got me only to Piccadilly; from there I took a taxi, but only after what seemed like an interminable wait.

In the flat I up-ended the telephone directories, leaving them splayed on the floor. My anger was so great that I knew it could not last, that I must act while it was at its height. But I was halted in my movements by a sudden feeling of faintness, and was obliged to sit on the floor until it passed. There was nothing mysterious about this; I had not eaten much on the previous day, and breakfast had consisted of a cup of coffee.

Sitting on the floor I examined Edmund's card, puzzling over it until my head cleared. It gave two addresses, one in Hampshire, one in London. The London address was presumably that of the house which Constance hated and which I had never seen. It was in a small square near the river, which I also did not know. The telephone number, I vaguely thought, was different from the one on Betsy's pad, but I was not sure of this, and blamed my passing malaise for my poor memory. When my head cleared I dialled the number on the card. There was no reply.

Almost instinctively I left the flat and made my way in the direction of the river. Never had the district seemed more inimical to me. The blazing sun had emptied the streets; blinds were pulled over the windows of the houses; cars crept by almost noiselessly. I longed for this day to end, yet did not want to face another like it. I felt involved in something that was too difficult for me, perhaps too difficult for anyone. Yet the sadness that this might have invoked was absent, had leaked away, leaving only a numb resolution. I tried to revive the anger I had felt; that too was now in default.

I found the small square as if I had been directed there. Again it seemed devoid of inhabitants, although two small boys were aimlessly kicking a ball on the corner. Soon they disappeared, no doubt discouraged by the heat. I had no trouble in finding the house. It advertised its presence insistently: there was a sign outside which proclaimed SOLD. The sign had been knocked slightly sideways, which may have indicated that it had been there for some time. This dereliction, into which it was becoming easier by the minute to descry a symbolic message, was now the only presence, though inanimate, in the deserted street. I hastened away from it, as if I had overheard a forbidden conversation, even a conspiracy, which sent an inscrutable message to those unfortunate enough to hear it. 'I know what has to be done,' he had said. There would be no need for explanation, for exegesis. All had been enacted, without our knowledge, let alone our consent. The decisiveness with which it had been done was, again, in character. Such decisiveness, such character were beyond my reach. There would be no time to tell the necessary lies. Thus, in a way that was almost acceptable, the matter had been taken care of. Betsy would not know of it; I hoped that she had been able to entertain, perhaps to welcome, an habitual illusion. For myself no illusion would be possible, not now, not ever. I knew the truth of the matter. And the truth of the matter was plain to see: from all our respective viewpoints, mine, Betsy's, even Edmund's, the case was closed.

19

Now, many years later, long after Betsy's death, long after Edmund's son had come off his motorbike and been killed by an oncoming car, I sit and think of these events as if they had taken place in another life. Strangely, or perhaps not so strangely, I mind David's death more than anything else, although I had hardly known the boy. But I remember his face, the reluctant smile that was a mirror image of Edmund's own, and perhaps of that of Constance, who smiled rarely. I am fifty-six, nearly fifty-seven. According to the tabloid which I now read over breakfast fifty is the new thirty. But this is not true: at thirty one still has expectations. I had been born a little too soon. I had been given the wrong instructions, by teachers, by novels. Betsy at least had chosen grander models. That was how I thought of her now, as a tragic heroine whose destiny it is to die. This brought a sense of symmetry to her end, and made it slightly easier to accommodate. But in fact everyone I know seems to have been prefigured somewhere, in pages which I do not take the trouble to trace. Even books can let you down.

I still see Nigel from time to time although the connection has been broken. Sometimes I join him on a walk in the park, which he suggests out of kindness, thinking me lonely. He senses distress of an order which he is not keen to investigate, nor could I explain it. It has something to do with the passing of time, which he does not seem to register, although he is older than I am. He no longer visits me, and I suspect that he has found an alternative arrangement. He is still a good-looking man, though now I must add, for his age.

Sometimes I walk, as I used to, in the early morning, or after dark. They welcome me kindly at the hospital, where I do voluntary work. I have made new friends there, but women, only women. I have caught Betsy's habit of gazing into children's faces: another sign of ageing. The time passes quickly now. There is just that failure of nerve around six o'clock, when I long to be summoned. But I sleep soundly, without dreams. Were I to dream I should find myself in the past again, at home, with my parents, or running to meet them, my face alight with joy, as it must have been, at the beginning of the world.